Praise for *The Bride Insists*

"Perfectly delightful Regency romance… Remarkably executed."

—*Publishers Weekly* Starred Review

"Ashford captures the reader's interest with her keen knowledge of the era and her deft writing. An engaging cast of characters…a charming plot, and just the right amount of sensuality will keep Ashford fans satisfied."

—*RT Book Reviews*, 4 Stars

"A marvelously engaging marriage of convenience tale, and Ashford's richly nuanced, realistically complex characters and impeccably crafted historical setting are bound to resonate with fans of Mary Balogh."

—*Booklist*

"Ashford establishes a union made for all the wrong reasons until trust and love can set things to rights… For all historical romance fans."

—*Library Journal Xpress*

"A solid historical…the heat is palpable."

—*Long and Short Reviews*

"A sweet historical romance that one can enjoy over a hot cup of happy and a warm blanket! Most assuredly a warm and fuzzy read!"

—*The Reading Café*

Praise for *Once Again a Bride*

"A near-perfect example of everything that makes this genre an escapist joy to read: unsought love triumphs despite difficult circumstances, unpleasantness is resolved and mysteries cleared, and good people get the happy lives they deserve."

—*Publishers Weekly*

"A bit of gothic suspense, a double love story, and the right touches of humor and sensuality add up to this delightfully fast-paced read about second chances and love's redeeming power."

—*RT Book Reviews*, 4 Stars

"Ms. Ashford has written a superbly crafted story with elements of political unrest, some gothic suspense, and an interesting romance."

—*Fresh Fiction*

"Well-rendered, relatable characters, superb writing, an excellent sense of time and place, and gentle wit make this a romance that shouldn't be missed... Ashford returns with a Regency winner that will please her longtime fans and garner new ones."

—*Library Journal*

"Mystery entwines with the romance, as Ms. Ashford leads us astray... *Once Again a Bride* is great fun."

—*Historical Hilarity*

Praise for *The Marriage Wager*

"Exceptional characters and beautifully crafted historical details ensure a delightful read for Judith McNaught and Mary Balogh fans."

—*Publishers Weekly*

"Lively, well-written Regency romance sparkles with wonderful dialogue, witty scenes, and just the right touch of humor, adventure, and repartee."

—*RT Book Reviews*, Nominated for Best Regency Historical Romance

"A riveting, emotional romance that will garner a place of prominence on anyone's keeper shelf."

—*Rendezvous*

"You're really going to enjoy *The Marriage Wager*. It is one of the finest marriage of convenience stories I've read."

—*All About Romance*

"Entertaining, colorful characters, romantic... An engaging and entertaining read."

—*Caffeinated Book Reviewer*

"An enjoyable Regency romance with complex characters."

—*Book Lover and Procrastinator*

"Fast-paced and thoroughly enjoyable."

—*Nook Book Lady*

Also by Jane Ashford

The Headstrong Ward

Jane Ashford

sourcebooks
casablanca

Published by Sourcebooks Casablanca, an imprint of Sourcebooks,
Inc.
P.O. Box 4410, Naperville, Illinois 60567-4410
(630) 961-3900
Fax: (630) 961-2168
www.sourcebooks.com

Originally published in 1983 by Signet, a division of The New
American Library, Inc., New York.

Printed and bound in Canada.
WC 10 9 8 7 6 5 4 3 2 1

One

CHARLES VINCENT DEBENHAM, FIFTH VISCOUNT Wrenley, stood before his library fire with a glass of Madeira in his hand and looked from one to the other of his two younger brothers. His expression was not particularly pleasant. "If that is all you have to contribute, Edward," he told the youngest, "you may as well keep your tongue between your teeth."

"I like that," retorted Captain Edward Debenham, an officer in the exclusive Horse Guards regiment. "Why ask for our opinions if you don't want to hear 'em?"

The viscount eyed him with distaste. "I begin to wonder why."

"Here, now, don't start to quarrel," put in Reverend Laurence Debenham, at twenty-seven the middle brother and accustomed to mediating disputes between the twenty-four-year-old Edward and the head of the family. "We shan't get anywhere if you do that."

"But Charles enjoys it so," responded Edward,

an irrepressible spark of mischief in his eye. "I hate to disappoint him. He *expects* it of me." When Lord Wrenley looked sharply at him, he grinned.

The viscount surveyed his brothers. An impartial observer might have pronounced all three men uncommonly handsome. The Debenhams were tall and well-made, with very pale blond hair and eyes of clear gray. Each possessed the arched, aquiline Debenham nose, which could be seen repeated in the portrait gallery on the first floor of Wrenley, their country seat. But here the resemblance ended. Charles added to these outlines a raised eyebrow and a faint sneer, which lent his rather thin face a haughty distance. At thirty-one, he dressed with the austere elegance of a Corinthian, and had the shoulders and leg to carry it off. Laurence, as befitted his clerical profession, was more quietly attired; his pleasant face was rounder than his brothers', and his gray eyes showed more kindness. He had particularly attractive hands, elegant and well-shaped, inherited from their gentle mother. Edward set off his dashing costume with a rakish air and careless manner that often irritated his eldest brother. He was the tallest of the three by an inch and had a spare, loose-knit frame. His crooked grin and wicked twinkle had been the downfall of many young ladies in all walks of society.

"You called us here to Wrenley," continued Laurence hurriedly, before Charles could make the caustic remark so evident in his expression, "to help you decide what is to be done about Anne."

"There is no need to repeat my own words back to me. And frankly, I begin to think I made a mistake. It is obvious that neither of you is going to be the least use."

Laurence frowned, but Edward merely laughed. "You might have known that, Charles. We none of us know the first thing about schoolgirls."

"No?" The viscount eyed him coldly. "From what I hear of your career in town, you, at least, know a deal too much."

Edward's eyes danced. "Not schoolgirls, Charles!"

The other turned away in disgust, taking a vermeil snuffbox from his waistcoat pocket and flipping it open with a practiced thumb.

"When does Anne arrive here?" asked Laurence. "I haven't seen her since Mother died. It must be…why, three years."

"She is to return from school next week."

"Funny to think of little Anne grown up," said Edward. "She must be…by Jove, she's nineteen this year, ain't she? What has she been doing in school all this time?" He looked apprehensive. "I say, Charles, she's not a bluestocking, is she?"

"On the contrary, her school reports suggest that she is hardly literate. I left her there an additional year in the hope she might improve." The viscount's chiseled lips turned down. "She did not."

"Did you truly hope so," responded Edward, "or did you wish to put off being saddled with a chit of a 'ward'?" He grinned as Charles glared at him.

"Is she…is she at all, ah, changed?" put in Laurence.

For one rare moment, the Debenham brothers were in complete sympathy as they heaved a collective sigh. Lady Anne Tremayne had been introduced into their household when she was barely a year old, after the tragic death of both her parents at sea. Their mother, Lady Wrenley, was the child's godmother, and when no blood relation stepped forward to claim Anne, she had informally adopted her, eventually providing for her in her will. But almost from the moment of the girl's arrival, she had been the despair of her new family. Suddenly blessed with three much older "brothers," Anne had asked for nothing better than to follow their example in everything. For boys of six, nine, and thirteen, this had been a continuing trial, and moreover, it had made Anne an unusual, intractable girl. She had ridden and shot and hunted from the earliest possible age with a concentrated abandon that no scolding could eradicate. Lady Wrenley gradually took refuge in an invalid's couch and a murmured stream of complaint, particularly after her husband's premature death when his eldest son was barely sixteen. Charles, overwhelmed by his new responsibilities, had had increasingly acrimonious quarrels with Anne, until, at last, he insisted that she be sent to school to learn manners. This had accordingly been done when the girl was barely fourteen. And her ladyship's death two years later had simply confirmed the arrangement.

The brothers sighed again as they thought of her.

In a remarkably handsome family, Anne had been an anomaly since her little-girl prettiness gave way to a gawky, awkward adolescence. They all remembered her, vividly, as a tall unattractive girl, all knees and elbows and unkempt red-blond hair, distressingly likely to indulge in fits of temper at the slightest provocation.

"I haven't the faintest notion," drawled Lord Wrenley.

"What do you mean?" Laurence stared at him. "How was she when you last visited the school?"

"I have not visited it."

Even Edward looked surprised.

"Not this year, you mean?" added Laurence.

"Not at all."

They gazed at him incredulously. "B-but...during her holidays?"

"She has always asked leave to spend them with one of her school friends since Mama died. I saw no reason to deny her."

"My dear Charles, you cannot mean that you have not seen Anne since our mother died?"

"Can I not?"

"But that is more than three years! Has no one been to visit her in three years?"

Lord Wrenley shrugged, looking slightly self-conscious. "She would not have welcomed a visit from me. We did not part on good terms, you know. And in any case, we hardly knew one another even before that."

"Hardly...? You are her guardian! And she was a

child when she left. I daresay she has changed a great deal. It was your duty—"

"Don't prate to *me* of duty," interrupted the viscount in a dangerous tone, and Laurence subsided. He knew that his brother harbored a lamentable bitterness over his premature family responsibilities. At sixteen, Charles had stolidly taken over for his dead father, but he had rid himself of each task as soon as practicable, and he had never shown any signs of enjoying his new position. On the contrary, it had changed him all out of recognition, in Laurence's opinion. In the place of an indulgently superior older brother, there had appeared a rigid, distant disciplinarian who had seemed only too eager to dispense with the encumbrance of their presence. Flashes of the old Charles occasionally appeared, but with decreasing regularity.

"I would have been happy to visit Anne," Laurence dared to add, before being silenced by the viscount's hard look.

"Well, I don't see that it matters now," said Edward unheedingly. "Anne's coming home. What's to be done with her?"

Lord Wrenley turned away from his brothers and looked down at the fire, mastering his anger with a visible effort. The prospect of being saddled with a schoolgirl, just now when he had succeeded in ordering his life to his own satisfaction, filled him with rage. "That, Edward, is what I asked you both down to Wrenley to discuss," he drawled finally.

"Yes, well…" The military branch of the Debenham family seemed at a loss.

"She must be brought out, of course," said Laurence. "That is the customary procedure."

"That's it," agreed Edward. "Find her a husband. Mama left her a tidy fortune, so it shouldn't be difficult to get someone." Laurence frowned, but his younger brother didn't notice. "Do you remember the day Anne came upon that party from the Grange down by the trout stream? One of the ladies frightened her horse; I forget how. They say the squire still hasn't recovered from the language she used. It positively set his hair on end. And she had a great purple bruise over her eye where she had fallen from the apple tree." He chuckled reminiscently; Laurence groaned.

"She always swore she'd be a jockey," continued Captain Debenham, "and I have to admit, she *could* ride. But, you know, Anne in a drawing room…" His voice trailed away, and he shook his head. "Her clothes were always thrown on by guess, and if she ever put a comb to her hair, *I* couldn't tell it. She hated dancing lessons, too."

"We must suppose that five years in a young ladies' seminary have changed that, at least," replied the viscount.

"Yes, but you know, Charles," continued the other, "she ain't at all pretty. It's odd, because she was very well when she was small, I remember. But after she was eleven, she went all gawky. Anne may have learned manners—mind, I say *may*—but…" He trailed off again, and all of them fell silent, imagining the Lady Anne Tremayne they remembered a deb in the London season.

Laurence groaned softly again. "Poor child."

Lord Wrenley raised his eyebrows. "Granting these things, can either of you suggest an alternative to presenting Anne this season?"

Edward grimaced, then shook his head. Laurence stared frowning at the carpet for a moment, then slowly did likewise.

"I see. We must suppose it settled, then." Charles sounded far from pleased.

"Will you use the town house?" asked Laurence.

"Where else?"

"Well, yes, but I mean…"

"I shall have to find a chaperone, of course."

Edward laughed. "You'd better find a tartar. Lord, what a comedy it will be."

"This is no laughing matter," chided Laurence.

"Well, if I don't joke, I shall dashed well weep. When I think of puffing Anne off in a London drawing room…" He grimaced eloquently again. "You don't care; you're safely settled here in the country. But Charles and I are in for a grim few months. Lord!"

The viscount smiled. "Oh, Laurence must come up to town for the season. We shall want his, er, counsel."

"Here, I say…" sputtered Laurence.

Edward gave a shout of laughter, as Charles blandly

took a pinch of snuff. "I shall find a chaperone," added the latter, "and Anne shall come out this season with *all* of us to support her."

"My clerical duties…" attempted Laurence.

"You have a curate."

Reverend Debenham's face fell, then brightened. "What about Lydia? I can't leave her right now. We are only just engaged."

Edward made a face indicating extreme distaste. Lord Wrenley remained impassive, but something in his tone as he replied, "I thought Miss Branwell was to be in London this season," suggested that he shared his youngest brother's low opinion of Laurence's affianced bride.

"Oh," answered Laurence. "Oh, yes, that's true."

"Splendid. You will not then be bereft of her charming company."

Edward made a derisive noise, and Laurence glared at him. "We shall be one great happy family." He snorted, unabashed. "The *ton* won't know what to make of it."

"Indeed," responded Charles quellingly. "Laurence will give Anne the benefit of his, er, guidance, and you will bring all your dashing friends round to meet her."

"No, here, I say, Charles!"

Lord Wrenley raised an eyebrow.

"They'll never forgive me!"

"Which might be for the best, considering some of the company you have been keeping."

"And what will *you* do, Charles?" retorted the other, stung.

"I shall lend you all my countenance."

Edward sniffed. "What about *your* friends?"

"They are far too old for a chit fresh from the schoolroom. Indeed, we shall have to rely upon you to squire Anne about, Edward. You are nearest her age and know all the younger crowd."

"Charles!"

Something like a twinkle appeared briefly in the viscount's gray eyes. "You have a duty to your family, Edward. It is high time you realized that."

❧

Some seventy miles west of Lord Wrenley's elegant library, on the outskirts of the city of Bath, the subject of these remarks was just then mounting a hired post chaise, which already contained one other young lady. She plumped alarmingly down on the cushions, waved a hand to the postilions to signal their readiness to depart, and grinned at her companion as the horses started forward. "Isn't this splendid!" she said. "We are really off at last. I could shout with joy!"

The other, a diminutive brunette with large, soft brown eyes, looked apprehensive.

"But I shan't, goose, so there's no need to wonder how you can dissuade me." Lady Anne Tremayne laughed. "I declare, Arabella, you are positively transparent."

Miss Arabella Castleton dimpled. "Well, so are you. And I daresay you *would* have shouted, and shocked the postboys horridly, if I weren't here to restrain you."

Anne wrinkled her nose at the girl who had been her dearest friend for the last three years. "And if I had not insisted, you would have remained at that beastly school for another week. For no earthly reason."

Slowly Arabella nodded. "Though we did have some good times there, didn't we? Particularly toward the end. Indeed, if you had left last year as you should have, I don't know how I could have endured my final year. I would have missed you dreadfully."

Lady Anne grimaced. "That was the only thing which kept me from *demanding* I be allowed to leave. And I will always think it a shabby trick. A whole extra year of school! But what else can one expect from a selfish beast like Charles?"

Miss Castleton eyed her friend doubtfully. Since the moment Arabella had arrived at the Millington Seminary for Young Ladies, as a frightened, homesick fifteen-year-old, she had regarded Anne with awed admiration. The older girl had befriended her and guided her kindly through the first daunting days at the school, saying that she knew only too well how hard it was to be thrown among so many strangers when one is missing one's home and family. It had seemed to Arabella that Anne possessed all the qualities so lamentably lacking in herself. Anne never hesitated to say what she thought or to ask for what she wanted, even when she was not at all likely to get it, and she excelled at the outdoor pursuits that Arabella had always found terrifying. Indeed, Anne's seat on a horse was said to be the admiration of the whole county. And when one was feeling melancholy or dismally at odds with the world, it needed only one of Anne's great gusts of laughter to dissipate the black mood and make all seem pleasant and interesting once again.

But though she was quiet and shy, Miss Castleton was by no means unintelligent, and she soon realized that there were corresponding flaws in her idol's character. Lady Anne's exuberance often carried her too far, and her impatience with the small niceties of polite society, aggravated by a lightning-hot temper, often offended even those well acquainted with it. By degrees, Arabella had found herself first remarking on these traits, then exerting her growing influence to moderate them. Their teachers had been well pleased to see the friendship grow between these two diametric opposites. Lady Anne drew Arabella out and taught her a new assurance and confidence in herself, and the younger girl had a marked quieting effect on Anne. By the third year of their association, both were much changed, and the Millington Seminary released them to the world with a degree of complacent satisfaction it would never have imagined possible after Lady Anne Tremayne's turbulent—almost legendary—first year.

"Oh, look!" said Anne, leaning perilously far out the carriage window. "There is the London mail coach.

With three passengers outside. I *still* think it would have been a splendid way to travel up to town, Bella."

"It would have been crowded and slow, and you would have tired of it after the first stage," replied her friend calmly. "And anyway, Mama would never have consented."

Lady Anne pulled her head in, revealing a bonnet little improved by the wind, and turned to grin at her. "We need not have told her."

"Anne!"

"Oh, I am only bamming you. You are such an easy mark, Bella. Perhaps that is why I like you so much." Miss Castleton stuck out her tongue, and Anne laughed. "It is certainly no time to offend your mother," she added, "as if I should ever wish to. I need her help far too much to indulge in any of what she calls my 'distempered freaks.'"

Arabella nodded. "But you know, Anne, I still think you should have written to your family and told them you mean to spend a few days with us in London before you go home. It seems wrong not to—"

"They are *not* my family!" snapped the other.

Miss Castleton shrank back a little.

"I'm sorry. I did not mean to shout at you. But Charles and Laurence and Edward are *not* my family, Bella. Lady Wrenley *was*, but she is gone. I haven't any family left."

"But, Anne…"

"We have been over all of this before. None of the

Debenhams, except Lady Wrenley, ever had the least affection for me. The boys mocked me and ignored me by turns. We did nothing but wrangle from the moment I could speak. And it is not as if we were at all related."

"But brothers and sisters often quarrel," murmured Arabella diffidently. "My older sisters and I—"

"They are not my brothers," interrupted Lady Anne. "I don't wish to talk of this, Bella. You are not going to change my opinion, as you must know by this time."

Recognizing her mood, Miss Castleton abandoned the subject. "Well, I do wish you might spend the season with us, then. It would be so much more comfortable."

Her eyes lighting mischievously, the older girl replied, "I wonder if your mother would think so."

"Mama is very fond of you!"

"Oh, yes. But I am not certain she finds me 'comfortable.'"

Arabella started to protest again, then paused.

"Exactly so!"

She laughed. "Well, but the season! All those balls and evening parties and strangers to be faced. *I* should be more comfortable if you were beside me."

"Nonsense! You will be an instant success without any help whatsoever."

"I? Oh, no. If I can but get through the first days without stammering or saying something bird-witted, I shall be satisfied."

Smiling, Lady Anne surveyed her friend. Not for the first time, she wondered at Arabella's low valuation of her own attractions, for Miss Castleton was a very pretty girl indeed. Though not tall, she carried herself well and had a lovely slim figure. Her deep brown hair showed red highlights, and her dark eyes were thickly lashed and expressive. Add to this a creamy skin, a perfectly sculpted pink mouth, and a shy smile that had already had a noticeable effect on more than one young gentleman in the streets of Bath, and it became hard to see how Arabella could be unaware of her own beauty. Anne laughed. "We shall see," she said. "It is much more likely that you will be called upon to help *me*."

Miss Castleton opened her eyes very wide. "How?"

"Goose. A season in London is not at all like being in school with a pack of simpering girls. I shan't be able to dictate to the *ton*. Indeed, I doubt very much I shall 'take.' I am not pretty, you know. And my manners..." She grinned. "Well, even charitable people call them 'original.' You may have to push some of your unwanted admirers in my direction. Poor things!"

"You are pretty! That is, not exactly pretty, but..." Anne grinned again. "Yes?"

Arabella frowned. It was true that Anne did not fit the common ideal of beauty. She was far too tall, for one thing, and her thin figure did not show much feminine softness. She might have modified this physical impression by diffident behavior, but, of course, she did not. "You know you have beautiful hair," she replied severely, "and eyes."

"Very good, Bella! You always find something to praise in the least attractive subject." Lady Anne put a hand to her head. "My hair is all right, isn't it? Though it looks dreadful in braids, of course."

Arabella nodded. It was true that Anne's lovely red-gold mane lost much of its sparkle when confined in the flat braids favored by the Millington School. And the style did not flatter her thin face, either. Anne's angular features needed softening. "But we shall get it cut as soon as we arrive in town," maintained Arabella stoutly, "and then it will look splendid. And really, Anne, your eyes are wonderful."

The other focused these orbs on her friend. They were of a peculiar dark gray, shot through with hints of violet, and as changeable as her moods. "Oh, I think I will be well enough when I have the proper clothes and so on. Your mama has taught me some of the ways it may be done, and I mean to learn more before this week is out. It is all a great bore, but I shall make the effort. It is an effort for me, though, Bella, while you are lovely in rags."

Miss Castleton looked outraged for a moment, then shook her head and began to laugh. "Not *rags*."

Anne grinned. "Well, I have never seen you in rags, but I wager you would be. But you understand why I must go to London before I go home, Bella. I can't return like *this*." She grasped the sleeve of her unbecoming stuff gown. "I *won't*. And if Charles heard I was going to town, he might forbid me, and then where should I be? I want to look…stunning when they first see me again."

"Would you have gone home if he *did* order it?" asked Arabella curiously.

Anne frowned silently for a long moment. "We needn't worry about that; he hasn't."

"But he is your guardian, you know, and when you are home again, he will naturally order your routine." This topic had been worrying Arabella for some weeks, and she was glad of an opportunity to bring it to Anne's attention.

Her friend's frown deepened, but when she spoke, it was only to say, "I shall smarten myself up in London, and then I shall *show* him."

"You keep saying that," responded Arabella uneasily, "but I can never discover what it means."

Anne stared out the window. She was not at all certain she knew the answer to this herself. "You must wait and see."

The carriage slowed. They had entered a small village, and the narrow streets made progress difficult. As they ponderously turned a corner and started along a row of little shops, Anne's gray-violet eyes suddenly lit. "Stop!" she cried. "Driver, stop here." She knocked on the roof of the chaise and repeated her order.

With a jerk, the vehicle came to a halt, the driver peering down at them in perplexity. "Yes, just here," approved Lady Anne, pushing open the carriage door and preparing to climb down. "I shan't be a moment."

"Where are you going?" cried Arabella.

"Into that shop. I'll be right back, Bella. Wait here."

"I shall do no such thing." Miss Castleton scrambled out behind her. "You cannot wander about a strange village alone."

"I'm not going to wander about."

"What are you going to do?" Long experience of Anne's sudden impulses made Arabella frown up at her.

Lady Anne gazed down; Arabella's head barely reached her shoulder, but she could tell when argument was useless. "Oh, come along if you like, then." She strode across the pavement and into the tiny shop she had seen from the chaise window. Arabella followed, mystified; she could see nothing of interest in the display. It appeared to be a secondhand-furniture shop.

"I will give you a good price," Anne was saying when her friend entered. "It is just what I want."

A gnarled old man stood behind the counter. He wore a neckerchief tied around his head and had somehow lost most of his teeth. He made Arabella think of pirates and other unsavory characters and, as usual, she wondered at her friend's fearless assurance. "Hadn't rightly considered selling," the man replied. "But now's you ask…" He looked toward the corner of the shop. "Five pounds."

"Five! Nonsense. I said a good price, not a ridiculous one. It is not worth ten shillings." The man started to protest, and Anne added, "But I will give you a pound."

"Not a penny less than five," growled the old man.

Lady Anne shrugged. "Very well. I am on my way to London and can no doubt find what I want at a much lower price there. Good day." She turned away.

"Wait," said the shopkeeper. "You can have 'im for a pound."

Smiling, Anne took a pound note from her reticule and laid it on the counter.

"It's highway robbery, mind," added the man, walking around the counter to the front of the shop. "But you seem a nice lass. You'll be good to 'im."

To Arabella's horror, he reached up and detached a large cage from a hook on the wall. In it sat a red-and-blue parrot who looked rather the worse for wear and who eyed the girls with an intimidatingly crafty malevolence. "Here you be," said the old man, handing the cage to Lady Anne.

"Anne," protested Arabella in a strangled voice.

"Thank you," said her friend, turning toward the door.

Stunned, Arabella followed. In the doorway, Anne paused and looked back. "Does he swear?" she asked.

"'Im?" The shopkeeper spread his hands and gazed at her with elaborately contrived innocence. "Pure as the driven snow, miss."

Anne eyed him for a moment, then grinned and nodded. "Splendid." She climbed back into the chaise, ignoring the scandalized glances of the driver and the postboys, set the cage on the front seat, and gave Arabella a hand up. Waving the coach forward, she turned to survey her purchase. "Isn't he wonderful, Bella?"

Her friend stared. The chaise lurched forward, and the parrot, startled, ruffled his feathers and croaked, "Damn your eyes, ye heathen!"

Lady Anne Tremayne fell back on the cushions in an ecstasy of laughter. "And won't Charles *adore* him," she added unevenly.

Two

A LITTLE MORE THAN A WEEK LATER, ANNE TREMAYNE was once again sitting in a post chaise traveling across the countryside. But in every other respect, save that the parrot's cage again occupied the forward seat, her circumstances were greatly changed. She had used her time in London to advantage. In that short period, with the help of Arabella's mother, she had acquired a new wardrobe, a fashionable haircut, and an experienced lady's maid to help her take care of them.

The latter was very necessary. Anne had never in her life paid much heed to her appearance. As a little girl, she had had no interest in the matter, and when she grew older, she found the effort involved in looking well irksome. She much preferred riding to hounds or a spirited walk to primping endlessly before the mirror. She had learned something of the principles of fashion at school, and her taste was good, but she was hopeless in practice. She had never minded the Millington School's braids and stuff gowns, even though they became her so ill, because they meant that she need not waste thought on her dress.

Now, however, her attitude had changed. She was determined to look as well as possible and to endure whatever tedium this required. Mrs. Castleton had thrown herself into the project. Not only had she been urging Anne in this direction for a year, she had already launched two daughters into society, and she knew all the tricks of fashion. And despite some friction over the unfortunate parrot, she had achieved marvels in the short period allowed her.

The Anne who sat gazing out the chaise window today was very different from the angular schoolgirl who had driven to London so lately. Her magnificent red-gold hair had been cropped and dressed in a cloud of curls, showing its fullness to advantage and softening the lines of her face until she hardly recognized her reflection in a mirror. Indeed, her hair, which had been Anne's despair since she was ten, always escaping the tightest bands and writhing wildly about her shoulders, was now her glory. She wore a new gown of pale primrose muslin sprigged with gold and violet flowers; it brought out the violet lights in her gray eyes, and the skillful modiste favored by Mrs. Castleton had cut it, and the five other dresses she and her staff had made up in record time, so as to de-emphasize Anne's thinness and height. All in all, Lady Anne was very pleased, though she could not help thinking at intervals that she had been much more comfortable in her old, unbecoming gown.

"How much farther is it now, my lady?" asked Crane.

Anne turned to look at her new abigail. The woman was middle-aged, with gray hair and an awesome primness. Anne was almost afraid of her. "Not far now. Perhaps another half hour."

Crane nodded. "Wrenley is a fine old house, I understand. The viscount will be there, I suppose?"

The girl nodded silently. She had no intention of talking about Charles. A sudden lurch threw her against the side panel of the chaise; it also rocked the parrot's cage, and she reached across to steady it. The bird was by no means reconciled to the inconveniences of travel. He squawked harshly, "Blast ye! Devil take ye all!"

Anne giggled. Crane, unable to draw herself up, since she was already sitting ramrod straight, made an outraged sound. "I cannot see, my lady," she said, "what you want with that disgusting creature. It is a very improper pet for you."

The parrot, who had had several run-ins with Crane already, leered at her cordially. Anne struggled with her laughter.

Goaded, Crane added, "We shall see what Lord Wrenley has to say about bringing that thing into his house."

Anne sobered immediately. "He will have nothing to say. Augustus is mine!"

"Augustus," sniffed the maid. But the flash of temper in Anne's eyes kept her from continuing.

Lady Anne sank back in her seat and, for the first time in days, allowed herself to consider what she would find when she arrived at Wrenley. She had not been to the home of her childhood in three years, and the last visit had been horribly melancholy and lonely, after the death of Lady Wrenley. Her memories of the place were ambivalent. She had had good times, racing headlong across the fields, surrounded by as many horses and dogs as even she could wish, and her adopted mother had been kind and, in her timid way, affectionate. But Anne had also often been unhappy, more sensitive than her active interests led anyone to believe, and desperately anxious to emulate and please her three "brothers," whose constant teasing had many times sent her to her room for a solitary cry. No one saw it; she made sure of that. But it hurt nonetheless.

Anne's jaw tightened. Charles had always been the worst. He had never had time for a girl twelve years his junior, which was more or less understandable, but it seemed to Anne that he had also encouraged the others to mock her by his sarcastic example and then treated her with unforgivable harshness in the matter of school. She had begged him not to send her away. The thought of living among strangers had terrified her, and she had promised to become a model of meekness and decorum if allowed to remain. But he had brushed her aside, not even listening, so that she could not go on to tell him what she barely sensed herself—that the memory of abandonment somehow clung from her earliest years, and that this further exile was almost more than she could bear.

Anne shuddered slightly. She *would* not think of her first year at Millington. It had been dreadful, but it was long over, and she had adjusted. With the death of Lady Wrenley, she had realized that she was alone in the world. None of the Debenhams could spare even a few hours for a visit. Well, let that be so, then. She had a tidy fortune, and she meant to order her own life at last. Charles must be shown this at once. He cared nothing for her, and, thus, he had no authority over her. She would come out—indeed, she was looking forward to the balls and parties—and then they would see.

Anne tossed her red-gold head. The Debenham brothers needed a lesson, and she was determined to give it to them.

"Is that the house, my lady?" asked Crane.

Anne leaned forward. A gap in the trees along the lane opened a long vista to the east, and there, at the bottom of a hill, stood Wrenley, a jumble of gray stone with a host of windows glittering in the afternoon sun. To Anne's astonishment, her throat grew tight and she felt tears start in her eyes. She nodded and furiously fought to control herself.

"A fine edifice," replied Crane, complacently. "I daresay there are twenty bedrooms."

"Into bed, lass," squawked Augustus, inspired.

Crane gasped. Anne choked and turned her head

quickly away. "That bird must be disposed of," said the maid in outraged accents.

"No, no," sputtered Anne. "He will be a…a model of propriety as soon as he is out of the carriage. He hates traveling."

"Hates…!" Crane sniffed and tossed her head indignantly.

The chaise turned off the road and into the avenue that led to Wrenley. Anne saw no one near the lodge, but as they drove through the park, every tree and bush seemed familiar. She had not thought she would remember it so well. Soon they were pulling up before the tall double doors, which were flung open at once, and Anne was jumping down to hurl herself into the embrace of a stout elderly woman who stood on the threshold and crying, "Brigs!"

Mrs. Brigham, housekeeper at Wrenley for the past twenty years, returned her hug. "Lady Anne. It's good to have you home, my lady."

Anne turned to the tall thin figure beside them and held out a hand. "And how are you, Fallow?"

"Very well, my lady," replied the butler, his austere face breaking into an uncharacteristic smile. "And may I add my sentiments to Mrs. Brigham's. We're all glad to see you back after so long."

"Thank you." The rest of the party had by now descended. "This is Crane, my abigail." The servants acknowledged one another warily. "And that is Augustus."

Brigham and Fallow gazed at the parrot. "Is it, my lady?" said the former.

Anne nodded, her eyes twinkling.

Fallow noticed it first. Summoning a footman to take charge of the cage, he said, "Well, my lady, I thought you were changed all out of recognition, but I see some of the old mischief is still there. Where were you thinking of keeping this, er, creature? In your bedchamber?"

"Oh, no. The drawing room."

Crane stared at her, aghast. The others, blissfully unaware, merely exchanged doubtful glances before moving to follow her orders.

"Charles is here?" added Anne.

"Yes, my lady. In the library," responded Fallow. "Shall I take you there at once, or…"

"No, I'll go upstairs first." It was just like Charles, thought Anne as she walked up the stairs, not to bestir himself and come to greet her. He could hardly have failed to hear her arrival. Well, she could play that game too. She would go to the library when she was ready, and not an instant before.

But half an hour later, when Anne was walking along the corridor toward the library door, she was stopped by Fallow and informed that Lord Wrenley had been called away by his bailiff. Fallow conveyed his lordship's apologies and the message that he would certainly join her for dinner, but Anne's only response was to pick up her skirts and stalk furiously back to her room.

By dinnertime, she had regained her equanimity. She had also changed into an evening dress of pale violet and allowed Crane to rearrange her curls and place a gauzy wrap over her elbows. As she sat in the drawing room awaiting the viscount, she rehearsed to herself the cool distant way she would greet him. Looking into a mirror on the far wall, she raised her red-gold eyebrows slightly and inclined her head. That should show Charles what she thought of his manners!

Ten minutes before the dinner hour, the door opened, and Lord Wrenley strolled into the room. Anne had maliciously hoped that he would appear in his riding dress, giving her an opportunity to overlook his gaffe in the most noticeable way possible, but he was impeccably dressed in buff pantaloons and an exquisitely cut dark blue coat. He looked so elegant, in fact, that Anne was slightly taken aback. She had not remembered that Charles was so fashionable. Involuntarily she stood as he came toward her.

"Anne." Politely he held out a hand. "You look very dashing. Millington did well by you."

Lady Anne, about to give him her hand, snatched it back. "Millington had nothing to do with it!" she snapped, outraged that he should dare to refer to the place of her exile so blithely.

"Indeed? I admit I wondered how you acquired such a gown at a girls' school. Have you been raiding the Bath shops?"

Anne took a deep breath and made a heroic attempt

to control her temper. She knew from past experience that if she gave way to anger, she was lost. "Bath?" she replied lightly. "Oh, lud, no. I bought a few things in London before I came here."

"London?" Lord Wrenley raised an eyebrow. "Do you mean you have been up to town?"

"Last week." Anne continued to speak airily. She sat down again and pretended to be absorbed in untangling the fringe of her wrap.

"You did not inform me of this."

She raised *her* eyebrows, just as she had practiced doing, and looked at him.

The viscount frowned. He had emphatically not wanted the responsibility of a schoolgirl ward, but as he had it, he must do his duty. "While you are under my care—" he began wearily.

"Your *care*!" interrupted Anne in as biting a tone as she could manage.

The man looked startled for a moment; then his eyes narrowed and he surveyed her. Anne met them squarely; pale gray eyes locked with violet-flecked ones. She concentrated on putting all her dislike of him in that long glance. "Ah," he said at last. "So that's the way of it, is it?" And to Anne's astonishment and chagrin, he smiled. Perhaps he could find some mild amusement in his new burden, he thought to himself. The girl was almost as easy to bait as Edward.

"Mr. Laurence," said Fallow from the doorway,

and the Reverend Laurence Debenham walked into the room.

His brother greeted him cordially. "And here, you see," he added, "is little Anne back from school."

His tone made this introduction almost insulting, and Laurence frowned at him before coming to shake Anne's hand. "How are you?" he said. "I am very pleased to see you home. And may I say that I am exceedingly sorry I never visited your school. If I had known—"

"Anne does not wish to talk of school," said Charles. "You are being clumsy, Laurence. You should rather compliment her on her gown. She has been up to London adorning herself for our meeting."

This was too close to the mark for comfort. Anne colored a little and looked down. There was no one on earth as abominable as Charles, she decided. She remembered that odiously mocking tone only too well.

"To…to London?" Laurence seemed at a loss. "Well, ah, to be sure, it is a lovely dress. You look very, er, striking, Anne."

"Fie, Laurence! A sickly compliment. You can do better than that."

"I know very well I am not pretty," Anne was goaded into saying. "You needn't make up compliments for *me*."

"No, you aren't," agreed Charles, causing Anne to draw herself up very straight. "But I am surprised to discover that you have a quality worth twice that.

Laurence was actually quite right. You are striking. You have a presence."

Before Anne could recover from her astonishment, Fallow came in to announce dinner. Lord Wrenley offered his arm, and she took it, still speechless. As they started toward the door, there was a scuffling sound from the corner of the room, and a raucous voice croaked, "For God's sake, get me a drink!"

The viscount stopped short and looked around. "What," he said, "was *that*?"

Anne gazed up at him, her chin high. "My parrot. Augustus."

"Your...parrot?"

She nodded.

"Does he often say such things?" inquired Laurence with concern.

"Oh...oh, no."

Lord Wrenley did not take his eyes from Anne's face, and she reddened slightly again under his amused and speculative gaze.

"Because, you know, it could be dashed embarrassing," continued Laurence. "And not fit for your ears, besides."

"Damn your eyes!" exclaimed Augustus.

"Here, now, really. Where did you get that bird, Anne? You must have been grossly deceived. We will dispose of it for you, won't we, Charles?"

Before Anne could voice the protest that rose hotly

to her lips, the viscount said, "Dispose of Anne's pet? Whatever can you be thinking of, Laurence?"

"But...but the thing...Anne can't have known..."

Lord Wrenley met the girl's eyes once again. "Oh, I think she did. I believe you underestimate her, Laurence."

"But, Charles..."

Anne frowned uneasily up at the viscount.

"Blighter!" screeched Augustus emphatically.

Three

THE FOLLOWING AFTERNOON, LADY ANNE SAT ALONE in the drawing room at Wrenley, her expression profoundly thoughtful. It now appeared to her that she had been inadequately prepared for her homecoming, and she had retired here to order her impressions of the past evening and morning and, if possible, to revise her plan of campaign. Charles was out, and Laurence had returned to his own home at the village rectory. She did not expect to be disturbed.

For some time, the only sound was the ticking of the clock on the mantel. Anne stared blindly up at it, chewing on her lower lip, an aid to concentration which had been repeatedly condemned at Millington, without noticeable effect. At last she rose and began to pace about the room. Her sudden movement startled Augustus in the corner, and he squawked.

The girl walked over to his cage. "That's all very well," she told the bird, "but I am not certain now that you will serve, you know."

The parrot gazed at her from one malignant green eye.

"Charles was amused by you," continued his mistress. "I swear it was amusement. And I am not trying to amuse him. Quite the contrary!"

"Give us a drink, sweetheart," urged Augustus.

Anne smiled. "Yes, well, perhaps you are comic. But I did not expect Charles to think so. If I am to give him his own again, as I am *determined* to do after the way he has treated me, I must find some other methods. The matter is more complicated than I realized."

"Lackwit!" screeched the parrot.

Anne grimaced at him. "Unfair! How was I to know anything, after being shut up for years and years at school? It is true I visited the Castletons, but I never met anyone like Charles *there*." She paced a bit more. "I admit I am at a stand. I don't see just how I should proceed. The thing to do is draw back a little and consider and observe. It will take a bit longer, but I shall find a way to show Charles." She smiled thinly. "Indeed, I shall."

Augustus merely croaked in response.

"Laurence is kinder, I think," mused Anne. "I believed him when he said he would have come to visit me. And he never teased as much as Edward. I shall leave him alone." She put an elbow on the mantelshelf and leaned there. "He is engaged, you know. He promised to bring his fiancée to call on me as soon as possible. He hoped we will be great friends. Isn't that kind of him? Miss Branwell is going to London for the season also."

Augustus, profoundly uninterested, was cracking seeds from his dish and scattering husks over the carpet.

"Yes," finished Anne. "I shall wait until we are settled in London before I make my big push. By then I should know what is best to do."

Hearing footsteps approaching the room, she removed her elbow from the mantel and went quickly to an armchair. Fallow came in, looking concerned. "Excuse me, my lady, but a, er, visitor has arrived, and I am not quite certain…"

Fallow was never uncertain in the matter of visitors. "Who is it?" asked Anne curiously.

"It is a…a lady. She gave her name as Mariah Postlewaite-Debenham. She said she had no card. I was not informed…"

"Oh, that is Charles's second cousin. She is to be my chaperone. He told me last night. But she is not supposed to arrive until next week. I'm sure he meant to tell you."

"Indeed. Perhaps she mistook the date." Fallow was clearly offended by his accidental ignorance.

"She must have. Bring her up here. I shall welcome her alone."

"Yes, my lady."

In a few moments, he returned, followed by one of the tiniest women Anne had ever seen. Mariah Postlewaite-Debenham could not have been even five feet in height, and her other dimensions were correspondingly slight. Rising and holding out her hand, Anne felt a giant. Her new chaperone had the Debenham coloring, a bit faded now, but not the nose. She wore a very plain gown of buff kerseymere, and in general looked like the sort of self-effacing, quiet person who is never remembered from one meeting to the next. Her manner as she looked about the room, a combination of vague surprise and disinterest, merely added to this impression.

"Good day," said Anne. "I am Anne Tremayne. Welcome to Wrenley."

Miss Postlewaite-Debenham raised pale gray eyes to hers. "Thank you, dear," she replied in an unexpectedly collected tone. "I am earlier than I said I would be, but the blight killed my pansies, and I saw no reason to linger."

"Oh. Ah…of course. Sit down, please."

"Well, for a moment, perhaps. But I want to walk around the park before teatime. Lord Wrenley said there were some remarkable perennial beds. Indeed, he assured me one was at least fifty years old." She drifted over to the front windows and looked earnestly out, as if in search of this fabulous bed.

"D-did he? I take it you are interested in gardening, ma'am?"

Miss Postlewaite-Debenham waved this aside as if unanswerable. "Call me Mariah, dear. You will have to. Postlewaite-Debenham is such a ridiculous mouthful. I always thought poor Mama misguided when she insisted upon it. And now I think I will go out, if you will excuse me."

"But...that is...wouldn't you like to see your room, or...or anything?"

The older woman seemed to really look at Anne for the first time. "What is the matter, dear?" she asked kindly. "You seem uneasy."

Anne, utterly disconcerted by this time, merely stared at her.

"Didn't Lord Wrenley speak to you about me?" continued the other.

"Oh, yes. He told me you would be my chaperone for the season, and that you were his cousin."

"Tch. He promised me that he would explain my position before I arrived. It was clearly agreed upon."

Fascinated, Anne could not stop staring at her diminutive companion. "Perhaps he meant to do so. We did not expect you until..."

"Yes, I see how it was. Well, it is vexing to have to repeat it all again, but I suppose it can't be helped." With a regretful glance out the window, Mariah walked over to the sofa and sat down. "Now, you mustn't be offended by what I am about to tell you, dear, because it has nothing to do with you, but as I told Lord Wrenley, I was very reluctant to leave my own house and come to stay with you in town. Indeed, I refused, until he insisted he could find no one else. I do understand that you must have a chaperone, and I am prepared to do my best for one season—no more. I am not fond of company; my garden is enough to content me, as I think it might anyone. And I came only on the understanding that I should be free to bring some of my plants and things along and tend them for part of each day."

"In...in London?" managed Anne.

"Lord Wrenley promised to set aside a room for my plants in his town house. It is very awkward, of course, but I must do my duty to the family. I have made arrangements for some of my things to be taken there after we arrive."

"I...I see. I apologize for being the unconscious cause of..."

"No, no. You mustn't feel that way. But it is best to have everything clear, is it not?"

Anne nodded. "Do you mean to accompany me to parties and...and that sort of thing?"

"I shall do whatever is necessary," replied Mariah Postlewaite-Debenham in the voice of a much-tried martyr.

"Th-thank you." Anne was by now exerting every effort not to laugh.

"But as I told Lord Wrenley, I will not spend half my days primping and trying on gowns. You must take me as I am."

With this, at least, Anne was wholly in sympathy. "I shall certainly do that," she replied.

Mariah surveyed her approvingly. "There! We shall

get on very well, I'm sure. You seem a sensible girl. Are you at all interested in gardening?"

"I fear I have never done any."

"Yes, but would you like to, that's the point?"

The fanatic light in her eye made Anne cautious. "I really think I prefer riding," she answered meekly.

"Horses? I see." Her tone implied that she saw a great deal, and did not much care for the vision. "Well, I must go out to the park. If I don't return in time for tea, send someone after me, dear. I am always forgetting the time."

Thinking this an ominous trait in a chaperone, Anne nodded. "Shall I ask Fallow to summon the head gardener to show you about?"

"The head gardener?" tittered Mariah. "No indeed! I haven't yet come to *that*." And before Anne could do more than wonder what she could possibly mean, she was gone.

The girl sat down with a bump. "Well, Augustus, what do you think of my chaperone? It will be an interesting season."

The parrot, uncharacteristically, said nothing.

By teatime, Anne was feeling rather bored. Charles had not come in, and there had been no further sign of Mariah. For a girl accustomed to having a large group of young ladies to talk to, it seemed a very slow afternoon. Anne resolved to ask Charles about a mount as soon as possible. She would not mope about in this foolish fashion another day. And immediately after tea, she would take a brisk walk.

With Fallow and the tea tray came diversion, however, in the form of Laurence Debenham, his fiancée, Lydia Branwell, and Lydia's mother. Anne was at first delighted. Laurence had painted a glowing picture of Lydia at dinner the previous evening, and Miss Branwell initially seemed to justify it completely. She was a fine-looking girl, not as tall as Anne, but above medium height and with a better figure. Her hair was a lustrous black and her skin very pale. She held herself well up, a habit that her arched brows and aquiline nose seemed to emphasize. Her eyes were an alert hazel.

They all sat down, and Anne moved, a bit uncertainly, to pour the tea. Indeed, she had almost asked Mrs. Branwell to perform this service, but the older woman sank into her chair with such self-effacing timidity that she changed her mind. Laurence, after a quick glance about the room, was at once up again and striding toward Augustus's corner. "Is this the cover for the cage?" he asked after a moment's search.

He looked so uneasy that Anne had to suppress a smile. She nodded.

"Laurence tells me," said Miss Branwell, "that your parrot has been taught some, ah, indelicate expressions." Her voice was low and musical, and she spoke slowly, carefully enunciating each word.

"I fear he has," agreed Anne. "I…I hope I may wean him from them."

Lydia Branwell shook her head sadly. "I *so*

disapprove of that sort of thing. Men have a duty to treat dumb animals with consideration and restraint. I think there should be laws against abusing them; those who do so deserve prison."

"You are always so tenderhearted, Lydia," said Laurence, coming back to his chair. The two exchanged a tender smile.

Anne looked from one to the other. Laurence had told her that Lydia was the daughter of the bishop in the neighboring cathedral town. Certainly the Branwells' clothing, along with other remarks Laurence had made, showed that they were a wealthy family. It was in all respects a fine match. And Laurence seemed to care for the girl. But Anne was beginning to feel certain doubts. "Do you think it brutal," she asked, "to teach a bird a few warm phrases?" She smiled slightly.

"Indeed, yes," replied Lydia, leaning earnestly forward. "Both brutal and malicious. Not only is one corrupting an innocent creature; one is thereby making it an instrument for the corruption of mankind. That is very, very wrong."

"But a parrot does not understand what he says," argued Anne, becoming a bit interested in the subject. "How, then, can one call him corrupted? He speaks in all innocence, whatever he says."

Lydia smiled pityingly at her, then looked at Laurence with wide eyes. "We poor women must admit our ignorance of these complex ethical questions," she said sweetly, "and appeal to one who can settle the matter. What do you think, Laurence?"

"I think you are perfectly right," responded Reverend Debenham.

Lydia turned back to Anne with a triumphant smile.

The corners of Anne's mouth turned down. "How far is your house from us?" she asked Mrs. Branwell, pointedly turning away from the others. "I have not yet visited the town."

Lydia's mother looked almost frightened at being addressed. "Not far," she managed to reply. "About six miles."

"You had a lovely day for a drive."

Mrs. Branwell merely nodded, without raising her eyes again.

"What have you done this morning, Anne?" asked Laurence. "Have you found it difficult to amuse yourself at Wrenley? It is very different from school, I suppose."

"I have been a little restless," admitted Anne. "I mean to go riding tomorrow."

"It is strange," put in Lydia Branwell, "but I have never been bored in my life. I have heard people talk of boredom, but I really do not understand it. There are always a thousand useful tasks ready to hand. Or one can read."

This effectively stopped the conversation.

"Are you fond of reading, Lady Anne?" added the other girl after a short silence.

"Not particularly. My friends at school were always passing around some novel or other, but I never found them very interesting."

Lydia looked shocked. "I did not mean... That is..."

"Lydia does not read novels," explained Laurence.

His fiancée shook her head. "No, indeed... I would never... I was referring to *improving* books."

"I see," said Anne dryly.

"My father has just published a volume of his sermons," continued the other eagerly. "It is a truly uplifting work. I will send you a copy if you like."

"Oh, ah, thank you."

Miss Branwell smiled complacently. "I think you will find it far more useful than any novel."

"I'm sure I shall."

Something in Anne's tone made Laurence turn sharply to look at her. She saw it from the corner of her eye, but made no sign. However, her initial happiness at having visitors was fading rapidly. "I wonder what has become of Mariah?" she said. "I sent a footman after her a quarter hour ago."

"Mariah?" asked Laurence.

"Oh, yes. I forgot to tell you. Miss Mariah Postlewaite-Debenham arrived this morning, my chaperone."

"Did she indeed? How fortunate that she should be early."

Anne smiled.

"Did you like her?" added Laurence, seeing her expression.

"Yes indeed."

"But where has she gone? Why isn't she down to tea?"

"She is outside. It seems that she is fond of gardening, and she wanted to look over the park."

"Ah. I believe Charles did say something about that."

"I wager he did," murmured Anne.

"What?"

She shook her head, and was spared from answering further by sounds on the staircase outside. As these increased in volume, it was apparent that several persons were approaching, and in another moment Mariah herself stalked in, followed by Fallow and a young man in coarse homespuns.

Mariah marched directly up to Laurence. "Are you my cousin Charles?" she demanded. Without waiting for an answer, she added, "I wish to tell you that *this* young man"—she pointed to the youth behind Fallow, and he cringed—"has no more idea of trenching than a sparrow. I found him filling in a border which had not been dug more than six inches!"

Laurence goggled at her.

"And if you intend to keep your park in any sort of condition, you must *do* something," continued Mariah. "Shallow trenching is *ruinous*."

"I, ah..." Reverend Debenham swiveled an anguished eye to Fallow.

The butler rose to the challenge. "This is not Lord Wrenley," he said. "As I informed you, Lord Wrenley is out for the day. This is Mr. Laurence Debenham, rector of Wrenley church. Miss Postlewaite-Debenham, sir."

Mariah heaved a sigh. "And I suppose none of you cares a farthing about trenching. Well, I shall simply have to show the boy myself, then."

She turned as if to go away again. "Won't you have some tea first, Mariah?" asked Anne. "That can wait, surely."

"Wait?" The other's outrage was patent.

Once again, Fallow stepped into the breach. "If I might mention, ma'am. Jack has just started in the gardens this week. He is inexperienced. I am sure Ames, the head gardener, means to educate him in the proper method of, er, trenching."

Mariah snorted. "Head gardener! Stuff and nonsense."

Fallow drew himself up and stared coldly over the company's heads.

"Come, Mariah, do have some tea," coaxed Anne. "It will be dark soon in any case, and we have visitors."

After a visible struggle with herself, the other gave in and came toward them. As she sank into an armchair, Fallow drew the unfortunate gardener's boy out of the room. Anne furnished her chaperone with tea and bread and butter and introduced their callers. "Branwell?" responded Mariah. "Family of Bishop Branwell?"

"Yes," said Lydia eagerly. "He is my father."

Mariah sniffed. "I am sorry for you, then. The man's views are unsound, completely unsound."

Lydia sank back with a gasp, and Laurence stared.

"Thinks roses should be pruned twice a year," continued Mariah. "I saw his article in *The Horticultural Gazette*. Never read such poppycock. A good thorough pruning in the autumn is what roses want, not some lunatic half-measure in October and another dose in November. Idiocy!"

Lydia was obviously speechless with outrage, though she was showing signs of recovering her tongue. Laurence seemed stunned, and Mrs. Branwell was shrinking back in her chair as if terrified. "Well, Mariah," ventured Anne, "I suppose there are differences of opinion in matters of gardening, as in everything else. I know my teachers said—"

"Nonsense!" interrupted the other. "There is a right way and a wrong way, and that is that. The bishop should stick to what he knows. I don't tell him how to preach a sermon; he shouldn't try to tell me how to prune my roses." She laughed abruptly. "Particularly since he knows nothing whatsoever about the matter."

"My father has won prizes for his roses!" snapped Lydia. "They are considered the finest in the county."

Mariah shook her head. "That is one of the wonders of nature. Abuse plants as you will, often as not they blossom anyway."

Miss Branwell sprang to her feet. "I think it's time we went, Mother," she said loftily.

Laurence hurried to her side as her mother joined her. "Lydia, you mustn't take this too seriously. After all..."

With a look that would have withered the roses in question, she turned away from him. "Good day, Lady Anne. I am so pleased to have met you. We are leaving for London in three days, but I shall see you there, of course."

Anne had also risen, though Mariah kept her seat. "Yes indeed, I shall look forward to meeting again soon."

Lydia bowed her head majestically and departed, her mother and Laurence close on her heels.

"Unpleasant girl," said Mariah, reaching for another piece of bread and butter. "It was plain she knows nothing at all about roses."

"Perhaps you were a little harsh, however," suggested Anne.

Mariah fixed her with a disconcerting twinkle. "You mean rude. Well, I warned you. I told Charles I wouldn't make a proper chaperone. This is the sort of person I am, and you must make the best of it."

Anne, returning to her seat and pouring out another cup of tea, thought that that might be more difficult than she had first thought. She also wondered whether Laurence could *really* be in love with Lydia and, uneasily, whether Bishop Branwell was accompanying his wife and daughter to London.

Four

AT DINNER THAT EVENING, LORD WRENLEY FOREVER alienated his second cousin Mariah by informing her that he had no interest in trenching and did not care a fig how it was done in his park. When he referred her to the head gardener, Anne knew that all was lost, but Charles seemed blandly unaware of Mariah's outrage, as of her eccentricities, which he ignored. Anne had been curious to see how he would respond to her unconventional chaperone, but she was disappointed. Whatever his thoughts, he kept them to himself.

Near the end of the meal, he turned to her and said, "I had planned to go up to London next week, but since Miss Postlewaite-Debenham has arrived, I see no reason to delay. I suppose you are ready to go?"

"Yes indeed. I am eager."

"Good. The season will not really get started for another two or three weeks, but you will be able to fill your time, I imagine."

"I have several friends in town for their come-outs,"

she agreed. She eyed him. "And I can call on Miss Branwell, of course."

"I heard she had been here. By all means, call upon her."

Anne sensed mockery, though she could see no signs of it in his face. She became even more interested in his opinion of Laurence's fiancée. "Miss Branwell seems a very *sincere* girl."

Lord Wrenley raised one blond eyebrow, his gray eyes glinting. "How well you put it. She is, isn't she?"

Confident that he shared her doubts, Anne replied, "Do you think she and Laurence will suit? Really, I mean?"

He shrugged.

Thinking he hadn't fully understood her, Anne added, "I was wondering, that is, whether he will be truly happy with her."

"I think it extremely unlikely," answered the viscount in an indifferent tone.

The girl's gray-violet eyes widened. "You sound as if you didn't care."

"It is none of my affair if Laurence chooses to saddle himself with a simpering, self-righteous wife. *I* shan't see much of her, you may be sure."

"None of your affair? Your brother's happiness?" Anne was both astonished and outraged by this indifference. And she could not quite believe it, even of Charles. Though she had always understood that the Debenham brothers cared little for *her*, she had thought they loved each other.

Her emotion seemed to amuse Charles. "Laurence is a grown man. He is not, any longer, my responsibility. He must make of his life what he can."

"But you are older, more experienced. You should help him!"

The viscount's mouth turned down. "How do you suggest I do so? Tell him my opinion of his fiancée? I assure you he would not listen. In fact, he would be extremely annoyed."

"Not if you spoke to him properly."

Lord Wrenley sighed. "You have a distorted view of brotherly exchanges, Anne. You must take my word for it, Laurence would not brook my interference. Allow that I know more of my family than you."

This callous remark brought back all Anne's personal grievances. She pushed back her chair and rose. "You *should*," she cried. "You were allowed to live in it!" She picked up her skirts and ran from the dining room.

Mariah, who had been placidly eating a Chantilly creme through this exchange, looked up in time to see the door slam. She shook her head and turned to gaze at Charles. He looked exasperated. "You know as little about handling young girls as you do about gardening," she commented, rising from her place.

"No doubt," retorted the viscount bitterly. "And I can only say I was very happy in my ignorance."

"Indeed?" Mariah's gray eyes twinkled. "I wonder how long that will last." And she followed Anne out of the room.

Lord Wrenley, left to himself, rang for the port and, when it came, poured it out savagely. This was just what he had expected—his peace cut up by emotional scenes, his temper roused by foolish chatter, and his pleasant routine disrupted by annoying trivialities. His predictions about Anne's arrival had been dead on the mark. The only thing to do now was get to London as soon as possible, where he could hand her over to Laurence and Edward and wash his hands of the whole dreary matter.

The Debenham party set off for town four days later, making quite a caravan on the high road. Charles and Laurence rode. Anne and Mariah occupied the traveling chaise. And the servants and baggage took up two other vehicles behind. The viscount was irritable, and the others avoided him, but Laurence did everything in his power to make up for it by being pleasant and attentive to the ladies' wishes. He joined them for several stages in the chaise, and by the time they reached London, Anne felt she knew him fairly well, and liked him better.

They pulled up before the Debenham town house in the late afternoon. Anne had never seen it before and was curious about all its fittings. Since Charles disappeared as soon as they arrived, Laurence showed her over it, and she praised the light elegance of the furnishings until he said, "Yes, Charles has done a splendid job on the place. He has fine taste."

"Your mother did not decorate it?"

"Years ago, yes. But she rarely came to London after Father died, you know, so Charles had the place refurbished."

Just like him, thought Anne.

"Edward is coming over to dinner," continued the other, "so we shall have all the family together again."

"How touching," replied Anne. Her tone made Laurence glance sharply at her, and she hurriedly added, "How is Edward?"

"Well." He chuckled. "Very dashing. He is a captain in the Horse Guards, you know, and extremely pleased about it. He is well fitted for a military career."

"As you are for the church?" Anne watched him closely.

"I hope so," answered Laurence, surprised. "I do my best."

"Did Charles decide what you and Edward would do?"

"Charles?" He laughed a little. "No indeed. He sent us both off to Oxford with ample allowances and obvious relief and told us to choose a profession. I have never heard him remark on the outcome."

"He seems strangely uninterested in his family."

"Ah, well, it was a case of too much too soon, I suppose."

Anne frowned, not understanding, but before she could inquire further, a gong sounded below.

"We must change for dinner," added Laurence.

"That was the half hour bell. Can you find your way back to your bedchamber?"

"Oh, yes."

"Good. I will see you in the drawing room, then."

Anne walked slowly along the corridor to her room, thinking about Laurence. He seemed sincerely committed to the church; she had heard that in his voice, and she was glad. His kindness must make him a good clergyman. Anne frowned. But what about the influence of Miss Lydia Branwell? That would have to be investigated.

Anne changed into an evening dress of sea-green satin that was her favorite of all the dresses Mrs. Castleton's modiste had made for her. The skirt was cut in two tiers, to lessen her height, and lace softened the lines at the neck and sleeves. Crane rearranged her curls, threading a green ribbon through them, and clasped a pearl necklace around her throat. All in all, Anne was very satisfied with the reflection that looked back from the mirror when she was finished. It was, if not beautiful, extremely eye-catching.

She was the first down to the drawing room, so she walked over and lifted the cover off Augustus's cage. There had been a heated debate at Wrenley as to whether the parrot should accompany them to London. Laurence had argued against taking him with all his eloquence. But Charles had merely smiled, and Anne, who had grown unaccountably attached to the bird, had insisted he must be brought. Without support, Laurence had finally given in. But it had been agreed that Augustus's cage would be covered early each night, encouraging him to go to sleep rather than enliven the company with unsuitable comments. "How are you?" Anne asked him now. "Was the journey very uncomfortable?"

Augustus cocked his head and stared at her with one green eye.

"We shan't be traveling again for a long while," she assured him.

"Bacon-brain!" squawked the parrot cordially. "Rattle-pate. Numbskull."

"Good God," replied a male voice from the doorway. "My reputation has preceded me again."

Anne let the cage cover fall and turned to find a lanky blond Guards officer lounging against the jamb. "Edward."

"You see. You knew right away. I declare it is too bad of Charles and Laurence. They might have allowed me to make my own impression."

Anne laughed. "They did. Augustus is indiscriminate with his abuse, I assure you. He has said the same to Fallow."

"Has he, by Jove?" Edward strolled toward her. "I wish I might have seen that. But who is Augustus?"

She lifted the cloth again. "My parrot."

"Your…" Captain Debenham blinked at the bird, then stared at her. "But you can't be…that is…you are not *Anne*?"

She returned his gaze.

Very uncharacteristically, Edward flushed. "That is…of course, you must be. I should have seen it at once. But you look so… I thought you must be someone else…but then, the parrot… Anne *would* have…I mean…"

Anne fought a smile. "Talking of reputations preceding one, it seems I have the same problem."

With an engaging grin, Edward spread his hands. "I shan't try to redeem myself. I have never in my life made such a shocking blunder. But you have changed a good deal, you know." He surveyed her with more care and obvious approval. "You look splendid, in fact."

Something in his tone made Anne answer sweetly, "That must be a great relief to you."

"Yes, it… No, dash it, nothing of the kind."

Unable to restrain herself any longer, the girl burst into peals of laughter.

Edward grinned with relief. "I remember that laugh, at least. You may look different, but the old Anne is still there." He lifted the cage cover and peered in. "This bird is evidence of that."

"Bacon-brain!" screeched Augustus again.

"Very perceptive," agreed Lord Wrenley from the doorway. "The creature has more taste than I realized."

"He called *you* a heathen," Anne pointed out.

"No, did he really?" asked Edward. "And what did Charles do?" He dropped the cloth and joined the others in walking toward the fireplace.

"I very wisely ignored it," responded his brother, "realizing that a parrot can mean nothing when it speaks."

"That is not what Miss Branwell thinks." Anne grinned mischievously.

"Lord, have you met the Branwell already?" exclaimed Edward.

"I passed Laurence on the stairs," said Lord Wrenley, and in the next moment, the third Debenham brother indeed joined them. Anne flushed slightly. She hoped Laurence had not overheard her remark; its content had been inoffensive, but the tone was not.

"Well, here we all are," declared Edward.

"All but Cousin Mariah," agreed the viscount. "I wonder what can be keeping her."

"Cousin…? Oh, Anne's chaperone, eh? She here already?" Edward looked vaguely toward the door.

"In the house, yes," replied Charles caustically. "In the drawing room, obviously not."

His tone seemed exaggeratedly harsh to Anne. She looked from one to the other of the brothers, but none seemed surprised by the exchange.

In the next moment, Mariah joined them. "I am sorry to be late," she said as she walked in. "I was looking over the back parlor, the one you have given me for my plants, Charles, and I lost track of the time."

The viscount inclined his head briefly, then introduced Edward.

"Oh, yes," answered Mariah, holding out her hand. "You are the last of them. How do you do?"

Looking bemused, Captain Debenham shook her hand. "Very well, thank you."

She nodded absently and turned back to their host. "Are you certain that is the sunniest room in the house, Charles? The windows are not overlarge."

"No, the sunniest is the dining room, but you cannot have that."

Mariah's eyes narrowed, but then she shook her head regretfully. "No, I suppose that would be inconvenient."

"Very," agreed the viscount.

"Well, the parlor will have to do, then, but I shall have trouble with my borders."

"Your...borders?" echoed Edward, fascinated.

But just then, Fallow came in to announce dinner, and the subject was lost in the general exodus.

Anne found the meal a little strange. Her only real experience of family gatherings had been at the Castletons', and that noisy happy group was quite unlike the one around the Debenham table. Edward did laugh and joke, and Laurence kept up a stream of pleasant conversation, but the overall feeling of the occasion never matched the Castletons' warmth. Mariah remained distracted; she had brought a sheet of paper and a pencil to the table and was drawing arcane diagrams throughout dinner. And it seemed to Anne that Charles missed no opportunity to blight the others' efforts at conviviality. His smiles were all thin sarcastic ones and his remarks chilling. His presence seemed to cast a pall over both Edward and Laurence, in different ways. Laurence became more solemn than usual, and Edward more impudent and extravagant. By the time the ladies rose from the table, Anne felt she had a great deal to think over.

Since returning home, her ideas on a number of subjects had undergone revision. She still resented the way Charles had treated her, but she now realized that it had not been a personal vendetta. He was the same with his own brothers. And the whole family was shadowed by it. Something, decided Anne, ought to be done. But she did not know precisely what, or even where to begin finding out. Only one thing was clear to her: her own view had been narrow. She must observe and ponder before she would truly understand the Debenhams, or her own position among them.

The gentlemen joined them in the drawing room after a short interval. As he walked in, Edward said, "What are the plans for the season, Anne? You are to have a ball, of course."

"I don't know. We haven't discussed it." She looked to Lord Wrenley.

"A ball, certainly. In three or four weeks' time. I thought to leave the date to you."

"And the arrangements?" asked Edward maliciously.

"Will be put in competent hands."

"Not yours?"

"No, Edward, not mine." Lord Wrenley eyed his youngest brother with sardonic amusement.

"Well, you can't expect Anne to organize her own ball," persisted Captain Debenham.

"I'll wager I could," said Anne.

"No doubt," responded Charles, "but you will be far too busy to do so. Mrs. Brigham and Fallow are quite capable of handling the household arrangements, and Laurence will compile the guest list."

The latter looked up in surprise. "I?"

"No, let me do it, Charles," said Edward, his gray eyes sparkling.

"Laurence," repeated the viscount. "You are free to offer suggestions, but the final decision is his."

"But, Charles, I really don't think—"

"I'm sure you'll do a splendid job," finished Lord Wrenley.

Laurence grimaced, but dropped the subject.

"I'll help you," said Anne. "There are some friends I want to ask."

"What else have you planned, Charles?" asked Edward. "Have you thought of Almack's and that sort of nonsense?"

Lord Wrenley sighed, casting a fleeting glance at Mariah, who was still busy with her diagrams. "That must certainly be attended to. I'll speak to Sally Jersey. And I suppose we will have other entertainments." His tone clearly conveyed his weary distaste for this prospect. "Perhaps the three of you can decide that amongst yourselves."

Edward nodded. "I know one thing Anne will

want—a horse. I will take you riding in the park as soon as you are mounted, Anne."

"I should like that. Where may I get one?"

"Well, Charles may have something in his stables?" He looked to his brother, who shook his head. "No? I'll take you to Tattersall's, then, and you may choose something you like."

"Perhaps you could perform that service yourself," said Lord Wrenley.

"Yes, but I thought Anne might wish to pick her own mount."

"Indeed, I do!"

Seeing the light of battle in her eyes, the viscount shrugged and turned away. "As you like. But it is unusual for young girls to go to Tattersall's."

"I'll be with her," objected Captain Debenham.

"Precisely."

"I'm sure Lydia will be eager to see you," put in Laurence hastily. "I will take you to call tomorrow, if you wish. And I know the Branwells plan an evening party very soon. We will all receive invitations."

Edward groaned, earning glares from Laurence and Anne and a thin smile from Lord Wrenley. "Of course I will call," answered Anne with a real attempt at enthusiasm.

"But we are to go to Tattersall's tomorrow!"

"Oh, yes. Well, the next day, then, Laurence."

He bowed slightly. "Of course."

Anne remembered something. "Is Bishop Branwell

in town with his family?" she asked softly, so as not to attract Mariah's notice.

"Why, yes. You will have the chance to meet him when we call."

She frowned a bit as she nodded.

"He is a very learned man."

"And a prosy bore," added Captain Debenham.

"Edward!"

"It's the truth, Laurence. The man's a plague; they say so at his own club."

"'They' being your friends, I suppose? I am not surprised to hear that a pack of empty-headed rattles speak of the bishop in those terms."

"A leveler, Edward," commented the viscount, looking from one to the other with the air of a man watching a mildly interesting boxing match.

"Lord Alvanley says so," retorted Edward. "*He* is not a rattle."

"No, he is one of a set who ought to know better than to behave as frivolously as they do."

"Charles knows him well!"

"No, no, don't try to drag me into this," protested Lord Wrenley. "I declare neutral status."

Edward, who was becoming truly incensed, responded with another gibe, and Anne watched the three of them with astonishment and discomfort. How could they talk so to one another? It was wholly unbrotherly. Yet she also had the sense that it was not uncommon. They all seemed to have fallen into habitual roles, and none appeared disturbed by the pattern. As she listened to their continuing hot debate, Anne nearly winced. This was not right! And later, when the group had broken up and she lay in bed, the girl determined that the Debenhams must be shown the wrongness of their conduct. And since it seemed no one else was available to show them, it was up to her.

Five

ANNE WAS AWAKENED AT AN UNREASONABLY EARLY hour the following morning by heavy tramping on the stairs below. She lay in bed for a while, listening, and expecting the noise to cease, but it did not, so finally she rose, put on a dressing gown, and went out on the landing. Looking over the rail, she could see the entire spiral of the staircase; it was empty. But the steady sound continued. "Can it be the back stairs?" wondered Anne. It was very odd that she should hear anything from so far away. But she walked along the corridor to the rear of the house, opened a door there, and walked out onto the landing of the back stairs. The noise immediately intensified.

Peering over this rail, Anne could see two men trudging up the steps far below her. Each carried a large sack over his back. As she watched, the leader reached the first floor and disappeared through the doorway there. But another man appeared to replace him at the very bottom of the stairs, also bearing a sack. "Whatever can they be delivering?" said Anne aloud. "And so early?"

"It's for Miss Pos...Miss Deb... It's for the older lady," replied a voice above her. Anne looked up sharply and saw a young housemaid leaning over the rail of the upper landing. She held a feather duster.

"They are delivering something to Miss Postlewaite-Debenham?" she asked. "But what?"

"I don't know, miss. My lady, I mean. I heard Fallow speak to Mrs. Brigham. Proper put out, he was. He told her the men would be coming today with the delivery. I didn't hear any more because I had to come up to do the dusting."

Anne looked over the rail again. The parade of delivery men continued. The bags they carried were really very large, and they looked extremely heavy.

Absently thanking the maid, Anne returned to her own room. She dressed as quickly as possible, not bothering to do more than run a comb through her red-gold curls, and hurried downstairs. On the first floor, she started back toward the rear, where she had seen the men enter, but she did not have to go all the way to the back stairs. From the corridor she saw that the deliveries were being taken to one of the parlors, and she followed them there.

She heard Mariah's voice before she saw her. "Yes," she was saying. "Empty it there and go for another. We ought to have more help; this is terribly slow."

Anne came to the parlor doorway and looked in.

Her eyes widened, and she stood stock-still. A very large pile of earth sat in the far corner of the room, and the man she had followed in was even now adding to it from the sack on his back. Mariah stood nearby, watching him critically. She wore a worn old muslin gown and a broad apron, and she held a rake.

"Excuse me, miss," said a diffident male voice behind Anne. She started and turned. Another servant, with a sack, was waiting to come in. She moved hastily into the room and out of his path. He trudged to the pile of soil and began to empty his bag onto it.

"Mariah, what are you doing?" said Anne.

The older woman noticed her and nodded. "Good morning, my dear. You are up early. I am beginning on my garden, as you can see."

"But…but…" Anne could not seem to frame a coherent sentence. She merely stared at the accumulation of earth. It was nearly four feet high, and the base covered a circle ten feet in diameter.

Mariah was making it larger with her rake. "Yes, dear?" she responded absently.

"A-all this dirt." Anne gestured. "What are you going…why are you putting it on the floor?"

Mariah stopped raking and turned to stare at her. "I can't grow anything without soil, Anne."

"N-no. But…I mean…I thought you would have pots with plants in them. Like…like a conservatory."

"Indeed not. That sort of planting is not at all good for the roots. They are constricted, and very often overwatered as well. No, it is much better to have open soil." As Anne continued to stare incredulously at her, Mariah frowned. "What is the matter? I had them remove all the furniture, and the carpet, of course. And we have covered the floor and the lower walls with oilcloth." She pointed. "They won't be harmed. I shall need only two feet of soil throughout the room. And I shall carefully block up the doorway to that height so that none falls into the corridor. I planned this all very carefully, Anne."

The girl swallowed. "Does...does Charles know about it?"

"Naturally. You know he does. He promised me a garden; I should not have come to London otherwise." Another workman entered, and she added, "Start piling it over there now, please." She indicated the other corner. "I will rake the piles smooth in the middle." The man nodded and went to empty his sack of earth; Mariah watched him complacently. "This goes slowly," she said. "I had not realized how long it would take. But I believe we can finish today. And then tomorrow I can begin putting in the plants. If only there were more light."

Anne looked up at the six broad windows, three on each of the back walls. With the hangings removed, they seemed to her to let in a flood of sunlight.

"Can't be helped," Mariah went on. "I'll put the shade plants in the front corner. I do hope it will serve. Was there something else you wanted, dear?"

Anne shook her head slowly.

"Well, then, I must get back to work. I shall be here all day if you need me." And she took up her rake once more.

Feeling slightly dazed, Anne walked away. At the front stairs, she paused, shook her head as if to clear it, and considered. It was no good going back to her room; she was fully awake now. She might as well have breakfast.

❧

Laurence was at the breakfast table. There was no sign of Charles. "Good morning, Anne," he said pleasantly when she entered. He rose and pulled out a chair for her. "You are up betimes. Are you an early riser, like me?"

"We always had to get up early at school," replied Anne, avoiding any mention of what had wakened her today.

"Ah, yes. A splendid habit, I think. I am always telling Charles so, but he refuses to leave his room before ten."

"D-does he?" She glanced at the mantel clock. It was only eight. Charles would not discover Mariah's activities for two hours, by which time she should be well along. She felt a twinge of amusement as well as a nagging apprehension. What would he do? She vowed to be on hand to see his reaction.

"Tea or coffee?" asked Laurence.

Anne pulled her chair closer to the table. Suddenly she was hungry. "Tea, please. And are those scones? I'll have one, and the jam."

Smiling, Laurence supplied these. "What time do you go to Tattersall's with Edward?"

"At eleven. Uh, Laurence, didn't you notice the noise this morning?"

"Noise?"

"Yes. On the back stairs. I heard tramping."

He shook his head. "The servants must have been carrying something up. I'll speak to them if you like. But my room is at the front of the house, next to Charles's. I would not hear anything quieter than a gunshot on the back stairs."

Anne nodded as she spread strawberry jam thickly over a hot scone.

"Do you want me to inquire about it?" asked Laurence curiously.

"Oh, no. It was nothing. Do you go to see Miss Branwell today?"

"Yes. This morning."

"Please give her my regards, and say I will call soon. When is your wedding to be; have you set a date?"

This diversion was so successful that Laurence talked of nothing but his plans through the rest of the meal, and by the time they separated in the hall, he was feeling very much in charity with Anne. His brothers never asked about Lydia. Indeed, if they spoke of her at all, it was slightingly. It was very pleasant to talk with someone who valued her as she deserved, and did not force one to defend her.

Anne returned to her room, to receive a scold from Crane for leaving it without ringing, and in a state, if one was to believe the maid, of complete and disgraceful disarray. The girl endured a lengthy rearrangement of her hair, a change of footgear, and the retying of the sash on her white sprigged-muslin gown, but then she sent Crane away and sat down at her writing desk to compose a note to Arabella Castleton. She longed to see Bella again, and she wanted to let her know she had arrived in town.

She made sure to finish well before ten, however, and a quarter hour before that time, she walked quietly down the stairs again and slipped into the drawing room, which was just down the corridor from Mariah's parlor. She wanted to be on hand for whatever happened when Charles came down.

She was greeted by a harsh squawk from Augustus. "Oh dear," she exclaimed. "Poor Augustus, I almost forgot you. Has someone given you breakfast?" She hurried over to look in his cage. "Yes. That's good."

"How about a drink, lass?" suggested the parrot.

Anne smiled. "You have water right in front of you. And it's far too early for anything else."

The bird repeated his request, and Anne laughed. "What am I to do with you? I begin to think I should have left you in that shop. I daresay you had more company there." She looked at Augustus; he stared back from one green eye. "I know. I will put you in Mariah's garden when she has finished it. You will like that. There will be green plants and a great deal of sunshine. I'll hang your cage in the window, where you can look out at the street."

"Damn your eyes!" replied Augustus.

"I must say I can see his point of view," added a voice from the doorway. "It sounds like a wearisome sort of existence."

Anne whirled to face Lord Wrenley. Clothed in impeccable town dress, he lounged against the doorjamb.

"I wager he would be far more content here," continued the viscount, "where he can shock the company. I do believe he enjoys that."

"I thought you would be glad to have him out of the way," answered Anne somewhat defensively.

"Ah, you were moving him for my sake? I am touched."

She glared at him. Charles's sarcastic tone never failed to anger her. Its careless mockery made it so clear that he did not care a straw for the person he spoke to. "I was thinking of Augustus," she retorted, "not you."

One side of his mouth turned up, and he bowed slightly. It was almost too easy to provoke Anne. But before he could speak again, they were both startled by a great thump which shook the very floor of the drawing room. "What the devil?" said Charles. He turned to look down the corridor as Anne hurried toward him. "What are you doing, man?" he added.

Peering around the door, Anne saw one of Mariah's workmen on his knees in the center of the hall carpet. He had dropped his burden, the sack had split, and moist earth now covered a sizable portion of the corridor. "B-beg pardon, sir," muttered the workman miserably. "It…it slipped out of me hands."

"What the deuce was it doing *in* your hands in my house?" asked Charles. "That is dirt, is it not? Good God!"

The workman cringed. "It is for Mariah's garden," put in Anne, hoping to spare him any further berating.

"I beg your pardon?"

The girl merely pointed to the parlor where Mariah worked. Charles strode toward it, a set expression on his handsome features. Anne followed more slowly. She watched him reach the parlor doorway, pause, then clench his fists and disappear inside. She hurried to the door and stationed herself there.

"Cousin Mariah," said the viscount, "what in God's name do you think you are doing?"

Mariah did not even stop raking. "I am preparing my garden, of course," she answered.

Anne saw Charles's back stiffen alarmingly; his fists grew even tighter. When he spoke, his voice held such exaggerated control that she was almost frightened. "You are planning to spread earth over this entire room?"

"Yes. I cannot have proper plantings without that." Mariah seemed to catch something of his mood. "You agreed that I should have a garden, Charles. It was a condition of my coming here."

"I had no idea you intended to fill my house with filth!" he exploded.

Mariah leaned on her rake and raised her slender blond brows. Charles towered over her. "That is fortunate, for you would have been quite mistaken. I have no such intention. Once this is planted, you will see nothing but green in this room."

"I shall see nothing but what was here before," snapped Lord Wrenley. "I want all of this…this"—he gestured, at a loss for words in his rage—"out of here at once. Do you understand me?"

Mariah nodded, unimpressed. "Clearly. I shall pack my bags at once."

Charles glared at her.

"That was our agreement," added Mariah placidly.

At this moment, Laurence came in, attracted by the shouting, and stopped beside Anne. After a wondering glance around the room, he said, "What is it? What is happening?"

"Mariah was making her garden," whispered Anne, "and Charles doesn't approve."

"I daresay he doesn't," replied Laurence feelingly.

"Our agreement is ended," said Lord Wrenley. "If I had known what you meant to do, I should never have made it. This is intolerable. Do you realize that the weight of this earth could damage the floor or even the supporting structure of the whole house?"

"I calculated the weight," responded Mariah, "and asked a builder about it. He said it would not."

The viscount made a peculiar sound, like a seltzer bottle about to burst. "I don't care what he said. I want this *out*!"

Mariah nodded. "I will see that it is removed before I leave."

Laurence went over to his brother. "Charles," he murmured, "you told us that Mariah was the only suitable chaperone you could find. I know she is not precisely what we would wish. But—"

"You are a master of understatement," interrupted Charles, "as well as a damned nuisance. I don't care what I said. I'll find someone else."

"Yes…but, Charles, you told us that your man of business had searched everywhere, and there was no one else."

The viscount ground his teeth. Mariah watched him with mild interest. Anne struggled between nervousness at the anger in his face and a desire to giggle.

"The deuce!" he burst out at last. "Leave it, then. What does it matter? My peace is entirely cut up as it is; one more annoyance will make no difference." He glared at Mariah again. "But if I see so much as a crumb of earth anywhere else in the house…"

"We shall be very tidy," said Mariah.

Lord Wrenley let out an enraged breath, turned on his heel, and stalked out. They heard him say, "Get out of my way, you," in the corridor, and then he was gone.

"Whew!" breathed Laurence. "I haven't seen Charles that angry since Edward took out his favorite gun without leave."

"A disgraceful exhibition of temper," agreed Mariah. "And over nothing at all."

Laurence opened his mouth to reply, but no words came out. Unable to control herself any longer, Anne started to laugh. The man turned to stare at her, even more incredulous, then slowly smiled. In another moment, he too was laughing, though with more nervousness than humor, Anne thought. "It is rather ridiculous," he murmured.

"Completely," agreed the girl.

"But Charles had some grounds…"

"Oh, yes."

Laurence sobered. "I wonder how we shall get through the season," he added. Before Anne could reply, Fallow came in to announce that Edward had come to take her to Tattersall's.

When Edward asked her, as they drove through the busy streets in his phaeton, how her morning had been, Anne could not resist telling him the full story of Mariah's garden. His reaction was much less cautious than Laurence's. He threw back his head and roared with laughter until Anne had to beg him to keep a better watch for pedestrians. "If I could have seen Charles's face," he gasped, "I would have paid a guinea—ten guineas—to have been there."

Anne gazed curiously across at him. "Don't you

like your brother? You always seem so pleased when he is annoyed."

Captain Debenham's grin did not fade, but he raised his blond eyebrows a little. "It's not a question of liking. It's just that Charles has had his own way so much, I enjoy seeing him thwarted now and then. I think it's good for him."

"Has he?"

"What?"

"Had his own way?"

"Well, of course he has. You know it as well as I. He took charge when Father died; Mama couldn't manage. He has been the head of the family since then."

"I wonder if he wished to be?" Edward stared at her, and Anne flushed a little. "It is just that I met the head of Arabella's family—her uncle Thomas—once, and he seemed to take great pleasure in his position. He meddled in everyone's affairs and tried to tell them what profession to take up and whom to marry. Yet Charles... Did he tell you to go into the army?"

"Are you joking? I have wanted that since I was in short coats."

"Have you?" Anne looked wistful. "I never knew. But you see, Charles does not act at all like Arabella's uncle. In fact, he seems to want nothing more than to be rid of all of us. You and me and Laurence, I mean."

Edward considered this, then shrugged. "Well, it don't make a particle of difference."

"But, Edward, it is very..." She stopped abruptly.

Her companion frowned. "Are you up to something, Anne? I know you're all grown up, and looking fine as fivepence, but I'd swear you haven't changed *that* much. I've seen that look in your eye—the one that means you're plotting mischief."

"Edward!"

"Oh, don't play the innocent; I *know* you. Indeed, Anne, I remember better than the others how you used to be. We shared a nursery for three years. So you needn't try to bamboozle me."

"Bamboozle? What does that mean?" She tried the word on her tongue again, and found it good.

"Oh, Lord, now they'll say I'm teaching you slang. You know perfectly well what it means, and you shan't do it to me."

Anne spread her hands. "Edward, I don't know what you mean."

He looked at her through narrowed eyes. "I don't care what you're up to, see, as long as you leave me out of it. You can do what you like with Charles and Laurence. Be good for them. But not me. Anyway, you'll have enough to occupy you with your come-out and finding yourself a…" He shut his mouth with a snap and reddened.

Anne grinned. "A husband?" she finished.

Edward scowled. "Not what I was going to say."

"Indeed it was. And you are right; it will be a great work. But as long as I am about it, perhaps I shall find you a wife as well." She looked sidelong at him.

"Me?" he gasped. "Good God, no!"

Anne began to laugh. "Why not? You are older than I, after all."

"That's different. Anne, swear to me that you will not try any such thing—or even think about it. The deuce! I never dreamed—"

"But, Edward," she interrupted teasingly, "you might *like* being married."

"I should as soon be shipped to the eastern plantations. Sooner! Anne, promise that you will *not*—"

"Is that Tattersall's?" asked the girl innocently, pointing to that establishment as they sped past it.

Cursing, Edward yanked back on the reins, and in the confusion that followed his attempt to turn the phaeton in the crowded street, their conversation lapsed.

Six

THE FOLLOWING MORNING WAS TO BE DEVOTED TO social calls. Mariah remained completely engrossed in her "garden," but Anne and Laurence set out at ten to visit the Branwells and the Castletons. Anne was in high spirits during the short drive, for Charles had informed her at the breakfast table that the Debenham group would attend the first evening party of the season that very night. Not even the prospect of seeing Lydia Branwell again could dampen her enthusiasm. "I wonder if Arabella is going," she said as they rode. "I can hardly wait to ask her."

Laurence, who had by this time heard all about Miss Castleton, was forced to admit ignorance. "Lydia and her mother will be present, I know," he offered.

"Oh. Splendid."

"There is to be music, and Lydia is passionately fond of music."

"I would have predicted that."

Laurence smiled. "She is a sensitive creature, is

she not? Charles and Edward will never see her true value."

"Well, I am not yet intimately acquainted with her, but I am sure you are right."

"You saw how distressed she was when Cousin Mariah criticized her father. She told me later that she nearly burst into tears."

Privately thinking that it had looked more like rage, Anne nodded.

"Lydia takes a great deal on herself, you know. Her mother is…not particularly interested in the bishop's work. Lydia helps him instead; indeed, it has kept her from many of the amusements common to young girls. She is extremely dedicated."

"Well, I am happy that she is to have a season in London, then. It sounds as if she deserves it."

"Oh, yes. Her father insisted."

Laurence sounded slightly dissatisfied, and Anne determined to examine Lydia Branwell carefully this morning. If, as she suspected, the bishop's daughter was false, she would make a real effort to show Laurence the truth. After that, he could make his own decisions.

The Branwells had hired a house near Berkeley Square. Anne and Laurence were admitted by a stately butler and taken directly up to the drawing room, where Lydia and her mother awaited them. Lydia rose as soon as they entered, and came forward with outstretched hands. "My dear Lady Anne," she cried, taking both of Anne's hands and pressing them gently.

"How wonderful to see you again. I have longed for your arrival."

"Thank you," replied Anne, extricating her fingers as politely as possible.

"It will be so good to meet someone with whom one can have a rational conversation at these endless *ton* parties," continued the other, tossing her black curls. "I find them unbearably tedious. All that gossip and empty chatter."

"Laurence!" exclaimed Anne. "Have you been gossiping to Miss Branwell? For shame!"

Lydia stared blankly at her, but Laurence smiled. "I hope Lydia excludes me from her denunciation." Seeing his fiancée's bewilderment, he added, "It was a joke, Lydia. Anne is bamming us."

"Oh. Oh, of course." Miss Branwell smiled thinly. "Very amusing. Laurence has told me about your lively sense of humor, Lady Anne."

"He flatters me."

"What have you done since you arrived in town?" asked Lydia, shifting the subject away from dangerous ground.

"Well, it has been only two days." Anne thought of Mariah's garden. She would not mention that to this girl. "I have bought some horses."

"Horses?"

"Yes, Edward took me to Tattersall's yesterday. I bought the sweetest little mare you can imagine for riding in the park, and I could not resist two hunters.

They were so fine-looking. Great shoulders and strong hocks. How I should like to try them at a fence."

"You...you hunt, then?" Lydia sounded rather as if she were asking about some indelicate eccentricity.

"Whenever I have the opportunity. I am very much hoping to get an invitation to Leicestershire this winter."

"From whom?"

"Anyone with a house in the neighborhood of the Quorn." Anne grinned.

"I shall have to see that you meet Lady Ellis." Laurence laughed. "She always gathers a large house party for the hunting."

"Do, by all means," encouraged Anne.

"I don't quite approve of hunting," murmured Lydia sweetly. "I feel so sorry for the poor little fox."

Anne raised one eyebrow. "That 'poor little fox' would soon destroy every covey in the county if he were left alone."

"And why not? I do not see why birds should be shot either."

Anne, seeing a dispute ahead, shrugged and would have abandoned the subject.

"My father is one of the strongest opponents of hunting and shooting," continued Lydia. "He feels they are unchristian."

"Well, you know, Lydia, I have always thought he goes a bit far," put in Laurence. "Hunting isn't all sport. It does help balance things on the land."

Miss Branwell drew herself up. Anne, with a slight smile, sat back in her chair.

"But, of course, the bishop knows more about it than I," added Laurence hastily. "I shall have to discuss it with him and learn his views."

"Oh, yes," breathed his fiancée, leaning forward and putting a hand over his where it lay on the chair arm. "Do, Laurence! He will convince you, I'm sure. He is so wise."

He nodded. But Anne saw his shoulders move impatiently beneath his coat, and her smile broadened a bit.

"Have you been shopping since you arrived in town?" Lydia asked Anne, eyeing her buff walking dress with approval.

"No, but some of the things I ordered last month have begun to arrive. I think I am fairly well equipped for now, thank heaven."

"You don't care for shopping?" Miss Branwell seemed surprised.

"I loathe it. I leave it for months, then I rush out and buy everything at once, half of it useless most of the time. But my new maid has been a great help, and the mother of one of my friends."

"Who is that?" Lydia cocked her head.

"Mrs. Castleton."

"Castleton." As Lydia considered this information, Anne was irresistibly reminded of one of the Wrenley dogs from her childhood. That hound had been celebrated for its discriminating sense of smell, as well as for the way it delicately tested the scent, then raised its head and seemed to compare it to all the others it had ever tried. "Is that the Dorset family?" concluded the other girl.

"Yes."

"Ah. A very good line, and extremely wealthy, I believe."

Anne nodded silently. "Speaking of them," she said, "we must go. I promised to call there this morning, and we have taken up too much of your time already."

"Not at all," answered Lydia, but she rose.

They took their leave of her and of the silent, inexplicable Mrs. Branwell and went downstairs to the carriage. When they had climbed in, Laurence said, "You do like Lydia, do you not?"

Anne hesitated. She had decided that she did not like Miss Branwell at all, and that Laurence was making a mistake. But to say this would only goad him into defending her and keep him from looking squarely at her deficiencies. She contented herself with, "She seems a thoughtful person."

"Yes." Laurence leaned forward. "It is very rare, you know, to find a girl who cares about serious things and can discuss them. Most of the London debs I have met are quite empty-headed. Lydia is exceptional."

"I'm sure she is," agreed Anne.

"Charles and Edward *won't* see that."

"Well, their opinions don't really matter, I suppose." She watched him curiously.

Laurence frowned. "No. No, of course not."

The Castleton town house was not far away. Again, they were admitted at once, but before they could mount the staircase, Arabella appeared on the landing and came running to meet them. "Anne!" she cried, hugging her. "Oh, how glad I am to see you. It seems an age. I called on you yesterday afternoon, but you were out." She gazed reproachfully up at her friend.

"I'm sorry. If I had known you were coming, I would have stayed home. Arabella, this is Laurence Debenham. Laurence, my friend Miss Arabella Castleton."

Arabella held out her hand, flushing a little at having betrayed such exuberance before a stranger. "Come upstairs," she said. "Mama is there."

Mrs. Castleton received them cordially, and they had a quarter hour's pleasant conversation. Anne retold the story of her visit to Tattersall's, in much greater detail this time, and soon had Arabella and her mother laughing. Laurence looked on appreciatively, clearly finding Anne's friend very pretty indeed, and occasionally added a comment on his brother's judgment of horseflesh. A little later, however, he rose. "You will want some private conversation with Miss Castleton," he told Anne, "and I have some business nearby. Shall I call for you in an hour, perhaps?"

"You needn't trouble, if you don't care to. I can go home alone in the carriage."

"No indeed. In an hour, then." He took punctilious leave of the Castleton ladies and went out.

"What a nice young man," said Mrs. Castleton. "So thoughtful. One hardly expects that these days."

Arabella nodded. "Come up to my room, Anne," she added, "where we can have a comfortable coze."

Her mother laughed. "You may have the drawing room. I must speak to Cook. But really, Arabella, you mustn't dismiss anyone besides me so abruptly. It would be very rude."

The girl's dark eyes widened. "Mama! I wouldn't…"

"All right, dear. Anne, good day. We will see you tonight."

When she was gone, the two girls settled on the sofa. "How is everything?" asked Arabella anxiously. "Are you getting on with the Debenhams?"

"Well enough. They are not quite…what I expected."

"What do you mean?"

Anne frowned. "It is hard to say."

"Well, what did Lord Wrenley say about the parrot? Has he been horrid?" She smiled. "Augustus, I mean."

"He said almost nothing. I think I made a mistake buying Augustus, Bella. It was a very childish thing to do."

The other stared at her, astonished to hear this from the madcap Anne Tremayne.

"In fact, I am rapidly coming to the conclusion that the Debenhams need my help," continued Anne. She grinned. "They have made a shocking mull of things without me."

"What can you mean?"

"I think—though I am not yet certain, mind—that I shall set the family in order." Her dimples showed again.

"Anne! What are you planning? You know it is disastrous when you try to interfere in other people's lives. Remember Miss Trevor!"

"That wasn't my fault. I bought her those books because she longed for them so. If she had not told the headmistress, she would not have been reprimanded."

"But she was asked where they came from. And everyone knew she hadn't the money to get them herself."

"Well, she should have said her uncle sent them, or something."

"The headmistress knew she hadn't any family either. Anne…"

"Well, it doesn't matter now. And besides, this is completely different."

"Yes. You are likely to get in much more trouble this time. Think how angry Lord Wrenley would be if he knew you planned to interfere."

Anne looked thoughtful. "I wonder."

"What precisely do you mean to do?" asked Arabella anxiously.

Her friend eyed her. "Have you met a Miss Lydia Branwell?"

"No."

"Well, I think I shall wait until you do to tell you." Anne rose. "Now I must go, Bella. I haven't decided what I will wear tonight, and Crane must do my hair, which takes *so* long. I shall see you at the party."

"But, Anne…"

"Good-bye." Waving a hand, Anne fled. Only when she was walking down the stairs did she remember that Laurence was to fetch her. "He can take a hack," she murmured to herself. "I want to go home." And giving these instructions to the Castletons' butler, she climbed into the carriage and did so.

❧

All three of the Debenham brothers gathered in the town house drawing room that evening, prepared to escort Anne to her first London party. And their mood was much lighter than they had predicted only three weeks ago. Indeed, Edward was ebullient, Laurence quietly optimistic, and even Charles blandly pleasant. Anne, pausing unobserved in the doorway to look at them, thought what a fine picture they made in their evening dress. Though Charles was by far the most elegant, Laurence was very handsome, and Edward had a certain careless grace that almost rivaled his oldest brother's austere perfection. The three seemed more in charity with one another than Anne had ever seen them as they stood before the fire discussing the latest political clash between supporters of the Regent and those of the poor old King.

Anne took a breath, smoothed the skirt of her dress, and said, "Good evening." The brothers turned as one and surveyed her. Crane had dressed her red-gold curls in an airy cloud around her head, with tendrils floating beside her face and softening it. She wore a gown of deep rich violet satin with an overdress of silver tissue and silver and violet ribbons. This combination, which had come to her dressmaker as a "revelation," echoed the shifting tints of her eyes admirably and set off the warm hue of her hair. Around her neck she wore amethysts and silver, and though her toilette could not impart classical beauty to her features or make her any less tall and slender, it was so enchanting that these flaws seemed to fade, leaving only the impression of glorious hair and eyes in a cloud of color.

"Whew!" exclaimed Edward.

"You look lovely, Anne," said Laurence.

She turned to look at Charles. For some reason, his opinion seemed more important than the others'.

"A stunning outfit," he responded with a nod.

"You'll break hearts tonight," added Edward. "Upon my soul, Anne, who would have thought you would turn out so elegant, after the way you used to race about the fields covered with mud and—"

"Tactful as ever, Edward," interrupted Lord Wrenley dryly.

"I'm sure it is a surprise," answered Anne. "I would be surprised myself, if I were not all in a quake over meeting so many strangers tonight."

"You?" Edward laughed. "You're roasting us. You've never been afraid of anything in your life."

"I assure you I have. But never as much as this. Do you really think I will do?"

"More than that," Laurence promised. "You will outshine them all."

"Come now, Anne," said Captain Debenham, "you don't mean to say that you are really nervy? Why, the girl who used to throw her heart over every fence as if it were nothing should snap her fingers at a mere evening party."

"Unless the reason for that throwing was that she was quaking in her boots." Anne laughed. She noticed Charles gazing at her with peculiar intensity. Probably he despised her for her fear. "But I shall do it again tonight. The *ton* cannot be any more frightening than the ditched hedge behind the squire's barn."

"It's a deal less so," answered Edward feelingly. "And when I recall how you took that jump on Dumpling—Dumpling!"

"And fell!"

"Yes, the first time. And the second. But you made it on the third try, by God. I don't think I've ever admired anything more than that last go."

Anne looked at him in surprise as Mariah entered the room.

"That was extremely dangerous," put in Laurence. "You should have stopped her, Edward."

"I? Stopped her? A Guards regiment might have done so; I could not."

"Well, I have learned something since then." Anne

laughed. "If you tried to stop me from going to this event tonight, I should agree at once."

"You haven't begun refusing your jumps!" exclaimed Edward.

"Alas, I may."

"Never!"

Anne laughed again. "Well, I *shall* go. But you must all help me over."

"That is our intention," replied Charles, in so serious a tone that the others all looked at him. He was a little surprised himself at his reaction to this new side of Anne. He had never thought her capable of such sensitivity, and seeing it now was something of a shock, for it suggested that he might have been mistaken about other facets of her character. Fleetingly he recalled her passionate pleas not to be sent to school. He had dismissed them as merely more evidence of her stubborn intractability and refusal of any guidance. Might he have been wrong? He shook off the thought impatiently. The school had done Anne a world of good.

"Dinner is served," said Fallow from the doorway. The viscount offered his arm, and Anne took it, gazing up at him curiously. The others followed them into the dining room, and the Debenhams sat down to a family meal with more cordiality than they had shown one another in years.

Two hours later, Anne stood in the center of an admiring circle of Guards officers, recounting another equestrian anecdote. "And so when Edward's horse wouldn't take the five-barred gate, it was really too much. He put her at it four times, but she was tired out, poor creature, and kept refusing. The hunt was well away by that time, but my mare had thrown a shoe, and I was leading her back. I came upon Edward just as he was promising the horse anything she could name if she would but *try* the gate. Of course, she couldn't name anything. I always wondered if he counted on that."

The gentlemen laughed. "For shame, Edward," said one. "Cheating a poor dumb beast."

Captain Debenham was smiling crookedly. "She didn't take me up. I had to open the gate and lead her through."

This was received with derisive snorts.

"It is too bad of them not to have dancing tonight," blurted a very young subaltern. "I should have asked you straightaway, Lady Anne."

"Ho, listen to Krebs," replied another officer. "This is a new start." The subaltern blushed hotly.

Anne smiled and thanked him, bringing on more rallying remarks. And though she felt sorry for Krebs, she could not help but acknowledge that she was enjoying herself very much. She had not dared hope to be a belle of the season; she knew she had little in common with conventional debs. But she was finding that her improved appearance, combined with her frank manner and humorous intelligence, was quite as effective as beauty in capturing the interest of young men. She had all the attention she could desire from Edward's friends, and had already received two invitations to ride in the park and several requests that she reserve a dance at the first ball she attended. "Oh, there is Arabella," she exclaimed suddenly. "I must go and speak to her."

There were protests from all sides. But one very enterprising lieutenant had the wit to ask which lady she referred to, and when Arabella was pointed out, to promptly offer his arm and his services as escort. He was heartily cursed when Anne accepted and started across the room toward Miss Castleton.

The two girls chatted with him for a few minutes and then escaped for a private conversation. When they had expressed mutual satisfaction with the party, Arabella said, "Now, where is this Miss Branwell? I haven't forgotten what you said, Anne."

"There she is, talking to Laurence."

Arabella looked in the indicated direction. "She is quite pretty."

"If you like the cold, chiseled type."

"Anne!"

"Well, come and I will present you. You can judge for yourself."

This was accordingly done. Miss Branwell received them with a sweet thin smile, and Laurence looked genuinely grateful for Anne's pointed notice of his fiancée.

"Have you ever endured such a tedious evening?" asked Lydia when the introductions were concluded. "I had thought the music might save it, but the little we have heard has been indifferently played."

"I must admit I have enjoyed meeting people and talking with them," replied Anne.

Miss Branwell's habitual smile turned pitying. "Oh, of course, Captain Debenham's fellow officers. They are considered very amusing by some, I believe." She gazed up at Laurence. "I myself find the military mind a trifle…vulgar."

Anne blinked. She did not know what she had done to earn Lydia Branwell's ire, but this was a clear slap at her. Laurence too seemed a bit taken aback.

"You have often said the same," added Lydia when the effect of her remark became obvious. "I remember how you deplored your brother's decision to join the Horse Guards regiment. You called it, let me see, 'one of the least sober and sensible.'"

Laurence looked self-conscious.

She turned to Arabella. "I understand that you too were fortunate in your morning callers today," she said archly. Anne's eyes narrowed. Could the girl be angry because she took Laurence to the Castletons'? Why?

Arabella appeared confused. "Fortunate? Well, of course, Anne called, with Mr. Debenham."

"Yes, they visited us as well. So charming of them, don't you think?"

Arabella merely gazed at her, puzzled.

"Bella," put in Anne, "I must present you to Mariah, my chaperone. If you will excuse us." There were no protests this time, and Anne led her friend across to where Mariah was sitting with the older women.

"What a very odd girl," said Arabella as they walked. "Now you see what I mean."

Miss Castleton frowned doubtfully, but they reached Mariah before she could protest.

They spent a quarter hour talking to Mariah about her garden, which was taking shape rapidly now. And when they left her again, Arabella said, "I shall call on you tomorrow, Anne, without fail. I want to see that garden."

"It is unusual, certainly."

"Unusual!"

Anne laughed. "Come and meet Edward, and then you will be finished with the Debenhams for tonight."

"What about Lord Wrenley?"

"Oh. I…I forgot him."

Bella stared at her.

"I mean, he went to the cardroom almost as soon as we arrived. I haven't seen him this evening." She looked away, then added hurriedly, "Here is Edward." Introductions were performed. Anne grinned wickedly when Captain Debenham threw her a nervous glance. Evidently he had not forgotten their conversation on the way to Tattersall's. And when Arabella was called away by her mother to meet some family friends, Anne said, "A charming girl, isn't she?"

"She's well enough," replied Edward. "Not really the type I favor, you know."

"Really? You are hard to please. What sort of girl do you prefer, so that I shall know?"

"Anne! I told you…"

"Celestial blonds, perhaps, like Miss Clayton? Or terribly intelligent ones, like Miss Archer? I admit I think Arabella perfect, but she is my best friend. I do not insist that you agree with me."

"You are *not* to be throwing girls at my head, Anne," protested Edward feverishly. "Miss Archer, good God!"

"As if I should do anything so pushing! But to give you the opportunity to meet a number of charming girls…"

"I've met all I want to. Anne, you must *promise* me…"

His companion burst out laughing. "Oh, Edward, you look so hunted and miserable."

He eyed her suspiciously. "And so would you, if you were in my place. Good Lord, Anne, I haven't any interest in marriage. Shan't have for years!"

Anne suppressed her laughter. "But that is only because you have not yet met the right woman. When you do—"

"No, it isn't," interrupted Captain Debenham. "It's a…a flaw in my character."

"Well, I'm sure it can be mended," answered the girl sweetly.

"Anne!"

"Look, there is Miss Georgia Daniels. I met her earlier. She seems a very sweet creature. Let us go and talk to her."

Captain Debenham shook his head vigorously and fled.

"Whatever were you saying to Edward?" asked Lord Wrenley. Anne started and turned to find him standing behind her. "I don't believe I have ever seen him look so harried."

She smiled slightly. "I was roasting him."

The viscount raised one eyebrow.

"I threatened to try to find him a bride."

"Did you? Why?"

"Oh, it is only a joke. That is, I *think* it is."

"You are not certain?"

"Well, no. It might be a good thing, though it seems unlikely."

"But why should you concern yourself with Edward's matrimonial plans? They are not your worry."

"But I should like to see him happy, of course."

"Why?"

Anne gazed up at him, frowning. "What do you mean?"

"You can hardly be said to know Edward. And his marriage will have no effect upon you. Why think about it?"

"Well…well, because…" She stopped, at a loss to explain her feelings.

Lord Wrenley shrugged, losing interest, as he

assumed Anne would when the season kept her busier with more personal concerns. "Have you enjoyed your first venture into London society?" he asked instead.

"Oh, yes. Edward presented several of his friends, and they were very kind. And I have met a number of others as well."

"Where is Cousin Mariah?" He scanned the crowd.

"Over there. With the other chaperones."

"I don't suppose she has been much help to you."

"I haven't required help," replied Anne a bit stiffly.

The viscount sighed. "I would have provided a better companion for you if I could have discovered one, Anne."

"I *like* Mariah!"

He shrugged again. "Well, that is something." He looked out over the crowd, as if dismissing the subject from his mind.

"H-have you enjoyed the evening?" ventured Anne.

Lord Wrenley's lip curled. "Not overmuch. We had a few hands of piquet, but they would have been better at White's."

"It...it was good of you to escort me."

He looked down at her, his light gray eyes meeting her darker ones. "Yes, it was."

His bland complacence made her angry. "You need not feel obliged to do so again," she snapped. "I daresay Laurence or Edward would be happy to take on that burden."

"That is my plan," he answered, unaffected by her sarcasm. "I am not much use at these deb parties, in any case."

Seething, Anne tried to think of some blighting remark, but nothing suitably withering came to mind.

"Are you nearly ready to go?" continued the viscount. "I confess I have been eager these two hours."

"Whenever you like," responded Anne icily.

"Good. I'll fetch Edward, and you speak to Laurence, will you?" He walked away; Anne watched him for a moment, her expression indignant, then stalked off to find Laurence.

Seven

RIGHT AFTER BREAKFAST THE NEXT MORNING, A
messenger brought a very large package for Anne.
It contained four gowns she had ordered from the
dressmaker on her earlier visit to London, and she had
them carried directly up to her bedchamber so that
she could try them. But as Crane fastened and adjusted
first one, then another, and Anne stood before the
long mirror to see the fit, she found herself thinking
not of gowns but of her conversation with Charles
the previous evening. This exchange had been in her
mind often since then. She had first of all forgiven him
for finding the party boring; a man who had seen at
least ten seasons come and go could not be expected
to enjoy such a commonplace gathering. But she still
could not understand his attitude toward his brothers,
and toward her interest in them. He had been truly
puzzled by her remarks on Edward's future, as he
had by her inquiries about Laurence's engagement.
Yet to Anne it seemed inevitable that she should be

concerned with these things, and incomprehensible that Charles was not.

"This ruffle drags in the back, my lady," said Crane. "The dress will have to be returned. Shoddy workmanship, I call it."

Diverted, Anne turned and looked in the mirror. "It is hardly an inch. We could alter that ourselves."

Crane looked outraged. "The dressmaker ought to correct her own mistakes, my lady. That is her job."

"But it is not really her fault. She told me I should have another fitting, but I could not go, and made her finish it without." She untied the ribbon sash in the front. "We will do it. If you don't care to sew it up…"

"I shall, of course, my lady, if you *wish* it." The maid was clearly unmollified.

But Anne had lost interest again. "Thank you, Crane," was her only reply, and she changed back into her blue muslin morning dress without further comment. Crane, picking up the offending garment as if it had a bad smell, left the room with her chin high, every line of her body expressing injured dignity.

Anne, finally noticing it as the door snapped shut, smiled a little. "Poor Crane," she murmured. "I must be a trial to her. I shall have to do something particularly nice to make up." But she did not pursue this thought. Her expression became thoughtful again, and after a moment she went downstairs and into the library. Charles often sat there in the mornings working over his papers. But the room was empty today.

Still preoccupied, Anne walked back into the corridor, where she encountered Mariah, struggling under the weight of a large leafy potted plant. "Mariah, let me help you!" she exclaimed and ran to hold one side of the container.

"Thank you, dear," replied the other, straightening up with the lessening of the weight. "It is a trifle heavy."

"Why didn't you ring for someone to carry it—one of the footmen? You should not be doing such heavy work."

"Nonsense. I do much more at home. And I didn't want to disturb any of the servants. They have quite enough to do without my garden added to it."

"Someone would have had time," insisted Anne.

"Perhaps, dear. But you see, I wanted it done *now*." Mariah smiled up at her, her diminutive frame and pale coloring very much at odds with the iron determination in her face. Her light gray eyes danced with mild self-mockery. "I always do, and it is so vexing to wait until someone is free to help."

Anne smiled. "Well, I am nearly always free. Ask me." She nodded down at the pot in their hands. "Let us take this in. It grows heavier by the moment."

Mariah laughed. "Very well."

They carried the plant down the hall to the "garden." Anne had not seen the room for a whole day, and when they reached the doorway, she drew a surprised breath. The transformation was amazing. The earth the workmen had carried in was smoothed over the floor in a uniform layer about two feet deep, confined by a wide plank at the door. In this, Mariah had already planted a number of green things, including, astonishingly, two small trees in the far corners. There were also beds of flowers started here and there.

"It is quite a sight, isn't it?" Mariah chuckled.

Anne nodded. "I had no idea it would look so... so real."

"Yes, it is a challenge. I am enjoying it much more than I thought I would. I think, when I finish, it will be unique."

"Indeed, it will."

"Come, we can put this down beyond the plank there. I haven't yet decided just where I shall plant it."

They heaved the pot onto the soil inside the door. Mariah eyed it critically. "I think I shall have everything in by tomorrow, or perhaps the next day. It depends upon when Robin arrives from my house with the last load."

"All this is coming from your garden at home?"

"Of course. Where else?"

"But what will you do when you return?"

Mariah stared at her. "Why, take it with me." Then she grinned. "Unless Charles wishes to keep it for himself. I shall ask him."

Anne couldn't restrain a smile at this prospect. Mariah stepped up over the plank and into the garden, immediately becoming engrossed in her work.

Anne watched her for a few minutes, then strolled to the drawing room. To her surprise, she found Charles there.

"Hello," he said. "I was just looking for you."

"For me?"

"Yes." He held out a stack of envelopes. "These invitations arrived with the morning post, the first of an avalanche, I suppose. Go through them and choose the ones you wish to accept."

"I?"

He raised one blond eyebrow. "Who else? You are the one coming out this season."

"But I don't know any of the people. How will I choose?"

"Oh, Laurence can help you with that," he replied carelessly.

"And do you not wish to be consulted?"

"No. I shall not be attending most of them. You and Laurence and Edward must go where you like."

She took the envelopes. "Very well." He nodded and turned to leave. "Charles?"

"Yes?"

"Are you…are you very busy? Might I talk to you for a moment?"

"I was on my way out." He met her eye and shrugged. "I can delay a short time, however."

"Thank you." She went to sit on the sofa. "I feel I must speak to you about Laurence. I am determined in my own mind, but it does not seem right to do anything without consulting you. You are the head of the family, after all."

Lord Wrenley's face hardened. "Consulting me?"

Anne nodded. She looked down at the pile of envelopes in her hands. "Charles, I am…convinced that Miss Branwell is not a proper match for Laurence. I thought so before, but now I am certain. They will *not* be happy."

The viscount's lips turned down. "And what do you expect me to do about it?" he answered coldly. "I warn you that I shall do nothing."

Anne gazed at him. There was no hint of emotion in his eyes. "I know your feelings on the subject," she agreed. "So I thought *I* would do something. But I wanted to tell you first."

The icy withdrawal in his face was softened by puzzlement. "You? But why should you? Laurence's happiness is not your responsibility."

"I cannot understand your complete lack of interest in these questions—for Edward as well."

"And I cannot understand your concern about them. Why should you care, Anne?"

Their eyes met in mutual incomprehension and held for a long moment. Charles was clearly intrigued. It was almost the first sign of real feeling Anne had seen him show. She sought words to explain. "I…I can't help but be concerned," she said at last. "Laurence has been kind to me; I have known him since I was a child. I want him to be happy."

Lord Wrenley continued to watch her.

"And…I want to do what I can to help him become so."

"Become?" He seemed to examine the word.

"Yes. And Edward, too."

"You believe, then, that they are *not* happy now?"

Anne blinked. "What…what do you mean?"

"You used the word 'become.' It implies that neither of my brothers is, in your view, happy now, if they must 'become' so."

She flushed. "I didn't mean… I wasn't thinking of that when I spoke."

"Precisely. You used it automatically." The viscount still gazed at her as if at some rare new breed of animal. It was astonishing to him that anyone should *wish* to shoulder the sort of responsibility that he had always found so irksome. To feel that another's happiness depended on one's actions—this had seemed a burden to him since the age of sixteen. He had thought Anne foolish to seek it, but he had also been convinced that she would soon change her mind; it was doubly surprising that she persisted.

Anne was looking down in confusion.

"And what of me?" added Lord Wrenley.

"You?"

"Do you include me in your program for happiness?" he asked, one eyebrow raised in habitual condescension.

Her flush deepening painfully, Anne stammered, "I did not think… I would not presume…"

"Good. In that case, you may meddle all you like,

as long as I am not bothered with the consequences. Does that satisfy your scruples?"

A spark of anger drove the blush from Anne's cheeks. "That is precisely what Edward said. Do you Debenhams care for no one but yourselves?"

Lord Wrenley frowned, the hint of interest in his eyes changing to a kind of self-conscious resentment. "I can only speak for myself, naturally. But I cared for my brothers throughout their adolescence, which seems to me quite enough for one lifetime."

"As you 'cared for' me?" retorted Anne. The moment the words were out, she regretted them.

His expression froze. "Precisely."

Anne's anger overbore her manners. "Then all I can say, Charles, is that you haven't the least idea of the meaning of the word 'care.'"

Silence fell: the two of them glared at one another across the Turkey carpet. Then, at the same time, Fallow came in to announce Arabella Castleton, and Augustus screeched, "At 'em, lads. Full forward!"

Anne blinked twice and started to laugh. Lord Wrenley looked toward the parrot, his expression less severe, but he said nothing, merely bowing slightly and striding out of the room. Anne shook her head. The man was impossible. "Send Miss Castleton right up," she told the butler, and she rose and walked over to Augustus's cage. "There are times," she told the bird, "when I cannot help but credit you with a particularly malicious sense of mischief."

"What has he done now?" asked Arabella from the doorway.

Anne turned, smiling. "Merely routed Charles with one well-chosen phrase, which is more than most people could do."

"Oh, dear, did he make him angry?"

"No, I did that. I've never needed any help to exasperate Charles."

"Anne."

"Don't look so despairing, goose. It wasn't at all important. Come, I have decided to move Augustus into Mariah's garden. If she will allow it, that is. Let us go and ask her. You can see the place at the same time."

Looking rather anxious, Arabella followed her friend down the hall. They found Mariah digging energetically in the corner of the parlor and had no trouble obtaining permission to move the parrot. "I'm fond of birds," said Mariah. "They're pleasant creatures. *Quite* unlike moles—and rabbits! A rabbit will eat a green shoot as soon as look at it."

"I'll bring him in a little while," replied Anne.

"Very well, my dear. I shall be here."

"He…ah…he talks, you know."

"Does he?" Mariah did not seem to be really listening; she was lowering the plant they had carried into the soil.

"You heard him, remember?"

The other looked up, then smiled. "Oh, yes. A most interesting bird. I shall enjoy his company."

Anne smiled back at her and nodded. With a sign to Arabella, she walked out.

"What an extraordinary place," said the latter, who had gazed openmouthed at the transformed parlor the whole time she stood there.

"Isn't it? I am beginning to admire Mariah's single-mindedness."

When they returned to the drawing room, they found Laurence there, looking for Anne. "Charles told me you wanted my advice on some invitations?" he said. His diffident tone made it a question.

"Yes indeed." She pointed to the pile on the table. "I am to choose among these, but I don't know anyone in London. I know; let us all go through them—the three of us. It will be great fun." They sat down and Anne reached for an envelope. "A Venetian breakfast at the Drews'. I know no one by that name."

"Yes, you do," replied Arabella. "You met Mrs. Drew and her daughter last night."

"I don't recall. What do they look like?"

Arabella glanced doubtfully at Laurence. "Well, they don't much resemble each other. Mrs. Drew is…tall."

"And her daughter is not, I suppose. Come, Bella, you are not usually so reticent. Do you know the Drews, Laurence?"

"I do." He grimaced faintly. "Edward calls them Friday-faced."

Arabella stifled a giggle, and Anne said, "I

remember them now. A bony predatory woman with a little mouse of a girl in tow. They talked to me of dukes."

Laurence looked puzzled. "Dukes?"

"I couldn't make head nor tail of it. But they seemed enamored of some duke or other and were singing his praises for a quarter hour. It took all my address to escape them."

Arabella burst out laughing.

"Now, Bella. Is that kind? I do have *some* social address."

Laurence smiled.

"I know," gasped Miss Castleton. "It was just the way you said it. And the duke is the Duke of Cumberland. He asked them to one of his levees."

"They were praising Cumberland for a quarter hour!" Laurence shook his head. "Refuse the invitation, Anne."

Arabella giggled again, and Laurence grinned at her.

"I certainly shall. And I want to hear all about the Duke of Cumberland later. Now we must deal with these other cards." She tore open another envelope. "Oh, a ball! Given by a duchess, the Duchess of Rutland."

"You must go to that," said Arabella. "Her entertainments are famous. We will be there."

"That is settled, then. Laurence?"

"I agree completely."

"Good. I will make separate piles for acceptances

and refusals. Now, here is an evening party at the Smythes'. What have you to say of them?"

Arabella shook her head. "I haven't met them." Both girls turned to Laurence, expectant.

He smiled a little. "I don't know them well, but the family seems pleasant. There is a daughter coming out this season, I believe. And there is at least one son."

"Well, we will go and test your judgment," answered Anne. "But I warn you, if they are not pleasant, we will not let you forget it."

"I shall await your decision with fear and trembling." Arabella laughed again, and Laurence smiled down at her.

Anne opened another envelope. "A musical evening at the Branwells'. We shall of course accept that. And next, a waltzing party at Lord Dunn's."

Laurence had looked gratified at her first remark, but now he frowned. "I'm afraid you must refuse the second. You cannot waltz until you are approved by one of the patronesses of Almack's."

"What? How ridiculous. I have been longing to learn the waltz for a year!"

"No, Anne, he is right," said Arabella. "You must wait."

"But why? Do they ever refuse to allow one to waltz?"

Laurence cocked his head. "No, not if they admit you to Almack's."

"And if they do not, it cannot matter to me what they think. So…"

"Yes, but if you waltz before you are approved, they will *not* admit you," responded Arabella. "And you *must* be admitted, Anne."

"Must I?" She looked mischievous. "Oh, yes. Almack's is also called 'the marriage mart,' isn't it?"

At the same moment, Arabella and Laurence exclaimed, "Anne!" in shocked tones. Their expressions were so identically aghast that Anne burst out laughing and pointed to the mirror behind the sofa. The others looked, saw their own reflections, and reluctantly began to smile.

"How easy it is to scandalize you two." Anne laughed. "I knew I could roast Bella, but I did not think I would catch you as well, Laurence. Oh, what a picture you made."

Arabella and Laurence exchanged understanding glances, smiling ruefully at each other. Seeing them, Anne was suddenly struck by a new idea. It was of such blinding beauty that her eyes widened and darkened to full violet and she pressed her lips together to keep from exclaiming aloud. In the next moment, when the other two turned back, she was looking down and reaching for another envelope. But if they could have seen the sparkle in her eyes, they might have once more united in uneasy inquiry.

The afternoon passed in this pleasant way. They had tea when they finished with the invitations, and a little while later, Arabella took her leave. As Anne and Laurence walked upstairs to change for dinner, he said,

"Your friend is charming. It must have been a help to you to have her at your school."

"Yes indeed," answered Anne, looking at the carpet. "Arabella got me through any number of scrapes. The teachers thought her a good influence on me."

Laurence merely nodded, but Anne felt she had sown a promising seed.

Eight

ANNE'S FIRST BALL CAME TWO WEEKS LATER. IN THE intervening time, she had attended a variety of lesser entertainments and made many new acquaintances. Laurence was tireless in escorting her, and Edward turned up with a group of his friends at nearly every one. Thus, she soon began to feel very much at home in London's drawing rooms and to cease worrying whether she would be a miserable failure as a deb. She was not one of the toasts of the season, as indeed she had never dreamed of being. But she was a creditable success, and more than one young officer showed signs of susceptibility to her charms. Arabella was even more sought after, and both girls were very pleased and excited.

Charles joined Laurence in squiring Anne to the Duchess of Rutland's ball. She had seen little of him lately; he seldom attended the deb parties, and he often dined away from home. Thus, she had the sense that their quarrel was not made up; it was merely ignored.

Yet whenever they encountered one another, Charles was politely solicitous. He asked if she were enjoying herself and if there was anything she needed. But she did not believe he was really interested in the answers. And Anne herself remained a little angry. Charles had no excuse for his cold treatment of others. She told herself that not only did she not miss his company, she was glad he avoided her. It considerably lessened the tension in her life.

This ball, however, was one of the major events of the season. Everyone would be there, and Charles could hardly refuse to join Laurence and Anne in the Debenham carriage. They pulled up before the duchess's house at ten and were ushered into the hall, where footmen took their cloaks. Anne had chosen a striking gown of coquelicot satin, which matched the color of her hair admirably, and she wore ornaments of twisted gold. The brothers were elegantly handsome in knee breeches and black coats, Charles particularly striking in evening dress. They greeted their hostess on the landing and moved into the ballroom, which had been hung with yards of blue cloth, tied up with garlands of flowers, for the occasion. The dancing had begun, and Anne was soon asked to join a set. Laurence went in search of Lydia Branwell, and Charles strolled over to speak to some of his friends. He rarely danced himself.

The first three sets passed very quickly and pleasantly for Anne. She danced, and between times managed to snatch a few words of conversation with

Arabella. But the fourth was a waltz, and as she had not yet received her all-important nod of approval from Almack's mighty patronesses, she was forced to sit out. This did not please her, particularly when she looked around to find that nearly everyone she knew *was* dancing. Even Arabella had passed into the select company of waltzers, by virtue of her mother's prompt efforts with Lady Jersey.

Anne grimaced and searched for someone to talk to. She was not going to sit alone in one of the gilt chairs by the wall and advertise her exile. But the only person she saw was Charles, standing with some of his friends in the corner of the ballroom. Anne hesitated a moment, then shrugged. Even Charles was better than solitude. She walked around the floor and joined his group. No one seemed to notice her—Charles was slightly turned away—but she did not mind. For as she came close to them, she had realized that she was entering exalted company. Lord Wrenley was chatting with Lord Alvanley, Sir James Steadham and his wife, and another couple who, though unknown to Anne, had the same air of fashion and elegance as the others. These were the very cream of the *haut ton*, and she was suddenly uncertain of her welcome.

No one made any remark, however, though she was certain Lord Alvanley, at least, saw her arrive. Anne wished that Charles would turn and say something, but he was engrossed in conversation with the woman she did not know.

"But you *must* remember, Charles," she was saying. "That night we all went to Vauxhall in dominoes and bet Prinny he could not tell who we were. He couldn't, and he had to buy us all champagne. You can't have forgotten. Teddy remembers. Don't you, Teddy?" She took her partner's arm and looked up into his face with open affection.

"Of course," responded Teddy promptly.

"You would 'remember' anything your wife asked you to." Charles laughed. His tone was so easy and friendly that Anne started in surprise. "I have no memory of the incident. It must have been someone else with you, Elaine. Indeed, I cannot imagine indulging in such a prank."

Elaine opened her blue eyes very wide. "You? And who was it replaced Teddy's splendid claret with a *very* inferior wine just before it was served at dinner? I don't believe our butler has recovered from it yet."

Charles laughed again, throwing back his head.

"He did not!" exclaimed Sir James Steadham. "Charles, that was my joke. You stole it!"

"I had to," replied the viscount. "It was too good not to repeat. I don't know whether I laughed more at Teddy's expression when he tasted it, or when you told me the story the first time."

"Who was your victim, James?" asked Lord Alvanley.

"Bob Pritcher."

"No! He is forever prosing on about his wine cellar."

"He was that night, too. That's what made me do

it. And you know the cream of the jest." He looked around the group, beaming. "Pritcher didn't even notice the difference. He drank this beastly port and praised it to us as if it were nectar."

"He did not!"

"I tell you he did, Alvanley. That was the moment I decided I wasn't the least sorry for the trick. The man knows nothing about wine, for all his boasting."

Lady Steadham shook her exquisitely coiffed head. "It was amazing. He really didn't know."

"I suppose that means you think I know nothing about wine," growled Teddy with mock ferocity. "Wrenley, I believe I will call you out."

"Peace. I didn't think anything of the kind." Charles grinned engagingly at the other man. "And you noticed at the first sip, didn't you? I was after Beckwith, not you."

"Beckwith?" Teddy frowned.

"He was one of our dinner guests, dear," said his wife. "You remember, that fat little man Mama wanted us to invite."

Teddy shook his head in bewilderment.

"I didn't know him either," said Charles, "but he insisted he was a better judge of wine than any man in the room, and I wanted to shut him up."

"Did he notice the switch?" asked Sir James.

Charles smiled ruefully. "Yes. As soon as anyone."

Steadham broke into laughter. "So it backfired on you."

Smiling, Charles nodded. "I haven't your finesse, James."

Throughout this exchange, Anne had been standing openmouthed on the fringes of the group. Here was a Charles she had never seen and hardly recognized. His smile was warm and genuine, lighting his thin face and cool eyes and revealing an entirely unsuspected facet of his personality. He was amusing, witty, and obviously attached to these friends, with whom he had clearly shared many pleasant times. He joked and laughingly mocked himself. She could scarcely believe her ears. And yet none of the others seemed to see anything out of the ordinary in his behavior. They were obviously as accustomed to this Charles as she was to the stern, distant man of her youth. It was so startling that Anne could not keep the astonishment from her expression.

Just then, Charles turned a little and saw her. In an instant, his face changed, the smile dying and the twinkling eyes going bland. "Anne, I didn't see you," he said with perfect politeness. "Did you want something?"

The transformation was so rapid, and so total, that Anne could hardly speak. "N-no. That is…I wasn't dancing, so I…" She flushed, feeling horridly young and clumsy before this glittering group.

"For shame, Charles," said Lady Steadham, "leaving your, ah, ward without a partner."

Her tone was kindly, and Anne knew that she

meant well, but this teasing remark merely made her blush more hotly.

"Yes indeed," agreed Elaine. "And as a punishment, you should dance the next set with her yourself." Turning to Anne, she quickly added, "I only say punishment because Charles hates dancing. Any man in his senses would consider it a reward."

By now desperately embarrassed, and wishing with all her heart that she had sat alone by the wall through this stupid waltz, Anne could not muster a reply. She merely pressed her lips together and fought back tears.

Charles bowed. "You do me an injustice. I should be delighted to dance with Anne. Shall we? It is a country dance."

He did not sound delighted, but Anne was ready to seize any escape. She took his arm and allowed him to lead her onto the floor. Once out of earshot, however, she stammered, "You needn't dance. It is all right. I don't want... I didn't mean..."

"Nonsense. Of course we shall dance," replied Charles, and he bowed her into the set forming nearby. But though he showed no sign of annoyance or anger at her intrusion, neither did he exhibit the easy friendliness and affection he had shown with his friends. The old Charles was back again. Indeed, he was feeling more than usually annoyed. He had been thoroughly enjoying himself with Alvanley and the others, only to be jerked away by responsibility to

Anne. Well, he would do his duty, but he would not pretend to enjoy it. He never had.

Anne was only too glad to escape him at the end of half an hour. Their dances had been ponderously polite and, for her, almost unendurable. She felt terribly confused, and since it was impossible to retreat and think things out alone, she longed to put this incident from her mind and not have to wonder why her chief emotion at the moment was envy of Steadham, Alvanley, and the rest.

She noticed Arabella leaving the set, and joined her, bidding Charles a firm farewell. He departed, showing neither eagerness nor regret, and the two girls walked toward the sofa where Mrs. Castleton was sitting with Mariah.

"What is the matter, Anne?" asked Arabella immediately. "You look as if you had seen a ghost."

"Perhaps I have."

"What?" But they reached the chaperones before Arabella could press her further, and she had to content herself with a frown and a concerned gaze. Mrs. Castleton greeted them contentedly. She had seen Arabella achieve a solid success, and more than one eligible young man had shown signs of serious interest. Though Mrs. Castleton's ideas and desires certainly went far beyond these heights, she could not help but feel gratified and relieved. Arabella was her youngest daughter, and the third she had presented in four years.

"Are you enjoying yourselves?" she asked both girls.

They nodded. Another waltz was beginning, and Anne took the vacant place on the sofa with a sigh. "I mustn't dance. Again!"

Arabella laughed. "It won't be for long. You go to Almack's this week, do you not?"

Anne nodded.

"Well, then. But I will stay with you if you like."

"No, indeed." Anne looked about them. Gentlemen were choosing partners around the room. One appeared to be approaching their group, but Anne suddenly saw Laurence standing nearby, with Mrs. Branwell and a large beefy man Anne took to be the bishop. Lydia had left them and was joining the dancers on the arm of another massive churchman. Smiling slightly, Anne beckoned to Laurence. He noticed at once, excused himself, and came toward them. Anne unobtrusively indicated Arabella, and Laurence nodded slightly, earning the girl's admiration. No word was spoken between them. Laurence simply stopped before Arabella, bowed, and requested the pleasure of a dance. Arabella, smiling, agreed, and Anne watched them walk onto the floor. Her pleasure was not lessened by the fact that Lydia Branwell threw them an exceedingly sharp look before the music began.

This gave Anne another idea. Turning, she looked again for the Branwells. The bishop had moved away when Laurence did, leaving Mrs. Branwell alone in a gilt chair by the wall. This was exactly what Anne had

hoped. She rose and went to join her. "Good evening,
Mrs. Branwell," she opened brightly. "May I sit with
you for a moment? As you can see, I am still barred
from waltzing. I find it a trial; it looks so lovely." She
pretended to gaze out over the dance floor, but looked
sidelong at the older woman beside her.

Mrs. Branwell seemed very nervous, almost unbe-
lievably so. She kept her eyes on the floor and fidgeted
with a handkerchief in her lap, saying nothing.

"Lydia dances very well," offered Anne, thinking
that a compliment to her only child must rouse the
woman to speech. But Mrs. Branwell merely raised
her eyes quickly, then looked down again with something that might be construed as a nod. Anne stared
at her. She had never met anyone so timid. Could
the woman really have reached such a mature age and
established social position and still be so painfully shy
with strangers? It didn't seem possible. "Do you enjoy
these balls?" she asked, determined to force at least one
word from her timorous companion.

Mrs. Branwell looked around as if hoping for
rescue, then seemed to capitulate. "Oh, yes," she murmured, so low that Anne could hardly hear, "of…of
course." Her voice was thin and high, and it somehow
made even the positive opinion she expressed sound
tentative and worried.

"I admit I do," replied Anne cordially. "But
that is because of the dancing. I should hate sitting
here the whole evening." She got no answer to her

inquiring pause. "Lydia is making her debut this season, is she not? I suppose it is your first in town for some time, then?"

Mrs. Branwell made a distressed sound, though Anne could not see why her rather commonplace question should have elicited it, and murmured, "I have never been to London before."

"Indeed? We are in the same case, then. What do you think of town life?"

The other squeaked again, and before she could do anything else, a resonant bass voice intoned, "Elvira." Mrs. Branwell started visibly and jerked her eyes upward, reminding Anne of a rabbit cornered by a pack of dogs. She too looked up, to find that the bishop had rejoined them. "Pray present me to your charming companion," continued this gentleman, smiling a broad professional smile.

Mrs. Branwell managed to whisper Anne's name. The bishop bowed over her hand. "My dear Lady Anne," he boomed. "A pleasure, a true pleasure. My daughter has mentioned you."

"How kind of her." Anne examined the bishop with interest. He was indeed a large man, tall and with a matching bulk. His impressive figure seemed to cry out for a surplice and chasuble, and she would have wagered a good deal that he was high-church. He had Lydia's black hair, noticeably thinning, a narrow prominent nose, and comfortable jowls. But the most striking thing about him at first acquaintance was his voice. He had just the sort of voice one imagined a bishop should have—melodious, deep, and possessing a broad range of tones.

Just now, it was confiding. "You are the foster sister of our dear Laurence. We have long looked forward to meeting you."

"Thank you." Anne ventured a glance at Mrs. Branwell, and saw that she had once more retreated into silence and handkerchief-twisting.

The bishop followed her gaze. "Elvira," he said, at once soft and somehow cutting, "you are ruining your kerchief."

Mrs. Branwell started violently again, raised her eyes, dropped them, and hurriedly let go of the cloth.

Anne turned away, puzzled and rather upset by her behavior. Was the man a domestic tyrant? That would explain his wife's manner to him, at least. She would be careful not to draw his attention in that direction again. "I understand this is your family's first season in London," she said.

He gestured expansively. "My family's, yes. But not, of course, mine. I have spent a good deal of time in town, what with one thing and another. I am a member of a number of societies which meet in London, and I naturally have a large acquaintance here."

"Yes." Anne was at a loss for a moment. "You must be very busy."

The bishop folded his arms under his coattails and tossed his head back, looking smugly satisfied. "I am indeed. Very busy. The calls of my profession are, of course, heavy, and yet I cannot neglect those other interests which have been important to me since before I attained my present position."

"N-no." Anne frowned, searching for some better reply. Suddenly she remembered something. "You are interested in gardening, I believe?"

"Deeply." He gazed down at her. "Do you also…?"

"Oh, no." Belatedly Anne also recalled why this subject should not be pursued. She tried to shift the conversation. "What other groups do you belong to?"

Bishop Branwell waved this aside. "Gardening occupies much of my leisure time. I have just finished adding substantially to my succession houses. In the spring I shall initiate a series of experiments in hybridization of roses. They will be quite scientific. I believe one should be rigorously exact even in one's hobbies, perhaps particularly so there. Don't you agree, Lady Anne?"

Anne was saved from answering by the end of the set and the return of Lydia. The latter's fine eyes were sparkling with some emotion Anne found difficult to identify until they were focused on herself; Miss Branwell was annoyed with her. Anne looked around and discovered Laurence and Arabella in animated, and obviously happy, conversation on the far side of the room. She started to smile, then thought better of it.

"Papa!" said Lydia. "And Lady Anne. How glad I am that you have met at last. Have you had a good talk?"

The bishop nodded complacently. "We have been discussing gardening. Lady Anne is interested in my hybridization plan."

"I'm sure she is." Miss Branwell cast Anne a glittering glance. "Has she told you that her chaperone is a great gardening expert?"

"No!" Her father looked to Anne eagerly.

"Ah. That is just her modesty, I suppose. You must meet Miss Postlewaite-Debenham." And Lydia took his arm and began to guide him across to the sofa where Mariah still sat.

"Oh, dear," murmured Anne, rising. "Will you excuse me please, Mrs. Branwell. Or perhaps you would like to come?"

The other woman stared as if she thought Anne had suddenly lost her mind, and quickly shook her head. With a wry smile of agreement, Anne moved across to Mariah.

Lydia had already initiated hostilities when she caught up with them. The subject under discussion was pruning. "My dear Miss Postlewaite-Debenham," the bishop was crooning, "you must admit that the vital juices retreat gradually from the stems, and therefore—"

"I admit nothing of the kind," snapped Mariah, clearly annoyed, though whether by the man's argument or his manner, Anne couldn't tell. "Roses have done quite well with one pruning for hundreds of years. I see no reason for a change."

"But, madam, change is not always an evil in itself.

It may be good as well as bad." The bishop's vowels were rotund. "Think, for example, of the—"

"I know roses," interrupted Mariah. "And I daresay mine are finer than yours, with only one pruning."

Branwell's mouth fell open, and his generous jowls shook. He was obviously not accustomed to being interrupted, and still less to having his opinions and plantations denigrated. Anne looked from his slowly empurpling countenance to his daughter's smugly satisfied one. Both of them were primed for the annihilation of the unfortunate Mariah—the one to do the deed, and the other to savor it. Hurriedly she looked for Laurence. He was still with Arabella, but their conversation was less intense. She tried to catch his eye, failed, and, with a quick look at the group around her, strode across to fetch him. He must hear this.

In a moment, the three of them were back. They had missed the bishop's opening salvo, but they were in time to hear him say patronizingly, "The ladies must always have the last word, of course. But it makes them perhaps a *little* deaf to wiser counsel. They are always so eager to cap the latest remark."

Mariah looked at him with contempt, and not a sign of the chagrin he no doubt expected her to feel. Laurence raised his eyebrows a bit.

"Yes indeed," added Lydia Branwell in strident accusatory tones, "we should listen to the opinions of those who know more about a subject than we." Her remark was so clearly directed at Mariah, and so clearly unfriendly, that Mrs. Castleton frowned and started to speak.

But Mariah was before her. "Oh, I am always ready to do *that*," she said. Before anyone could reply, she rose. "And now, if you will excuse me, I must speak to Charles about something."

She was gone before Lydia and her father recovered. Anne had to stifle a giggle. The bishop looked exactly like a large fish out of water.

"Whatever was that about?" asked Laurence in the silence that followed.

Lydia turned, saw him, and glared at Anne. Then she slipped her hand through her father's arm and said, "We must go back to Mama. Come, Laurence, I will tell you all about it." She swept off, and Laurence, still frowning, hesitated a moment, then followed.

When they were out of earshot, Anne sank onto the sofa. "Whew!" she said.

The Castletons looked at her. "You are up to something, aren't you, Anne?" asked Mrs. Castleton.

"I?"

The older woman smiled. "And I have an idea what it is."

Anne gazed uneasily at her, but she merely smiled and nodded. After a moment, Anne smiled back.

"Well, I don't know whether I like it," said Arabella. "You know what happens whenever you meddle, Anne."

"*This* time, it is necessary," replied the other firmly.

Her friend continued to look doubtful, but another set was starting up, and she was solicited for it. As she walked away with her partner, Edward Debenham approached Anne. "Come and dance," he said.

"I should love to."

They took their places, and the music started. "How can you bear talking to those poisonous Branwells?" asked Edward. "I wouldn't come near you until they took themselves off. Can't abide them, particularly the bishop."

Anne shrugged noncommittally.

"Oh, come. You can't convince me that you like them. I've seen your eyes when you talk of the fair Lydia. What a horror that girl is. I cannot understand Laurence's blindness, as I have told him more than once."

"I know," retorted Anne acidly, "and you would be much better advised to hold your tongue."

He stared down at her. "What do you mean? You don't want Laurence to *marry* that Friday-faced creature, do you?"

She bit her bottom lip. She had not meant to be so vehement. Meeting Edward's pale gray gaze, she eyed him speculatively.

"Whatever it is, no," he said.

"What do you mean?"

"I know mischief when I see it, Anne, and I want no part of it."

But Anne had made up her mind. "I *don't* want to see Laurence marry Miss Branwell," she said.

"Who could?" agreed Edward cautiously.

"And I mean to do something about it, unlike you and your brother. I don't call that mischief!"

"I've been doing something," replied Edward, aggrieved. "I've been telling him since he offered for her that she was a poor bargain."

Anne gazed up at him, her gray-violet eyes wide. "How," she wondered, "can men be so stupid?"

Edward looked surprised.

"Can't you see that that is *precisely* the wrong way to go about it? What would you do if Laurence criticized one of your decisions, a serious one, mind?"

"Why I should tell him to…" Edward paused.

"I know. I have seen you do it. All of you. So for you to snipe at Miss Branwell simply makes Laurence defend her the more. It is the worst possible course of action."

Edward looked both irritated and amused. "I suppose you have a better idea?"

"Oh, yes."

"What?"

"I mean to show Laurence what sort of girl Lydia Branwell really is. I shall be very polite to her and agree with all Laurence's praises, but I shall make opportunities for her to show her true colors. I did so once tonight. And you know, Edward, you could help me."

He gazed down at her, bemused.

"It is not always easy to gather all the right people together," continued Anne. "If I had someone to help, I daresay I could find many more chances."

"You are quite serious, aren't you?"

"Well, of course I am."

"But what you plan could be very unpleasant. Miss Branwell isn't stupid, you know. She will eventually see what you are doing, and then I daresay she will be after *you*."

"What does that signify?" asked Anne impatiently.

"Well, I mean, she's a tartar. She might…" Edward groped for an example. "She might do something dashed uncomfortable."

Anne shrugged. "I am not frightened. And what could be *more* uncomfortable than having her married to Laurence?"

"Yes." He seemed much struck.

"Will you help me, then?"

"Ah, well, I don't know, Anne. Laurence won't relish interference."

"He won't know anything about it."

"Yes, but—"

"Oh, you are just like your brother. You don't care a whit about Laurence; you are too selfish."

He goggled. "Did you ask *Charles* to help you?"

Anne laughed shortly. "No indeed, not after I had spoken to him on this subject. He cares nothing about it. I did not expect you to be the same."

"Yes, but, Anne—"

"Abandoning your brother to that sort of…of *managing* female. He deserves better from you."

"But—"

"I daresay he has done you a score of services, and you cannot so much as lift a finger when he needs your help."

"Would *he* say he needed it, though?" asked Edward bluntly.

Anne shrugged and turned her face away, but her companion did not notice. He was frowning and considering her argument. After a short silence, one side of his mouth quirked up and he murmured, "Good old Laurence."

"What?"

"I was just thinking of something that happened while I was up at Oxford. Here, Anne, I'll tell you what. I will help you if you promise I shan't have to spend much time with the Branwell. I cannot abide that girl."

Anne smiled brilliantly up at him. "You won't. I shall take care of that."

He nodded. "Very well. I'm your man."

"Oh, Edward, you won't regret this."

"I rather think I shall, actually, but a man can't turn cow-hearted when it's a question of his own brother, can he?"

"No indeed. I knew you would see it so!"

"Yes…but, Anne, I'm going to ask something in return."

"Of course. What is it?"

"You are to promise not to be pushing girls at me and grinning in that terrifying way, as you have been doing."

She grinned now.

"That's it. That's the look," added Edward.

"But, Edward, I worry about *your* happiness, too," she teased.

"Well, don't. I ain't Laurence, and I'm perfectly able to manage my own...uh...er..."

Anne laughed ringingly. "All right, Edward. I promise."

He breathed a sigh of relief. "Thank God. Now, what exactly do you plan to do?"

The music was ending. "Come and sit down, and I will tell you," answered Anne.

"I daresay I shall regret this before the evening is out," said Edward as he followed her from the floor.

Nine

THE NEXT FEW DAYS WERE BUSY ONES FOR ANNE. BY
this time, she had social engagements nearly every
night; she attended another ball, joined a party at
Vauxhall Gardens, and went to the theater with
Laurence and Edward. Mariah accompanied her
when there was no other chaperone, but she made it
clear that she did not relish the outings. And when a
substitute was available, she excused herself at once.
Charles did not appear at any of these functions.
Indeed, he was out a good deal during the whole
week. But Anne found herself thinking of him often.
She could not get the memory of his "other self" out
of her mind.

She had thought she knew Charles; she had had
years to observe him, from a distance, and to draw her
conclusions, and she had done so. She thought of him
as a distant, cold disciplinarian who cared for nothing
and no one but himself. This opinion had been only
slightly modified after her return from school. She saw

that her view had been childishly exaggerated, but the basic judgment remained unchanged.

But now she was forced to question it. The Charles she had glimpsed at the Duchess of Rutland's ball was charming and warm. He laughed and joked in a way she would have declared impossible if she had not seen it herself. Indeed, had she met this Charles as a stranger, she would have pronounced him one of the most attractive members of London society.

His smile, his open look, his affectionate tone—all had drawn her.

And this, of course, made the contrast even harder to accept. Why did Charles treat his friends so well and his family so badly? Anne could not understand it. It was puzzling enough that he should have these two opposite faces, but why should the pleasant one be turned outward, toward strangers? To Anne, whose limited notions about family life came from her reading and short visits to the Castletons', his behavior seemed reprehensible. A man's family, she felt, ought to be the people closest to him, ought to be treated with the utmost consideration. But Charles turned this around.

And why? Anne pondered this question the longest. She could find no reason. Laurence and Edward, though not of course perfect individuals, were certainly above the common average. Laurence could be a little pompous, but he was also very kind and considerate; Edward, though sometimes heedless and a bit wild, was charming and, at bottom, sound. Why should Charles treat them with such cold disinterest? She did not include herself; she was not, after all, a real member of Charles's family.

Before the ball, the answer to these questions had been clear: Charles was a cold, rather disagreeable man. He might have sophistication and wit, but he was not the sort of person Anne admired or liked. Now she could not decide what to think. The only thing she was sure of, to her chagrin, was that she was jealous of the strangers who knew the "other" Charles. She longed to know him better herself, but because of who she was, this appeared impossible.

These meditations did not leave her in a pleasant mood. And Arabella several times commented on Anne's unaccustomed taciturnity. By the end of the week, as the date of the Branwells' musical evening approached, Anne had determined to put the whole matter from her mind. There was nothing she could do about it, and it was not improving her temper. The best thing for her to do, she decided, was to ignore Charles and his eccentric behavior, as he was ignoring all of them.

The whole Debenham household was, perforce, to attend the Branwells' entertainment. Laurence's engagement made this attention mandatory. Anne went up to put the finishing touches on her toilette directly after dinner, leaving the three brothers over their wine. She had chosen a simple gown of white

sarcenet, trimmed with white ribbons and a single
white rose. The pale background made her red-gold
hair and changing eyes even more vivid. Crane awaited
her in her room, ready to tidy any stray curl or readjust
a flounce. As she walked up the stairs, Anne considered
the meal just past. It had been unusually pleasant. She
and Laurence and Edward had gotten into an animated
discussion about dogs, and the only disputes between
the other two had been laughing ones. Edward was on
his best behavior and did not make even one slighting
remark about the Branwells. Charles had looked on
with cool approval and, Anne thought, some surprise,
but he had not added much to the conversation. She
could not decide whether this was an advantage or a
disappointment. Charles had several times evinced a
weary resignation about this evening's entertainment,
and it was certainly good that he had not repeated that.
Yet she had a notion that he could have added a great
deal to their discussion if he had consented to do so,
and she rather resented his holding back.

These thoughts dissipated when Anne entered
her bedchamber to find Crane facing the door, arms
akimbo, brows drawn together. "What is it, Crane?"
she asked, recognizing her maid's look of disapproval.
"Couldn't you find the paisley shawl? I did *not* leave it
at the Archers'. I know I did not."

"I found the shawl, my lady." Momentarily
diverted, Crane added, "It was crumpled in the
bottom of your wardrobe."

"Oh, dear. I can't think how that could have happened. I did not put it there."

Crane's lips merely tightened. "If I might speak to you about something, my lady?"

Anne's heart sank. "Of course."

"It's the bird."

For a moment, she could not think what Crane meant, and Anne had a lamentable desire to giggle. "Th-the bird? Oh, you mean Augustus?"

"Yes, my lady. No one else wished to inform you, but I feel it is my duty to tell you that he has bitten the housemaid."

"Oh, dear."

"Yes, my lady. She was giving the creature water, I understand, when he attacked her. She fell into a fit of the vapors and is not yet fully recovered."

"She is not badly hurt?"

"As to that, I couldn't say. The creature took a nasty chunk out of her thumb."

"Oh, dear," said Anne again.

"Yes, my lady. The girl is unable to work, and it is a great inconvenience to the whole household. Fallow did not wish to tell you about the incident, but I thought it better to do so." Crane looked smug. She and Fallow had not established a comfortable relationship.

"Well, I will apologize to the maid, of course. What is her name? And I will see to Augustus myself from now on. He will not bite *me*."

Crane drew herself up. "If I may say so, my lady,

I think it would be much better if you got rid of the creature. I've said it before, and I say it again—he is not a fit pet for you or for a gentleman's house."

"I know your views, Crane," replied Anne. "But I have become rather fond of Augustus and mean to keep him. What is the name of the girl he bit?"

"But, my lady…"

"Please, Crane."

Under Anne's direct gaze, the dresser fell silent, pressing her lips together disapprovingly. "Her name is Ellen, my lady."

"Thank you. I shall speak to her tomorrow. Now, I had best get ready. The others will be waiting for me."

Within half an hour the Debenham party was riding through the streets toward the Branwells' rented town house. Laurence, having been spared Edward's usual caustic remarks, was very cheerful, and he kept up a flow of talk, explaining the plans for the evening's entertainment. "They have got Madame Callini to sing," he told a rather unresponsive audience. "She has a wonderful voice. And there will be a chamber group as well. The violinist is the one the Prince had last summer in Brighton. Yes, I think I can promise you that the music will be memorable. Lydia arranged the whole; she is very fond of music, you know."

The others, who were not particularly fond of music, nodded dutifully. Edward directed a furtive grimace at Anne.

"It is unusual, at an entertainment such as this, to

find such quality," continued Laurence blithely. "Most of these musical evenings are simply excuses for gossip and flirtation. But Lydia means to show what can be done if the effort is made."

Thinking that this sounded like Lydia's own words, and afraid Edward would not be able to restrain a critical comment, Anne said, "Does she play herself?"

"Oh, yes. Both the pianoforte and the harp. Splendidly."

"We will hear her tonight also, perhaps?" Anne resolutely ignored another grimace from Edward.

"No. She says she will not inflict her performance on the guests when they have the opportunity of hearing such superior musicians. I told her that was nonsense, of course, but Lydia is very modest about her accomplishments."

"Ah," was all Anne could think of to reply, but they fortunately reached the house at that moment, and a footman opened the carriage door.

All three Branwells greeted them on the landing inside. Or rather, the bishop and Lydia did so. Mrs. Branwell merely stood between them, looking tired. "You will want to go directly to the drawing room," said Lydia. "A great many people have already arrived, and the good seats are being taken. I set aside yours in the first row, but someone may usurp them if you do not go right in."

Laurence agreed, and the party moved off. In the drawing-room doorway, however, Charles paused.

"There are the Steadhams. I must speak to them," he said, starting to turn away.

"But our seats," objected Laurence.

"Oh, keep mine for me, by all means, Laurence." The younger man's cheek reddened at his mocking tone as the viscount walked away.

"There's Kelso," added Edward hurriedly and a bit guiltily. "Have something important to ask him." And he too left them, before Laurence could speak.

"Isn't there someone *you* must see, Anne?" he said then, looking annoyed.

She smiled at him. "No, I am ready to go to my seat. Laurence, you know they don't care for music. It is too much to expect that they sit in the first row. Besides, Edward might fall asleep and disgrace you before everyone."

He smiled reluctantly. "He might indeed. Come, we shall give their seats away to more deserving persons at the first opportunity."

"A splendid idea." They walked up the room together. The furniture had been removed and replaced by rows of gilt chairs set before an elevated platform containing a pianoforte and several music stands. They nodded to various acquaintances as they went. "Oh, there is Arabella," said Anne. She waved to her friend, struck by an idea. "Talking of deserving persons, Laurence, Bella is extremely fond of music. She plays also. Let us offer her one of our favored seats."

Laurence agreed enthusiastically, and in a moment

this was done and the three of them were settling in the front row of chairs. Laurence repeated his catalog of the coming treats to Arabella, who received it with much more interest than his family had shown. Soon they were engrossed in a discussion about the singers to be heard in London this season, and Anne was free to look about the room.

She was beginning to recognize certain signs in a crowded drawing room, and they told her that this group was unusual. It seemed to be divided between a small number of very earnest guests, who huddled in animated discussion and almost none of whom she knew, and a large proportion of bored fashionables, who swung their fans idly or raised quizzing glasses in jaundiced weariness. Anne smiled slightly. It was fortunate that Mariah had convinced Charles she need not come. She would not care for this party.

The Branwells came in, escorting several late arrivals, and made their way to the front of the room. Mrs. Branwell sank into a chair at once, but the bishop made a show of establishing his daughter on the raised platform and capturing the guests' attention. Lydia waited with her fine head held high. Anne saw Charles sit down with a group of his friends near the back of the room—she hadn't expected him to join them—and smiled as Edward slipped out with some fellow officers, no doubt in search of a quiet place and a hand of cards. Then, as Lydia began to speak, she turned to look at her.

"We have a great treat tonight," said Miss Branwell. "Madame Callini of Milan is with us and has promised to sing several of her justly celebrated arias. I won't delay that pleasure any longer, but will merely present…Madame Callini." She extended a hand and looked expectantly toward the rear doorway. The audience turned also.

There was a moment of silence. Someone giggled, then quickly controlled himself. "Madame Callini?" repeated Lydia, louder and with impatience in her voice. The doorway remained vacant. Whisperings started in the crowd.

Her eyes flashing, Miss Branwell glanced at her father, who looked thunderous, then stepped down and strode through the drawing room and out at the rear. As one, the guests began an avid discussion of this contretemps.

"I wonder what can be the matter?" said Laurence. "Perhaps I should offer Lydia my assistance?"

"Yes, indeed," replied Anne. "I wager she would be very grateful." To herself, she thought that this was a fine opportunity for Laurence to observe his fiancée's temper.

He rose. "I hope there hasn't been an accident."

"Oh, yes," agreed Arabella from his other side. "Poor Miss Branwell, she must be so worried."

Throwing her a warm look, Laurence departed. Anne watched him go with a faint smile, but just as he reached the doorway, Charles stopped him with a raised finger and called him over. As Anne frowned in annoyance, the viscount could be seen admonishing his brother and finally urging him into a chair nearby. "Stupid!" exclaimed Anne.

"What?" Arabella turned from the gentleman on her right and gazed at her friend.

"Nothing, nothing."

"What do you think is wrong?"

"I suppose Madame Callini is being temperamental. Singers are known for that, are they not?"

"Some are. But how dreadful for the Branwells—to have all these people waiting, and no…" She stopped as Lydia entered the drawing room again. There was no sign of Madame Callini, but four very cowed-looking male musicians trailed after her. Lydia appeared to be controlling her rage with great difficulty.

She made no further introductions, merely waving the men onto the platform and dropping into a chair beside her father. When the bishop leaned over to ask an irritable question, he received a glance of such burning outrage that even he drew back, daunted. "Why did Charles have to meddle?" murmured Anne savagely.

"What?" Arabella looked around for Laurence, then moved over into his seat as the musicians struck up. "What is the matter, Anne?"

The other sighed and leaned back in her chair. "Nothing, Bella, I promise."

"Shh," hissed Lydia, glaring at them as if everything

were their fault, and they fell silent, turning dutiful eyes to the players.

The program seemed rather long to Anne and, judging by the restless rustling that increased as time passed, to other members of the audience as well. The quartet no sooner finished one piece than they began another, hardly pausing for the audience to express appreciation. Anne concluded that they had received harsh orders from Lydia Branwell. At last, however, they ceased, and the bishop announced a buffet supper in the dining room. The guests filed out eagerly, as many turning toward the stairs, Anne noticed, as toward the food. The second part of the performance would be more sparsely attended.

Anne and Arabella walked to the dining room together and joined a table of young people near the door. A lively, noisy meal was in progress, the gentlemen fetching plate after plate of tidbits and vying for designation as most discriminating provider. Arabella laughingly agreed to judge between the lobster patties and the meringues, insisting that she liked them equally well, but Anne refused to be pulled into the competition. She was looking around for Charles, determined to speak to him.

She did not find him at once, but at last a group of diners moved toward the buffet, and she saw him in the far corner. Rising despite the others' protests, she made her way across and caught him just as he was leaving a group there. "Charles, I want to talk to you."

He turned. "Of course."

Meeting his cool gray eyes, the blond brows slightly raised, Anne was at first uncertain how to begin. She had been very annoyed when he stopped Laurence from following Lydia, but now she felt only confused. "Why did you interfere?" she blurted finally and, at once, bit her lower lip in annoyance.

The eyebrows climbed higher. "I? Interfere?"

Anne raised her chin, determined to continue. "Yes. When I sent Laurence after Miss Branwell. You stopped him."

"I haven't spoken to Laurence since... Do you mean in the drawing room?"

She nodded.

"I see. I did not realize that you had 'sent' him."

"Well, I did. And you spoiled it. I wanted him to see her in a rage."

"Ah." Lord Wrenley's expression was wry. "I see. And I, in a misguided attempt to spare him that sight, forestalled you."

"Spare him?"

"Yes, Anne. I am not entirely unfeeling, you know. I may weary of my brothers' follies, but that does not mean that I wish them to endure the rages of a creature like Lydia Branwell. I was moved by, er, compassion to save him."

"But if he *saw*—"

"I understand now. No doubt you are quite correct. I apologize for 'interfering.' I shan't do so again."

He looked away. He had given some thought to Anne's remarks about Laurence, and decided that they had merit. And though nothing could be done about his brother's unfortunate choice, Charles had felt a moment's sympathy for him tonight and acted upon it. Predictably, this had only caused more problems. He wished he had left it alone.

He looked so strange, almost piqued, that Anne added, "I have a plan, you see, to show him the truth."

Charles bowed his head, coldly acknowledging her remark, but expressing no interest or approval.

"And when he knows, all will be at an end."

"Will it?"

"Well, of course. No one would wish to marry someone like Lydia Branwell if he realized what she is really like."

"Possibly not. But what has that to do with anything?"

Anne stared up at him. "What do you mean?"

"If you achieve this revelation for Laurence—as I suppose you must, the girl certainly offers ample opportunity—what do you expect him to do?"

"Why, break it off, of..." Anne shut her mouth abruptly. She raised her eyes to his. He looked inquiring. "He cannot break it off, can he?" she whispered after a while.

"It is certainly not the act of a gentleman."

"But... Oh, dear."

"It appears that your meddling is as misguided as mine. Perhaps we should both give it up."

Anne was thinking. "I shall have to find a way to make her cry off," she said to herself.

"An unlikely development."

"Yes, it will be much harder. I hadn't thought." She looked at him speculatively. "You might help me."

He shook his head, still rather offended. "My philanthropic impulses are erratic, and limited to such as you saw tonight."

"Very well, I shall do it myself, then. With Edward."

"He is unlikely to be of assistance."

"On the contrary, he has promised to help me."

"Indeed?" Lord Wrenley looked truly surprised. "Haven't the two of you enough to amuse yourselves with the season?"

"We are not *amusing* ourselves," retorted Anne fiercely. "Can't you see that?"

He looked down at her, frowning slightly. "The first time your crusade seriously inconveniences you, you may see matters differently."

Anne began a hot reply, then paused. Charles really could not understand how she felt, and this made her more sad than angry. "I won't," she answered with quiet conviction. "I like Laurence more and more. I *care* about him. I will do everything I can to further his happiness, whatever the inconvenience."

Their eyes met. Charles was genuinely puzzled. His bewildered expression made Anne smile faintly. "What if one of your friends were about to make a disastrous marriage?" she ventured daringly. "Would you not do something?"

"Of course not. It would be none of my affair."

"You never offer advice, then? Or any kind of help?"

He started to shake his head, then paused.

"You see? How can it be different for your own *family*?"

He frowned. "I have always fulfilled my responsibilities toward—"

"Oh, Charles, I am not talking about *responsibilities*. If that is all you can feel, then I pity you." And turning on her heel, she walked away.

Lord Wrenley watched her go, his frown deepening. He really could not imagine what the girl meant. His family had meant nothing *but* responsibility since he was sixteen. His duty had overshadowed all other emotions, and it had been a burden very nearly too heavy for an adolescent. Now that Laurence and Edward were older, he was only too glad to give them free rein. What more could Anne ask?

Raising his head, he looked at her from under lowered eyelids, trying to dismiss her remarks from his mind. But for some reason, this was very difficult. Her phrases and, particularly, her intense tone lingered in his thoughts. He could not, quite, still the echo of that outraged—"I am not talking about *responsibilities*."

Ten

TWO EVENINGS LATER, ANNE, MARIAH, AND Laurence set off after dinner for Almack's. This was to be Anne's first visit to that famous assembly, and she was eager to see the rooms she had heard so much of. Mariah, who had completed the planting of her parlor garden that afternoon and wanted nothing more from life than to work in it, was resigned to the outing but not inclined to talk, so the conversation during the drive was confined to Anne's questions about what she could see and Laurence's replies.

"I do wish Brummel were still in London," said Anne finally. "Mrs. Castleton was telling me about him yesterday. I should have liked to see him."

"Yes, we haven't anyone to match the Beau," agreed Laurence. "But perhaps the Prince will look in. He does sometimes, when he is in town."

Anne's eyes twinkled. "I understand he is a wondrous sight. They say his corsets creak."

Her escort smiled back at her but said, "Don't say such things to strangers, Anne. The Prince is sensitive."

"I won't. And I hope he does come. But even if he does not, at least I shall be able to waltz, *finally*."

"I hope you will."

"Is there any doubt of it?"

"Well, no, of course not."

"Do they sometimes leave one sitting at the side through *all* the waltzes?" she demanded, suspicions aroused.

"No. That is, hardly ever. Only when they...er..."

"When they don't like you," finished Anne. "And I trod on Lady Jersey's flounce at the Archers' ball and tore it! She will probably tell the others not to approve me. Oh, Laurence, if I have to sit by and watch everyone else dancing many more times, I shall...burst!"

"You won't. I'll...I'll speak to someone."

"Will you? Are you well acquainted with one of the patronesses?"

"Ah, no. But I..."

"Fiddle. I shall have to do something myself."

"No!" exclaimed Laurence, then quickly added, "I will take care of the matter, I promise."

She met his anxious eyes and almost giggled, he looked so afraid of what she might do. "Well, I will give you a chance to do so," she conceded, "but I warn you, I will not sit through every waltz again tonight."

He nodded.

"Is Miss Branwell coming to Almack's tonight?"

"Yes, I expect to see her there."

"I hope she has forgotten that unfortunate mix-up at their musical evening. Did they discover what had become of Madame Callini?"

"Yes." Laurence looked slightly self-conscious, much to Anne's satisfaction. "She…er…had another engagement."

"How heedless she must be, to make two appointments for the same evening. But the Branwells told her so, I suppose."

Looking unhappy, Laurence nodded again. He turned to look out the carriage window. "Here we are."

Anne leaned forward to look. "Mariah, here is Almack's. Look."

The other woman had been reclining in the corner of the chaise, lost in reflection, but now she started and sat up. "What? Oh, to be sure." She looked out the window. "Very pretty."

Anne smiled at her. "Aren't you the least bit excited to see it, Mariah?"

Cocking her head, she considered the question. "Well, dear, I don't believe I am. It is well enough, of course, and perhaps if I were younger I might feel differently, but as it is"—she looked again—"well, I fear I prefer my garden. Did I tell you that your parrot has learned to say 'boxwood'?"

"Yes, Mariah." The girl laughed as the carriage pulled up before the steps. "Perhaps you can reform his vocabulary. I know Laurence, at least, would be grateful."

All three of them laughed at that, and they made a merry picture as they climbed down from the coach. Laurence was handsome in the knee breeches and silk stockings required by Almack's. Mariah was neatly, if somberly, dressed in gray satin. And Anne wore an evening dress of pale green which by contrast brought out the violet shades in her eyes.

Inside, Anne duly admired the graceful proportions of the rooms, the scrolled molding on the walls, and the gleaming chandeliers. A set was forming, and she was asked to join it before she had time to do more. Mariah sat down with the chaperones by the wall, and Laurence went in search of the Branwell party. The first two sets, which were country dances, passed pleasantly; Anne saw Arabella and a number of other acquaintances and spoke to them during the interval. But for the third, the musicians struck up a waltz.

Grimacing, Anne retreated to the chairs along the wall. She looked around for Laurence, hoping that he was keeping his promise, but found him leading Lydia Branwell onto the floor. She saw no one she knew sitting out. With a sigh, she started to make her way across to Mariah.

"Lady Anne?" said an extremely aristocratic female voice behind her.

She turned, and found herself facing the Princess Lieven, Almack's haughtiest patroness, and Charles.

The former smiled graciously. "I cannot introduce Lord Wrenley to you as a suitable partner, since you know him quite well, of course. But I hope you will consent to waltz with him?"

Considerably startled, Anne nodded. The princess inclined her head; Charles offered his arm, and in the next moment they were whirling together round the floor.

When she was certain she had grasped the steps correctly, Anne raised her head and shook out her red-gold curls. The waltz was as exhilarating as it had appeared. She thought it rather like riding—two creatures moving in harmony through set paces. She tossed her head again.

"You look remarkably pleased," said Charles.

"I am! You know how I have longed to waltz. Oh, thank you for asking Princess Lieven to approve me."

"My pleasure."

She looked up at him questioningly, realizing that he had made an uncharacteristic effort to help her. "Is it?"

"Yes, Anne. But let us talk of something more interesting. What were you thinking a moment ago, when you looked so rapt?"

"Of how I enjoyed the dance, and how like riding it is."

His eyebrows came up. "Riding?" Slowly he nodded. "I suppose I see what you mean. But don't say so to anyone else, Anne."

"Why not?" she began, then realized that the comparison was perhaps a bit indelicate. She almost laughed; then, incomprehensibly, her cheeks started to burn and she felt suddenly awkward. She looked down. For some reason, she had become much more aware of Charles—his arm encircling her waist, his hand holding hers, his chest only inches from her chin. Her flush deepened.

"You know," said Charles conversationally, "I don't believe I have ever seen you embarrassed before. I was not certain you ever were."

A small spark of anger lessened her confusion. "Of course I am. What do you think me?"

"An interesting question. Do you know, I am not quite sure." His tone was meditative, because, in fact, he had asked himself this more than once over the past few days. He knew very clearly what he *had* thought of Anne. He had judged her an infuriating, intractable child and, when she returned from school much improved, an acceptable young lady. He had expected then to dismiss her from his mind. But this had not happened. First her obvious, rather juvenile hostility toward him had been mildly amusing. Then, her insistence upon Laurence's "happiness" and commitment to doing something about it had mystified him and, later, made him think. Indeed, he had not devoted so much thought to his family in years. Anne's questions about his reaction to a friend's trouble, as opposed to Laurence's, had remained in his mind. He still believed he was right not to meddle in his brother's affairs, but Anne had somehow become much more interesting to him. He had found himself wondering, often, what she would do next.

Anne gazed up at him. His face showed none of its usual mockery. Indeed, she could not interpret his look. As she continued to stare, his arm tightened slightly, and he whirled her in a sudden turn. Anne caught her breath and looked down again.

There was a silence between them. Finally Charles said, "How is your campaign to free Laurence coming along?"

"I…I haven't done anything else as yet."

"Ah." He looked around. "They seem in charity with one another."

Anne followed his gaze to Laurence and Lydia, dancing nearby. They were talking animatedly. "Yes. But he was shaken by her anger at the party; I could tell."

"Could you? And what is your next move?"

"I don't know. I have been trying to think of a way to draw Miss Branwell off. But it is difficult."

"So I should imagine."

"Perhaps you could suggest something? You know more of these things than I."

"You flatter me. I fear I haven't the smallest notion."

Anne nodded. "Well, you will tell me if you think of something, I hope."

He shrugged, looking a little distant. "That seems to me very unlikely." There was another pause. Anne was offended at his tone; he had begun the subject, after all. Finally he said, "Have you tried your mare in the park yet?"

"Yes."

"You are satisfied with her? You didn't sound particularly enthusiastic."

"Oh, yes," replied Anne warmly. "She is a sweet goer. Our only trouble is that we cannot have a gallop in the Row. I believe she finds trotting up and down as stupid as I do. I have seen it in her eye."

"You are well matched, then." Charles laughed.

"Yes indeed."

"Well, when you take her down to Wrenley, you can both have all the gallops you care for. Will you hunt her?"

With this, they plunged into a discussion of the hunt pack near Wrenley and of the various courses Charles had done with them in the last few years. This occupied them through the remainder of the set, and when the music stopped, Anne was surprised. She had not realized so much time had passed. As they walked across to the refreshment room to get a glass of ratafia, she marveled. Charles had been uncommonly pleasant to her, nearly as pleasant as to his friends on the night she watched him rally them. What had come over him? She could not remember enjoying a dance more in her life. And Charles had not even said he was coming to Almack's tonight.

They encountered Laurence and Lydia Branwell in the refreshment room and paused a moment beside them. Arabella came up with her partner, and the group chatted desultorily for several minutes. Anne could almost feel Charles becoming bored with Lydia's description of a concert she had attended the previous evening. The music started up again, and Arabella's partner excused himself, saying he was promised for this set. Lydia continued her story, oblivious of the increasing restlessness of her audience, including Laurence. Finally, when Arabella had been gazing into the ballroom for a full minute, her foot tapping in time to the music, Laurence smiled and asked if she would like to join the set. With a brilliant smile, she nodded.

"But I am talking, Laurence," interrupted Lydia, clearly displeased.

"You have told me about the concert already," he replied. "And Charles and Anne are here with you. I am sure you will excuse me."

"Are you?"

Laurence's smile started to fade. He seemed both puzzled and embarrassed. But before he could speak again, Lydia noticed his reaction and added, "Of course I do. Go on. I will be with Mama later."

Smile restored, Laurence bowed slightly and went off with Arabella on his arm. Lydia watched them go, her expression thunderous, and the others observed her curiously. When Miss Branwell turned back and became aware of their scrutiny, she produced a smile that was more like a snarl. "Such a charming girl, your *friend* Miss Castleton," she said to Anne.

But Anne had faced more frightening opponents than this. "Isn't she?" she responded, sternly keeping the amusement out of her voice and eyes.

"And you are so *kind* to her, presenting her to everyone."

"Well, of course I do that. But I hardly call it a kindness, unless to my friends. Arabella needs none of my help."

"Indeed? One can see that she has extremely *accommodating* manners. I hope they do not lead her into trouble one day."

Anne's gray-violet eyes blazed at the insinuation in her tone. She was about to make a blistering reply, which would no doubt be as ineffective as unwise, when Lord Wrenley said, "I think your choice of words inapt, Miss Branwell. But there are less attractive sorts of manners, even so."

Lydia's head jerked as if she had been slapped, and she turned to stare at Wrenley as if she had forgotten he was present. In an instant, her face changed, a smile effacing the annoyance so visible a moment before. "But of course, Lord Wrenley," she agreed. "I meant nothing. Perhaps my word choice was careless. Miss Castleton is the most delightful of girls. And now, if you will excuse me, I must speak to Mama." She walked away, the set of her back proclaiming the falseness of her apology.

Anne found that she was shaking, whether with rage or in reaction to this hostile exchange, or both, she was uncertain. She clenched her fists and opened them again.

"You will endure a lot more of that sort of thing, and worse, if you continue in your efforts to end the engagement," said Charles.

"She is an odious girl!" replied Anne.

"Undoubtedly. And because she is, she will always be willing to say more than you. She can make your encounters very unpleasant. Are you certain you wish to face that?"

"I don't wish to at all. But if I must to help Laurence, I shall, of course."

The viscount gazed down at her. She was still visibly shaking. "Are you serious?"

Anne glanced up, surprised. "Yes. But I must speak to Edward, and there he is. Excuse me."

He watched her approach the youngest Debenham, detach him from a group of fellow officers, and pull him to a vacant sofa. Lord Wrenley's face showed puzzlement and a dawning admiration.

"So you see," Anne was telling Captain Debenham, "my plan was not quite right. Laurence cannot be the one to cry off; she must. We must find a way to make her."

Edward scratched his head. "She won't do that. The bishop is keen on the 'family connection.'"

"How do you know that?"

"One of his cronies is father to a friend of mine. Heard the whole story."

"Hmm. Well, but surely there are other families?"

He shrugged. "But the girl likes Laurence, I suppose, hard as that may be to stomach."

Anne grimaced at him, but considered this possibility seriously. "I am not certain she does," she said finally. "She seems to want to manage him, but I haven't noticed any signs of real affection."

"Well, the only way to call *her* off is to dangle a better match before her." Edward grimaced in his turn. "A rum notion."

"Edward, you are brilliant. That is precisely what we will do. We will find someone better suited to Miss Branwell and throw them together!"

He shook his head. "No one's suited to that harpy. Wouldn't wish her on my worst enemy."

"N-no. But surely there is some man who would find her amiable."

"Laurence," suggested Captain Debenham pessimistically.

"Yes, but he is mistaken!"

"There you are."

"I mean someone who would admire her true qualities, someone who likes a woman to be..."

"It won't fadge, Anne. Who would?"

"Well, I don't care," snapped the girl impatiently. "It must be someone other than Laurence. I shall begin looking at once, and you are to do so too."

"I'll do my best, but I don't promise anything. Everyone I know avoids the Branwell like plague."

Anne waved this aside. "Is there nothing else we can try at the same time? Think!"

Edward frowned. "Might make a push to convince her that Laurence is unworthy of her regard."

"What do you mean?"

"Tell her something off-putting about him. Tell her he drinks too much."

"He does not!"

"No," admitted Edward rather regretfully. "And she wouldn't believe it, either. Have to think of something else."

"We are *not* going to tell lies about Laurence, not even to save him," said Anne firmly.

"All right." Edward shrugged. "Still, it's not a bad idea."

She ignored this. "We must consider what sort of man would draw Miss Branwell away from Laurence, and then find him. I suppose she wishes to marry a clergyman, as her father is a bishop. And you say they are concerned with a good family connection."

"She has money, too," added Edward. "Her father won't countenance a pauper."

"I should think a very serious young man," mused Anne. "Interested in music, and eager to have the management of his household taken wholly out of his hands. Yes."

Edward laughed. "Particularly that last. Find a wellborn churchman who wants to live under the cat's foot, and there's your man."

She could not help but giggle at this description. "That does not sound too difficult."

He snorted. "Sounds dashed impossible to me."

"Nonsense. We can begin looking tonight. Can you think of anyone who might be here?"

"At Almack's?"

"Laurence is here."

Edward frowned and pondered the question. After a while, he shook his head. "This'll never work, Anne."

"Of course it will. It has to. Come, let us walk about and examine the crowd."

"Looking for clergymen? Have you lost your wits?"

"Are you turning cow-hearted on me now, Edward?"

"I? Not a bit of it. But, Anne—"

"Good. Come along, then." She took his arm and urged him up from the sofa.

"See here, Anne…"

"Don't worry, we'll find someone. Now, who is that gentleman over there?"

With a sinking heart, Edward followed the direction of her gaze and embarked on the first of what was to be a long series of character sketches.

Eleven

THE FOLLOWING MORNING, ANNE WENT RIDING IN THE park with Edward. They had agreed upon this appointment at the end of an unsuccessful search at Almack's, in the hope that one or the other of them might think of a new scheme during the night. The day dawned fresh and clear, with air so cool and crisp that Anne could almost imagine that she was in the country again, and as she put on her dark blue riding habit, she said to herself, "We *will* solve this problem today; I'm sure of it."

And in fact, Edward's first words to her were, "I have hit upon something!"

She hurried down the stairs to join him in the front hall, but nothing more could be said until they had mounted their horses and started toward the park, the groom following at a distance. "What is it?" she asked then, easily holding her fresh mare alongside Edward's mount.

"It is the simplest thing. I don't know why I didn't think of it last night."

"What?"

"Well, we want to see the Branwell married to someone else, don't we?"

"Yes, Edward. Do come to the point."

"Give me a chance. Now, there is one very simple way of ensuring that she must do so."

"What?" said Anne impatiently again.

He gestured with his free hand. "We will arrange for her to be stranded overnight with the chap, someone we don't like. A bit of work on a carriage wheel ought to turn the trick. And then, you see, they will be forced to…" He trailed off in the face of Anne's wide, horrified gaze. "What's the matter?"

"The matter? Edward! You cannot be serious."

"Why not? The thing's a certainty."

"We *could* not be a party to such a shocking trick. I am…I hardly know what to say to you. How could you suggest such a thing?"

Edward moved his shoulders uneasily under her accusing stare. "I thought you wanted to separate her from Laurence," he said defensively. "This would do it, with the least trouble and sure success. I don't see why you're cutting up rough about it."

"Don't you?" She continued to gaze at him.

He shifted uncomfortably again and looked away. "It is unusual, of course, but…"

"Edward!"

"I was only trying to help," he burst out. "This was your scheme, and I think you might be more grateful for my ideas. *I* wasn't the one who decided to meddle."

Anne opened her mouth on a blistering rejoinder, then shut it again. He was right. The original plan had been hers. Edward's suggestion was outrageous, but perhaps her calm assumption that she knew what was best for Laurence, a man eight years her senior, and her headlong plunge into his affairs, was just as wrong. Edward's impossible scheme showed her the folly of her own actions. "You are right," she said, bowing her head. "How could I be so arrogant as to think I could order Laurence's life better than he? I rushed in without thinking again, and made my usual muddle."

"No, here, I say, Anne. I didn't mean—"

"We will forget the whole matter," she interrupted. "We won't speak of it or think of it again. Laurence must be allowed to make his own decisions." They had reached the park, and she turned her mare onto a gravel lane bordered with evergreens, spurring her to a trot.

Edward fell a bit behind, and it took him a moment to catch up. "But, Anne..." he began then.

"No. You aren't to mention the matter again." She looked away. "There are daffodils! See, through there."

He did not answer her, and she turned to look at him. Captain Debenham's handsome face showed a very uncharacteristic expression. He seemed lost in thought. As she watched, his brows came further together, he shook his head once, and looked up. "No, Anne," he said. "You are wrong."

She stared at him. He did not sound like the heed-less, teasing Edward.

"Not about my scheme," he continued. "I see that that is unsuitable. I suppose I was half joking anyway. But we cannot simply give up. I admit I wasn't keen on interfering when you first enlisted me, but now I am convinced. I've watched Laurence with that girl. She's got him blinkered and tied. He has no more idea of her true character than a cat—less! He thinks her a model of goodness. It ain't fair!"

Anne gazed at him, astonished.

"Dash it, Laurence and I disagree about scores of things, but he's a good fellow. He don't deserve that harpy. He needs a nice lively girl, to keep him from being stodgy."

"You…you care about him, don't you?" murmured Anne, who had been watching his face as he spoke.

"I?" Edward looked away, then down at the path before them. "He is my brother, dash it."

The girl smiled. "Yes. But do you think it is wrong to meddle in his affairs without telling him? I know it was my idea, but now…"

"Well, we certainly can't *tell* him what we mean to do," replied Edward sensibly. "He wouldn't stand for it."

"Exactly."

He eyed her. "Have you changed your opinion of Lydia Branwell all at once?"

Anne shook her head.

"Well, have you decided you don't care for Laurence after all? Perhaps you want to see him miserable?"

"No!"

"All right, then. We must go on with our plan."

"Y-yes. Oh, Edward. I don't know what is right. Perhaps we should ask Charles."

"Charles!" He stared as if she had suddenly lost her mind.

"He is older, more experienced."

"Don't you know what Charles would say to us if we ran to him with this?" Anne turned to look at him. "He would tell us we were both fools to worry over Laurence, and that Laurence was an even greater fool to have offered for the Branwell, *and* he would say that he has no patience with fools."

"But I did tell him…"

"No, Anne. This is up to us. What are we going to do?"

She frowned at him, feeling confused. "We are *not* going to compromise Miss Branwell."

"No, no. I told you I had done with that."

"Yes. Well…we must, uh, go back to our old plan, I suppose."

"A substitute for Laurence?"

She nodded, still far from satisfied with the way things stood.

"We can keep looking," he agreed. "But we need some alternatives, in case we can't find anyone. We must think."

The rest of their ride was taken up with discussing, and rejecting, various courses of action, and when they returned to the Debenham town house, they were no further along. As Anne bid Edward good-bye, she still felt distinctly uneasy. She had made so many mistakes in her life through being too impetuous, and she was afraid this was another. Edward's reassurance, and his new concern for his brother, gratified but did not calm her. He was far too much like herself to represent the steadying influence she knew to be vital in these cases.

She thought over their conversation again as she walked up the stairs, holding up the heavy skirts of her habit. It made her frown. But her gloomy meditations were interrupted dramatically on the first landing. One of the housemaids burst out of the corridor doorway, her arms flung over her head, shrieking. Close behind her flew Augustus, his gaudy red-and-blue plumage flashing against the pale blue walls. The maid did not pause upon seeing Anne, but ran down the stairs with dangerous speed, still screaming at the top of her lungs, and disappeared through the door leading to the kitchens, slamming it behind her. Augustus, thwarted, screeched, "Blast ye!" and spiraled up to settle on the hall chandelier, glaring down at Anne with malevolent glee.

At this moment Mariah appeared at one side of the landing, wearing a long earth-soiled apron and carrying a trowel, and Charles at the other, in impeccable yellow pantaloons and a light blue coat. Both of them followed Anne's stunned gaze to the chandelier. "Damn your eyes!" squawked the parrot, swaying back and forth among the crystal teardrops.

"How," inquired Charles calmly, "did he escape his cage? I presume it was not intentional?"

"If they would let me be," complained Mariah, "and not continually plague me with silly questions about this ball, it would not have happened."

The viscount turned to look at her.

"I let him out in the garden for some exercise," added Mariah. "Every creature needs exercise; birds are no exception. The door was tightly closed; there was no possibility of escape. Then that silly girl came in with some question about glasses. What do I know about glasses? Why do they send to me? She left the door standing open, and when Augustus saw it, he naturally flew out. He is not stupid. But he did *not* attack the girl. It was her screaming that excited *him*. I might have gotten him back into his cage by now if it weren't for that."

Anne bit her lower lip to keep from giggling.

"I see," replied Lord Wrenley. "Well, perhaps you might do so now."

Mariah snorted. "He will not come *now*. He is overstimulated and hysterical."

Charles looked up at Augustus, who returned his gaze impassively. "Is he?" They regarded one another.

Unable to restrain herself any longer, Anne burst out laughing. She laughed so hard that she had to lean against the stair rail.

The viscount turned to her. "Happy as I am to see you so amused," he added, "I cannot help but wish that you would remove your, er, pet from my chandelier."

This only made Anne laugh harder. She put a hand to her mouth and tried valiantly to stop. "I'm sorry," she gasped. "It was just the way you looked at each other." She lapsed into giggles.

Charles gazed up at Augustus, whose beady eye remained on the group below him, then back at Anne. A spark of amusement kindled in his gray eyes though his face showed nothing.

"She won't get him down either," said Mariah. "Leave him. He'll come when he's hungry."

"Possibly," agreed the viscount, "but I am not inclined to await that event. I cannot endure hours of shrieking housemaids or the, er, other inconveniences attendant upon Augustus's freedom." He noticed that Fallow had come into the hall below and was eyeing the parrot with dislike and apprehension. "Is that not right, Fallow?" he added.

"Absolutely, sir," agreed the butler.

"We must find some means of dislodging him," concluded Lord Wrenley, "and I think the task falls to Anne. The bird belongs to her."

Anne, who had finally gotten her giggling under control, replied, "*I* don't know how to get him down. Why, he is twenty feet from the floor. And I can't put a ladder against a chandelier."

"Call him," retorted Charles, a hint of irritation creeping into his voice.

Hearing it, Anne decided to oblige, though she had little hope of success. "Augustus! Come down at once. Down, sir." She held out her wrist as she had seen a woman do in an old picture of hawking. "Augustus!"

Lord Wrenley's lips twitched visibly. The parrot swayed from side to side on the chandelier and leered at Anne.

"Come down, Augustus! I will give you a seed cracker." She moved her wrist suggestively.

"Of course he won't," began Mariah, and Charles burst out laughing. Anne glanced sharply over at him, started to frown, then smiled instead. Their eyes met, and she was once again overcome by giggles. Mariah put her hands on her hips. "I shall be in the garden if you want me," she said disgustedly, and she turned on her heel and disappeared into the corridor.

Charles and Anne laughed until they were weak, he leaning against the door frame, she again draped over the stair rail. Fallow watched them with bewilderment for a while, then went to fetch a footman and a ladder. Augustus remained as he was.

Finally, exhausted, they fell silent. "Nevertheless, we must get him back to his cage, you know," said Charles then.

"Oh, yes. But how?"

Fallow returned with his henchmen. The tall-est footman placed the ladder against the wall and climbed up as far as he could, Fallow and another servant holding the base steady. It brought him nowhere near the parrot.

"I have an idea," said Charles. Anne turned to find a mischievous light in his eyes. "Wait here," he added, and ran lightly up the stairs and out of sight.

He was gone so long that Anne began to consider going after him. She could not imagine what he was doing. But after about half an hour, during which Augustus did not move and Fallow and the footmen gave up and took the ladder away again, he came down; in his hands were a long-handled net and a small cloth bag. "I thought this was still in the attics," he said with satisfaction, indicating the net. "It belonged to my father. He was a great salmon fisherman. I am only glad he is not here to see the use I mean to put it to."

"But it is not long enough to reach Augustus," replied Anne.

"No, but I have a plan. I shall stand on the stairs as near to the chandelier as possible, holding the net. You will dislodge the bird with *these*." He handed her the cloth bag, and she opened it.

"Checkers!"

He nodded, smiling. "They were also in the attic. I wanted something light enough to spare the crystal. Wooden checkers are just the ticket. How is your throwing arm? I remember it was once very accurate."

She wrinkled her nose at him. "If you are thinking

of the cricket ball that I threw at Edward, that was an accident."

"Naturally."

"And I haven't tried anything like it for years."

"But you are game?"

Anne weighed the bag of checkers in her hand; their eyes met. She smiled, bit her lower lip, and nodded.

"Good." He moved up a few steps and braced himself on the rail, grasping the net in both hands. "Fire when ready."

She moved up beside him, taking a checker and calculating the distance that separated her from Augustus. Her eyes narrowed as she cocked her hand back and threw. The missile struck the crystal teardrop beside the parrot's perch, causing it to swing dangerously, but it only made Augustus flap his wings and screech at them.

"Another!" said Charles.

She tried again, and this time her aim was perfect. The second checker struck the bird square in the chest. Outraged, he took wing, flying straight toward them. Charles made a massive swoop with the net, and missed by a hair! The momentum carried his upper body far out over the stair rail, and to Anne it seemed that he might fall over it altogether. Dropping the bag of checkers, she threw her arms around him and pulled back, but she realized at once that he had remained perfectly balanced. It was he who levered them both away from the drop. She tried to step back, her face crimson with embarrassment, and found that the buttons of her cuffs had become entangled with the strands of the net. "Excuse me," she blurted. "I…I thought you were going to fall."

He looked down into her eyes, only inches from his. "Thank you, I was taking care." He raised one eyebrow, as if inquiring why she did not move away.

Anne, acutely conscious of his gaze, and of his body against hers, stammered, "My buttons. Stuck."

"What? Ah. I see. Here, I will disentangle you." In a moment he had done so, and Anne stepped hastily back, her face still flushed. Blessedly, he turned away. "Augustus has returned to his place," he said, pointing. "Shall we try again?"

Anne bent to pick up the bag of checkers, grateful for the opportunity to hide her burning face. She nodded silently. Her first shot after this went wild, but the second again hit the parrot, and this time Charles managed to capture him in the fishing net. The parrot screeched with outrage and fought fiercely, but the strands held him immobile.

"I'll take him back to his cage," said Anne quickly, holding out a hand for the net. "I'm sorry you were disturbed."

Charles extended the handle, but kept his grip on it. This encounter had had a marked effect on him. When Anne looked up questioningly, he said, "Being 'disturbed' is not always unpleasant."

Abruptly, Anne's heart was beating very fast; her hands seemed frozen next to his on the net.

"I don't believe I had quite realized that before," added the viscount.

Anne's lips parted, but no sound came out. She could not think of anything to say; her brain was whirling. But before the silence could drag, Fallow came into the hall again. "You have caught him, sir," he said. "Thank heaven. Shall I call someone to return the creature to its cage?"

"No, no, I'm going," stammered Anne. She pulled slightly at the handle and Charles released it. "I'll see that he doesn't escape again," she blurted as she ran through the door and into the corridor.

Twelve

THE FOLLOWING THURSDAY WAS THE DAY SET FOR THE Debenham ball, and Anne was amazed to rise to a reasonably orderly household that morning. After the upsets and confusion of the previous week, she had expected disaster, but somehow everything seemed to have been settled and solved. There was still much to do, but she no longer had to anticipate hysterics among the maids, fisticuffs between footmen, or pistols at dawn for Mariah and the housekeeper. Her chaperone had been wholly uninterested in the preparations from the beginning, refusing to become embroiled in the various discussions about food and decorations or to join the disputes with tradesmen, and now she blandly accepted the successful completion of arrangements as if these things had never existed. Indeed, her blithe attitude suggested that she had not noticed most of them.

"My lavender is not getting enough light," was her first remark when Anne came into her garden at midmorning. "I was afraid of this. I told Charles I needed more windows." She eyed one of the windowless walls speculatively.

"I don't think that would be possible," replied Anne hurriedly. "All the other walls are interior."

Mariah sighed. "True."

"I wanted to ask you if you have everything you need for the ball tonight," added the girl. "I am driving to Bond Street, and I can get anything you like."

Cocking her head, Mariah smiled. In her outsized apron, she looked rather like a sparrow under a napkin. "No, no, I need nothing. I have more fripperies than I can manage now. You are taking Crane?"

Anne nodded.

"Good. I shall be very relieved when this ball nonsense is over and we can return to our normal routine in this house." Gripping her trowel, she turned back to the bed she had been digging.

"Aren't you at all excited by the idea of our own ball?" asked Anne, whose excitement had been growing through the week.

Mariah smiled again. "No, dear. If the graft takes on my new rosebush, *then* I shall be excited."

The girl laughed. "Well, don't forget that the dinner guests will begin to arrive at seven."

"No, dear," agreed Mariah, bending solicitously over her drooping lavender.

Anne did her shopping, exchanged a book at the library, and returned home to a solitary luncheon. She did not know where Charles and Laurence were, and Mariah never ate in the middle of the day. She could hardly sit still, and wished for someone to talk to. But no one appeared, either then or in the drawing room afterward, and the day passed with exasperating slowness for her. She did not want to read or write letters or sew; she wanted it to be evening and the ball under way.

At last it was time to go upstairs and dress. She still had not seen anyone, though she thought she had heard Charles come in and go to his study. She almost went to make certain, but though the viscount had been much pleasanter these past days, she still did not feel quite easy bursting in on him.

In her bedroom, Crane was waiting. She had spread Anne's dress out across the bed, and the girl could not help but take a deep breath when she saw it. She had devoted a great deal of thought to this gown for her own ball, and she was extremely pleased with the result. She had liked the combination of violet and silver used in one of her other dresses, and her dressmaker agreed that it was flattering. So when Anne suggested that they design a gown using several layers of gauze in these shades, the woman had been eager, and the result was a garment as lovely and changeable as the sea. The modiste had begun with a deep violet layer, then added a series of others shading through lavender to a shimmering silver. Each nearly transparent gauze allowed the previous hues to show through, and when

Anne moved, the effect was stunning. Otherwise, the design was simple—tiny puffed sleeves, a scooped neckline, and a ruffle at the hem that foamed about her silver slippers. Deep violet ribbons were used here and there as trim, and Anne's red-gold hair rose out of this creation like a glorious sunset.

When she was dressed, Anne could not restrain an ecstatic sigh. "Oh, Crane, it *is* a beautiful dress, is it not?"

Her charge's glowing looks had softened even the redoubtable Crane. "It is that, my lady," she replied. "I've never seen one to match it."

Anne smiled at her reflection in the mirror, turning this way and that to look at the dress. A tap on the door made her whirl; Crane admitted a footman laden with boxes. "Whatever are those?" wondered the girl, moving to open the top parcel. "Oh, flowers!"

There were five bouquets in all. Laurence and Edward had each sent one, and three of Anne's admirers and most frequent partners had also remembered. Crane took them from their boxes and set them in a row on the mantelpiece, looking smugly pleased.

"How shall I choose?" wailed Anne. "I cannot carry them all."

"Of course not, my lady. But there's no question of that. These pink roses won't do at all, nor will the yellow." Crane removed the offending blooms to the dressing table, eliminating the contributions of Edward Debenham and one of his fellow officers. "The white roses are suitable," continued the maid, moving down the row, but her tone suggested that she did not think much of this choice, "and the lilies, of course. The red roses are wrong." A third bouquet joined those set aside.

"I suppose the roses," Anne was beginning doubtfully, when there was another knock. Crane opened the door to reveal a footman with a single parcel. She took it and sent him on his way.

"Perhaps this one will be…" The maid stopped abruptly and drew in her breath.

"What is it?" Anne joined her just as Crane pulled the final bouquet from its wrappings. It was beautiful. In a filigree silver holder rested a great purple orchid surrounded by a wide border of violets and fern. Anne also caught her breath. "Who is it from?" she asked. Crane handed her the card. "Oh, it is Charles!" The girl took the flowers and turned to the mirror; they complimented her gown perfectly. "Did you tell him about my dress, Crane?"

"No, my lady." She began to gather up the rejected flowers. "I'll put these in water, shall I?"

"What? Oh, yes. I'm just going downstairs." But when Crane had gone, Anne remained where she was for a moment, gazing into the mirror. She read the card again, "Unusual blossoms for an unusual girl," and could not understand why this message made her heart beat so fast.

The Branwells, the Castletons, and Edward had

been invited to dinner before the ball, and Anne found the former family in the drawing room chatting with Laurence when she came down. Lydia looked very well in deep pink satin and pearls, and the bishop was massively solemn in his evening clothes. She had hardly greeted them when Arabella and her parents arrived, and Anne took the first opportunity to retire into a corner with her friend. "That gown is splendid!" exclaimed Arabella then. "And your bouquet is wonderful. Oh, Anne, you look just as I imagined you might. Extraordinary!"

"I shall take that as a compliment." Anne laughed. "Unlike you, I need an extraordinary dress to come up to standard. It is not everyone who can wear a mere slip of white satin and look pretty as a picture, you know."

Arabella objected to this description of her elegant ball gown. "If Papa could hear you! After the way he grumbled over the bill." But indeed the art of her dress was in its simplicity. It was a mere sheath of white, with the tiniest of sleeves and a plain round neck. Yet Arabella's dark sparkling eyes, perfect features, and creamy complexion provided all the ornament necessary. "Where did you get your bouquet?" she added.

"From Charles. Can you imagine?"

Clearly her friend found it difficult, but Anne did not elaborate. Edward came in, splendid in a new long-tailed coat, and Mariah followed close on his heels. She looked resigned to her fate. Their party was now complete, save the host. "I wonder where Charles can be," murmured Anne.

In the next moment, he appeared in the doorway, apologizing for his tardiness. He wore black knee pants and coat, with striped stockings, a snowy shirt, and a silver waistcoat; all in all, Anne could not recall having seen a more elegant, handsome figure in London. As she gazed across at him, he turned and met her eyes. There was an intensity in his gray ones that made her smile tremulously back at him. She glanced down at her bouquet, then up again, nodding slightly. Charles smiled and bowed his head before going to speak to the Castletons.

Fallow announced dinner, and the party went into the dining room. Anne was seated in the middle of the table, between Mr. Castleton and Edward. As their numbers were uneven, Arabella sat across between the bishop and his daughter, and looked none too happy about the arrangement. Mariah, at the foot of the table, addressed Mr. Castleton at once, and so Anne was free to talk with Edward. As soon as conversation became general, he leaned over and murmured, "I have found a candidate."

"What?"

"You know." He glanced significantly at Lydia Branwell.

"Oh! Who is it?"

"Harry Hargreaves. He's the brother of a friend of mine."

"Captain Hargreaves?"

"That's it. Both sons of Earl Chalham, you know. Harry went into the church. He's secretary to the Archbishop of Canterbury."

"Oh, Edward, that's splendid!"

"Ain't it? They say he has good prospects. *And* a tidy fortune."

"He sounds perfect."

Captain Debenham nodded. "Dull as ditchwater, too."

Anne frowned. "That sounds less promising."

"What do you mean? Just the sort of fellow she wants. Talks of nothing but the rates and the Catholic question, that kind of thing."

"But Laurence is not dull." Looking around hastily, Anne lowered her voice. "Quite the opposite."

"She'd like it if he were, though. Haven't you heard her?"

Anne looked doubtful.

"I tell you, Harry Hargreaves is our man."

"You've met him?"

"No. He lives in Canterbury." As Anne started to protest, he added, "*But* he's coming up to London for several weeks on church business, and Alec, his brother, has promised to present me." Edward grinned. "Nearly cost me my reputation to arrange that. Alec can't see why I want to meet a dull dog like his brother."

Smiling, Anne said, "You will bring him to call?"

"And we'll push him onto the Branwells at the first

opportunity," he agreed. "After that, I daresay things will take care of themselves."

Anne was less sanguine, but she nodded. She would be there to help them along if they did not. "I am impressed, Edward. How did you manage to find someone so quickly?"

"I asked." He grinned. "No one takes any heed of what I say. I can find out anything, and they forget they've told me."

She laughed. "I must keep that in mind."

Mr. Castleton ended his conversation with Mariah and turned to Anne, throwing Edward back upon Mrs. Branwell and her timorous silences. He made heavy work of that while Anne enjoyed a pleasant chat, and they had no more opportunity for private discussion through the rest of the meal. The party did not linger at table; the guests would begin to arrive right after dinner. And an hour later, Anne was standing on the stairs before the ballroom, flanked by Charles and Mariah, holding out her hand to the first of them.

The file seemed endless. All of London turned out for the first ball at the Debenham house in twenty years. Anne soon lost track of time and of the countless names she heard. She had been present at many of the tremendous "squeezes" of the season, but she had never before been required to greet so many people personally. Finally, when the flow of arrivals had begun to slow, Charles took her arm. "Come, you must open the dancing. I will present you to your partner."

"Present me?"

"Yes, you will be dancing with a duke's son."

"I don't know any dukes' sons."

He smiled slightly. "Does that signify?"

"Of course. I should much rather dance with a friend."

"Yes. But in this case, a duke's son will give your debut cachet, you see."

"Do I? I suppose so. Is he at least a charming duke's son?"

"I believe the duke is considered very charming."

"No, I meant… Oh, you know quite well." She wrinkled her nose at him, and he smiled down in response. Anne remembered her bouquet. "I must thank you for my flowers. They are exquisite. How did you know to get purple?"

"An inspired guess."

"No, really! I thought my gown such a secret."

"I assure you it was. Here is the marquess."

He presented Anne, and the couple took their places on the floor as Charles went to ask one of the older ladies for the set. Soon the room was filled with dancing couples. Anne found her partner rather dull, and she was not sorry when the dance ended and she could exchange him for one of Edward's officer friends. After that, the ball went merrily; she danced with two other Guards officers, Laurence, and Edward, and went down to supper with a third military man, joining a gay, noisy table which also included Arabella. After the interval, the two girls went upstairs, then returned to the ballroom together. "I *do* like dancing," said Anne as they walked. "I am having a splendid time; are you?"

"Oh, yes." Arabella's rose-pink cheeks were glowing. "I think I like balls better than any other sort of entertainment."

Anne laughed. "I am sure of it."

A waltz was beginning as they entered the ball-room, and Laurence came up to ask Arabella to join it. As they walked away together, Anne noticed Lydia Branwell coming toward her. She looked quickly about, but could not see any possibility of rescue. Short of obvious rudeness, she could not avoid her. With a sigh, Anne fixed a smile on her face. "Good evening," she said when Miss Branwell was closer. "Are you enjoying the ball?"

"I have decided," replied Lydia without preamble, "to tell you that I know precisely what you are doing."

Anne paled slightly. "I?"

"Oh, come!" The other girl gestured to Laurence and Arabella, whirling in a graceful waltz not far away. "And I shall tell you my reaction as well. Exactly who do you think you are, Lady Anne Tremayne?"

"I…I don't know…"

"You return from school, a mere child, and at once you begin interfering in matters which are none of your affair. Do you really think you have a right to do this? Or any justification? I should like to know. Tell me!"

Anne had begun to tremble before this unexpected attack. "I don't know what you mean."

"Nonsense! We both know quite well. If you wish to pretend ignorance—well, it is just another example of your lack of moral sense. What you are doing is *wicked*, Lady Anne. Meddling in others' lives is arrogant and wicked. No true Christian woman could do so."

"H-how dare you speak so to me?"

Lydia Branwell raised her eyebrows, a superior smile curving her thin lips. "I am perhaps in a position to offer guidance to one who has not had my advantages."

"Guidance? Why, you…"

"I believe this is our dance, Anne," drawled a male voice behind her. She turned to find Charles standing there, holding out a hand. Before she could do anything, he had taken one of hers and was leading her onto the floor. Anne was still trembling with outrage and shock as he swept her into the waltz. "You looked as if you might need rescuing," said the viscount. He held her shaking hand firmly. "Are you all right?"

"If you had waited a moment longer, it would not have been I that needed rescuing," she replied through clenched teeth.

He smiled. "Doubtless. But I did not want to see you reduce Miss Branwell to ribbons before this crowd, satisfying as it might have been for some of us."

Anne blinked and looked around. She had nearly

forgotten the other guests. When she thought of what she had been about to say to Lydia, she flushed.

"Precisely," added Charles, smiling down at her.

One side of Anne's mouth jerked. "I suppose you are right, though she *deserved* a tongue-lashing. But this is not the place."

"No. What did she say?"

"Oh, all sorts of intolerable things. She called me unchristian."

He raised one eyebrow.

"Well, I may not be a prating prig, but I am *not* unchristian!"

"Of course not."

"And she said I shouldn't interfere." Anne frowned. "I hope I am right to do so. I have worried about it, but Edward said—"

"Edward!"

"Yes." She gazed anxiously up at him. "What do *you* think? Do you believe it is wrong for me to try to help Laurence in…in the way I mean to?"

He surveyed her uneasy features; her hand still trembled slightly in his. "Does it really worry you so much?"

"Yes! I want to do what is right. Meddling is so… horrid sometimes. I don't want to be the sort of person who interferes with all her acquaintances and is moaned about in secret."

Lord Wrenley laughed. "You will never be that. You are too straightforward."

"But do you think I am wrong?"

He hesitated a moment longer, then slowly shook his head. He was gradually becoming convinced that Anne's view of the situation was indeed the correct one. He had seen more of Laurence, of both his brothers, this season than at any time in the past ten years. And he was surprised to find them very likable men. Gone were the untidy, demanding boys who had vied for his time and approval at a period when he found them very hard to give. He didn't know how Laurence and Edward had turned out so well; he certainly took no credit for it. But somehow, they had, and Lord Wrenley was more and more drawn to all of his family. He met Anne's eyes again. "I think your purpose is laudable, and your means have been fair."

Anne heaved a relieved sigh. "Thank you!"

He smiled again. "How do you progress?"

"Well, I think. Edward has found a substitute for Laurence."

"A…?"

"A man she will like better. We mean to bring them together." The music stopped, and Anne looked around the room. "Oh, no, Mariah is talking to Bishop Branwell again. I must separate them before they begin shouting. Excuse me."

She hurried off. Charles watched her take Mariah's arm and pull her away with some excuse. The bishop, who was indeed looking thunderous, held himself rigid for a long moment, then stalked over to sit beside his wife. Charles smiled wryly and turned away.

Thirteen

ANNE PASSED SEVERAL QUIET DAYS AFTER THE BALL. No important social events were scheduled, and the family had dined at home two nights running, a very unusual occurrence. She chatted with Mariah in her garden, did some necessary shopping, and called on Arabella. She found she welcomed the respite, as much as she would probably welcome the resumption of festivities with an evening party the following night.

On the third morning, she was sitting in the drawing room with a new novel when Edward came striding in. "I have met him," he said.

"Who?"

"Harry Hargreaves, of course. You can't have forgotten already."

Anne laid aside her book. "No indeed. What is he like?"

Captain Debenham grinned. "Perfect!"

"Really?" She laughed. "How? Tell me about him."

"He is the most pompous, sententious, solemn

chap I have ever had the misfortune to dine with. He cares about nothing but church matters and, I fancy, his own preferment. You should have seen how he brightened when I hinted that Charles has three livings in his gift. He asked me to dine in an instant."

Anne laughed again. "But if he is so pompous, I cannot believe Lydia Branwell will like him. She isn't stupid, Edward. And she likes Laurence, who is quite charming."

"She likes him because of his name and his prospects," retorted her companion. "Show her better ones, and she will forget about liking." He paused. "Besides, Laurence can be fairly pompous when encouraged."

"That seems harsh," murmured Anne. "How do we know that—"

"Anne." He fixed her with an intent look, all joking gone. "You know that I have been on the town for some years, since I was twenty."

"Yes, but..."

"And I've seen a deal of flirtation and a good many matches made in that time. I've even, er, had some encounters myself."

Anne grinned at him.

"So, well," he hurried on, "I can tell something about what a girl feels for the man she's engaged to. I've seen all sorts, and I'm certain that Lydia Branwell cares nothing for Laurence *himself*. In fact, from the look in her eye, I'd wager she means to change him all out of recognition as soon as she has him safely married."

Anne thought this over, remembering certain remarks she had overheard. "You may be right."

"I *am*. I tell you I've seen it a dozen times."

Meeting his gray eyes, she was suddenly convinced that he had. "Very well. We must put Mr. Hargreaves in her way, making certain that she knows all about him."

Edward nodded. "I shall get him an invitation to the Archers' rout party on Friday; they will be glad to have another man. We will present him then."

She nodded. "Bring him to call here before that."

"Why? He is an abominable slowtop, I promise you."

"Nonetheless, I should like to see him first."

"All right." Edward shrugged. "I daresay he'll be happy enough to come to Charles's house."

Anne dimpled. "I'll warn Charles to keep out of his way, so as not to be cajoled out of one of his livings."

"Charles!" He stared at her, then grimaced. "It's all very well to joke, but I have had a great deal of trouble over this. I missed Richard's dinner at the Daffy Club to fawn on this Hargreaves."

"You have been wonderful," replied Anne warmly. "I am very grateful to you, and Laurence will be also, someday."

"I hope so." Edward rose. "I must get back; I have duty this afternoon."

"Thank you for coming to tell me. And you will bring Mr. Hargreaves?"

"Yes, yes. Tomorrow."

She held out her hand. "I am proud of you, Edward."

He nodded, his expression a mixture of complacence and impatience, and took a hasty leave of her. When she sat down with her book again, Anne was smiling. Edward really was behaving splendidly, but it was comic to see his half-annoyed satisfaction with his good deeds.

The following day, Captain Debenham kept his promise; he and Harry Hargreaves arrived at midmorning and were taken directly up to the drawing room, where the latter was presented to Anne. She surveyed him with interest. Mr. Hargreaves was a tall, thin gentleman with sparse red hair and a great many freckles on his face and hands. Yet despite this, he was not ugly. His features were well-formed and his blue eyes large and expressive. Anne was thankful for this, for she could not imagine Lydia Branwell rejecting the handsome Laurence for an ugly man.

They all sat down, Mr. Hargreaves looking around the room as if searching for something. "You have just arrived in London, I understand, Mr. Hargreaves?" said Anne.

"That is correct. I am here on business for my employer, the Archbishop of Canterbury. I am his personal secretary."

"So Edward has told me. You must find your work very interesting."

"Indeed. Pardon me, Lady Anne, but is your companion out this morning? We certainly do not wish to embarrass you by an untimely call."

"My…? No, Mariah is here."

"Ah." Mr. Hargreaves leaned back a little. "No doubt she will join us directly, then. I feared we had intruded on you at an inconvenient moment, and I did not wish to allow politeness to stop me from righting the mistake."

Edward grimaced expressively at Anne.

"N-no. To be sure. I am, uh, grateful for your consideration. I'll just see what is keeping Mariah." Anne rose and hurried to the back parlor. Mariah was working on one of her floral borders. "Pardon me, Mariah," said the girl, "but I must ask you to come to the drawing room for a little while. A gentleman has called."

The other straightened and laid aside her trowel. "Of course, dear. You mustn't receive gentlemen alone."

Honesty forced Anne to add, "Edward is here."

In the act of pulling off her gardening gloves, Mariah paused. "He is? Then why must I come?"

"Well, the gentleman, the *other* gentleman, thinks it improper for me to sit with them alone."

Mariah smiled. "He does not sound like one of Edward's friends."

"No. He is not."

"Very well. I shall be along in a moment."

"Th-thank you. I am sorry to inconvenience you—"

"Nonsense, dear. I promised Charles I would look after you, and I shall. You were very right to fetch me."

Anne returned to the drawing room, where Edward

and Mr. Hargreaves were involved in a labored conversation about the painting over the mantel. Murmuring that Mariah would join them directly, she sank into her chair once more. Mr. Hargreaves looked serenely unaware of anything but his own concerns, she thought. Possibly he was pleased that the proprieties had now been satisfied. When Mariah entered a few moments later, he stood and greeted her punctiliously. Mariah's reply that she had been working in her garden made him hesitate, but he soon recovered and initiated a smooth flow of commonplaces that continued for precisely a quarter of an hour. After this very correct interval, he rose and made ready to depart. "Do you come with me, Debenham?" he asked.

"No, I shall stay a moment longer. But I will see you tomorrow at the Archers'."

"Of course." He bowed slightly. "Ladies."

They were all glad to see him go. "What a priggish young man," snorted Mariah almost before he was out of earshot. "Why did you bring him here, Edward? He is not at all your sort."

Captain Debenham grinned. "Anne wished to make his acquaintance."

Mariah frowned at Anne. "Well, I hope she has learned her lesson. I am going back to the garden. If any other gentlemen call, send them away."

Edward burst out laughing. "You may count on me." Mariah went out, and he turned back to Anne. "You see?"

"He is *very* pompous. Oh, Edward, I cannot believe Lydia will like him. Who could?"

"Wait and see. We will meet at the Archers' rout party, and carry out the next phase of our campaign. I must go." He rose.

"Do you *really* think it can succeed?"

"Not a doubt of it! Truly, Anne."

"I hope you are right."

He grimaced comically and with a wave of his hand went out. Anne stayed where she was, thinking over their plan and wondering whether they had made a mistake. Could *anyone* wish to marry Harry Hargreaves? She could not imagine it.

That evening, Laurence escorted Anne and Mariah to an evening party in Berkeley Square, at the house of Lady Mountjoy. The gathering was not particularly brilliant, but Arabella and some of Anne's other friends were there, and she had a pleasant time. About midway through the evening she encountered Charles as she came out of the small back drawing room into the crowded front one. They paused beside the doorway to exchange greetings. "I did not know you would be here tonight," said Anne.

"I did not intend to be. The friends with whom I dined dragged me with them afterward."

Enviously she wondered who these influential friends were. *She* could not have coaxed him to a party he did not wish to attend.

"They regret it already," he added lightly. "Have

you ever seen such a tedious group of people under one roof?"

"Yes, it is not a very interesting party."

"What is the matter?"

She glanced up quickly. "What do you mean?"

"You sounded so unhappy."

"I? I am not. Perhaps it is fatigue, or boredom."

"More likely the latter. You never tire."

"Don't I?" answered Anne wistfully.

Charles looked down at her with a frown. "You really are out of sorts, aren't you? Would you like some lemonade? Are you too hot?"

"No. I am perfectly all right." His questions were mere politeness, she thought. He really cared a thousand times more for his friends than for her.

He did not say any more, but he examined her face closely before remarking, "I understand that you have met your 'substitute.' Edward was telling me about him earlier."

Anne found this a little startling. "Was he?"

"I asked. The gentleman is not here this evening, evidently."

"No. But he will be at the Archers' rout party tomorrow night."

"I am tempted to come and have a look at him."

Even more surprised, she replied, "You won't like him."

"No, from what Edward said, I doubt that I shall. But will the lady? That is the important thing."

"I don't know. Edward says she will, but…"

Seeing her knotted brow, the viscount's gray eyes twinkled. "Edward is expert in these matters, I assure you."

"I… Is he?" Anne gazed up at him with a frown.

"Absolutely."

"That's what he said, but—"

"He did not! Not even my scapegrace brother would be such a coxcomb, surely?"

"He…he didn't use those words precisely, but I got the notion that he…"

Charles began to laugh. "Edward, Edward!"

She eyed him doubtfully.

"I am sorry. I shouldn't laugh."

"Shouldn't laugh with *me*, you mean?"

"What?"

"Never mind. You do laugh more often than I remembered. I expect my memory is at fault."

Surprised, he stared down at her, seeming uncharacteristically at a loss for a reply. Before either of them could speak again, a penetrating voice on the other side of the doorway said, "Yes, Laurence and I hope to be married in August."

"Lydia Branwell," murmured Anne. They could not see Miss Branwell, or the person she addressed, but they could hear her perfectly well.

"Oh, yes, a wonderful family," continued Lydia. "They have been very kind to me. You know Lord Wrenley, of course. A most distinguished man."

Anne wrinkled her nose at Charles, who smiled. He took her arm and whispered, "Let us go before we hear something worse."

She started to agree; then Lydia said, "Have you met Lady Anne? She must be counted as a member of the family, though of course she is not actually related to them." Anne pulled him back and bent her head to listen; Charles smiled again.

"A sweet girl," Miss Branwell went on. "A bit impetuous perhaps, but she is young. I hope to exert some influence in that quarter when we are married. Laurence thinks I can have a calming effect on her."

Anne grimaced and stuck out her tongue at the vacant doorway.

"Her choice of friends, for example, may have been a bit unwise. I do not mention anyone in particular, of course, but a little guidance is clearly in order."

"Do come away, Anne," urged Charles softly.

She shook her head, her lips firmly pressed together. "I *will* hear this!"

The inaudible second person had evidently begged Lydia to elaborate. "Well, I shouldn't say anything, but you are very discreet, I know. I was thinking of Miss Castleton, actually."

Anne's grip on the viscount's arm tightened convulsively.

"Yes, the little dark-haired girl. Have you met her? She is quite pretty, I believe."

"She *believes*," hissed Anne. "She knows very well

that Bella is ten times prettier than she is!" Lord Wrenley held her arm firmly.

"But a little…shall we say, *too* biddable," continued Lydia.

Her listener said something.

"Well, I *shouldn't*, but I know you will not spread the story about. I have heard that Miss Castleton's conduct was not quite all that it should be while she was at school. That is where Lady Anne met her, of course."

There was another pause as the other spoke, still inaudible.

"Oh, nothing definite. You understand that I heard this from someone who had gotten the details from the headmistress. But I didn't really care to listen. I believe there was some talk of an elopement. It was stopped, naturally, and the matter hushed up at once. I really don't know the truth of the matter. You mustn't take my word for anything."

Anne's nails were digging so deeply into the viscount's arm that he had to pull her hand away. He had felt her start to tremble, and now her face had gone dead white and her eyes dark violet, huge and burning with outrage. "I will kill her!" she hissed. "I will scratch her eyes out! How *dare* she? How dare she tell such lies about Bella?"

"Now, *don't*, I pray you, let this go any further, Lady Duncan," Lydia was finishing. "As you can see, it is the merest gossip. Probably inflated all out of proportion. Oh, there is Mama. Excuse me."

"Duncan," croaked Anne, so angry that she could hardly form words. "She is one of the greatest gossips in the *ton*. *Everyone* will hear that story before the night is out. Oh, I will kill her!"

"Come," said Charles, his firm grip forcing her to walk along the wall to a door and into a deserted corridor.

But once out of the crowd, she jerked away. "No! I must see that…viper Lydia Branwell. I will throw her lies in her teeth and *make* her retract them!"

"That would be very unwise."

"What do you mean?" She glared at him, her eyes still glittering with rage. "You don't believe it, surely!"

"I do not. But this is neither the time nor the place to do anything about it. You are too angry to think clearly, and there are far too many people present. To confront Miss Branwell now would merely draw more attention to the matter."

Anne clenched her fists at her sides, her whole body rigid. She had not stopped trembling, and now she had to grit her teeth to keep from shouting at Charles. Finally, when she had gained a little more control, she said, "You do not care. You hardly know Bella. *I* must do something, or I shall *burst*!"

"You are mistaken." He met her eyes, and she saw a spark of cold anger in his. "I do care. Miss Branwell's behavior was contemptible. I do not understand how she, or any woman, could sink so low. And I am not suggesting that you do nothing, only that you wait for a better time."

"But the story will be all over London by tomorrow! Bella will be ruined!"

He shook his head. "It will not be so bad as that. Some people ignore malicious gossip. But it will be unpleasant; I can't deny that. However, we cannot prevent the story from spreading just now."

"Why not? Only leave me alone with that spiteful creature for five minutes. I'll make her take back her vile story!"

"And confirm it," he replied quietly.

"What?"

"If you, Miss Castleton's best friend, leap to her aid in that obvious way, most people will say there must be some reason for it. They will conclude that there *is* some truth in the story, else why should you be so angry?"

"Am I not to be angry if it is a lie?"

"I am only telling you what will happen."

Anne's shoulders drooped. "You mean I must simply stand by and watch that dreadful rumor run round the *ton*? I cannot!" She raised her head again. "Charles, I cannot!"

"Of course you cannot."

She looked at him.

"We must plan a more suitable counterattack, that is all."

"More…?"

He nodded. "First, if you hear anyone repeating the tale, even tonight, you must look incredulous, then laugh as if it were the funniest joke you have ever heard."

"Laugh? I couldn't!"

"You can. And that is the best defense against gossip. Never let the gossips see that you care about anything they say. They will soon find you poor sport."

She merely stared at him.

"Second," he continued, "we must think of some way to squelch the rumors *and* to give Miss Branwell her own again. I admit I do not yet see how that may be done, but I shall think of something."

"You?"

Charles looked down at her, meeting wide inquiring eyes. "Is it so surprising that I mean to help you?"

"Well, no, but…that is, yes!"

He shrugged. "I like your friend Miss Castleton, and as I said, I think Miss Branwell's action contemptible. But chiefly I want to prevent you from doing something rash that you would regret for the rest of your life."

She continued to gaze up at him.

"If you will listen to me, I believe we can bring this matter to a satisfactory conclusion."

There was a momentary silence; then Anne said quietly, "I *will* listen to you."

"Thank you." Their eyes held, his a bit amused, hers still wide with surprise but softer than before.

A servant passing along the corridor broke the spell. Anne looked down at the floor. "But what will we *do*?" she asked him.

"I must think about that."

"Oh, if it had been *me* she libeled, I probably deserve it; I am so heedless sometimes. But Bella! You have no idea how fine she is."

"I am very glad it was *not* you," he replied in a hard voice. "Are you ready to go back in?"

Anne swallowed. "Yes, I think so."

"And you will remember what I told you? If you hear any mention of the story, laugh."

Her chin came up, and she squared her shoulders. "Yes. It will be one of the hardest things I have ever done, but I will. I would rather face a five-barred gate, however."

He smiled. "I will circulate among the gentlemen. They are more likely to repeat it here; the ladies will save it for the drawing room."

"Edward could help you."

"Yes. I will enlist his aid. But not tonight. He is too likely to fly into a rage and spoil all."

Anne smiled wryly. "As I nearly did? I suppose I must be glad you were with me."

He raised an eyebrow.

"I find it hard," she told him. "If you had not been, I should have had the exquisite pleasure of throttling Lydia Branwell. I daresay I would be sorry now. But I would feel vastly better for having done it."

He laughed. "We will try to ensure that you get an equally satisfying, if less violent, revenge." He offered his arm.

"It is only that thought which is keeping me from her throat," she replied, taking it. They strolled back into the crowded drawing room.

Fourteen

ANNE FACED THE ROUT PARTY THE FOLLOWING EVENING with a mixture of apprehension and eagerness. She was at once anxious and afraid to discover the results of Lydia Branwell's contemptible lie, and she remained concerned about what she might say if forced to converse with Laurence's fiancée. When she thought of her, she still clenched her jaw in rage. As Crane retied one of the bunches of blue ribbon that trimmed her white muslin gown, she met her own eyes in the mirror and tried for a cool, composed gaze. It was no good; they continued to flash with righteous indignation. She would simply have to avoid Lydia and hope Charles came up with a solution to the problem before she blurted out something she would regret.

"There you are, my lady," said Crane. She surveyed Anne's cloud of red-gold curls critically. "All set to rights."

"Thank you," replied Anne absently.

"You'd best go down. It's nearly nine."

"Oh. Yes. Thank you."

Charles, Laurence, and Mariah were waiting for her in the drawing room, and the group departed soon after. The viscount's presence was unusual enough to draw a comment from his brother, especially since the rout party was not an event he would customarily have attended, but Charles passed it off with a joke. They had, of course, said nothing to Laurence about Lydia's perfidy, but he seemed in low spirits as they drove the short distance to the Archers'. Only Mariah was as usual, and since she was habitually silent unless she had something important to say, the ride was quiet. Anne saw Charles glance at his brother several times, as if wondering what was the matter. She had an idea she knew, and could not decide whether to be glad or sorry.

The Archers' town house was brightly lighted, the pavement thronged with arriving guests, chairmen, link boys, and other attendants. They made their way in and greeted their host and hostess along with a stream of other fashionables, then moved on into the drawing room. As soon as they entered, Edward approached Anne and took her arm. "Come," he murmured, "all is ready, but you must be there." He drew her away from his brother.

"Ready for what?"

"For the introduction," he answered impatiently. "Hargreaves is there, and the Branwells came in five minutes ago. I was only waiting for you."

Anne drew back. "I can't. You...you go on; do it without me."

"What?" Captain Debenham looked disgusted. "That will look strange. It's well known I'm not overfond of the Branwell; I daresay she knows it herself. Why would I go out of my way to present her to anyone?"

"Edward, I can't face her. You don't know what she has done!"

"Nor do I care. If she has been up to her tricks again, all the more reason to go forward. Come!"

Slowly and reluctantly, Anne followed him across the floor. He was undoubtedly right; it was more important than ever that they carry out their plan. But she hated the idea of facing Lydia Branwell. And she did not want to present her to a potential husband; she did not want her to marry at all. No man deserved such a mate. No, she hoped Lydia would sink into a miserable crabbed old age and... At this point Anne remembered that it was much more likely that Lydia would marry Laurence, unless something was done, and she tried to gather the resolve to do it.

Harry Hargreaves greeted her ponderously. He was standing alone in the corner where Edward had left him, making no effort to speak to anyone. "I was observing the behavior of what is, I suppose, the *haut ton*," he told Anne. "There is much to deplore here, and little to admire, I fear."

"You may be right," agreed Anne. "But I should

like to present you to some friends of mine who are quite different—Bishop Branwell and his family."

Mr. Hargreaves was immediately at her service. "I should be delighted to meet the bishop," he replied.

The three of them made their way to the Branwell party. Laurence had already joined them and was standing—rather forlornly, Anne thought—at the edge of the group. Lydia was talking animatedly to another girl.

Anne performed the introductions. Both parties seemed extremely pleased. At the mention of the archbishop, Branwell's eyes sharpened, and he moved forward to engage Hargreaves in conversation. Lydia at once abandoned her female friend and sidled close to the newcomer, gazing up at his freckled face with a sweet smile. Anne, satisfied and glad to escape without speaking to Lydia, edged away with Edward. When they had definitely disassociated themselves from the group, he grinned widely and sauntered off into the crowd.

"What is the matter with Edward?" Laurence asked Anne.

She started; she had almost forgotten him. "Matter?"

"Why was he grinning in that idiotic way?"

"Oh, just a joke. I am going to find the Castletons, Laurence. Why not come with me?"

He swallowed, glanced back at the Branwells, and shook his head. "No. I must stay here just now."

"But they are very busy talking." Indeed, the trio had become engrossed in a discussion of the poor rates.

Laurence shook his head again and turned away. Anne did not press him further; she was rather pleased than otherwise with his reaction.

Arabella and her mother were not far away. They greeted Anne cordially as she sat down beside them, but the former was frowning. "I just had the oddest encounter with Jane Thorndale," she said, referring to the daughter of one of the highest sticklers in the *ton*. "She went right by me without speaking, though I am certain she saw me. I wonder if she has the headache again? She is horridly plagued by them."

Anne stiffened. Had the gossip already begun to have an effect? As she returned some light answer, she scanned the room carefully. It did seem that an unusual number of people were looking in their direction. She clenched her fists. What could she do? She looked for Charles. He was chatting with friends and appeared blithely unconcerned. How could he?

"Oh, there is Alice Worth," said Arabella. "Let us go and speak to her, Anne. She told me she had some beautiful new dress patterns."

Anne obediently rose, praying that Bella would not meet another snub, but as they walked across toward Miss Worth, they encountered Laurence coming in the opposite direction with a glass of lemonade.

He could not avoid greeting them, but he looked rather self-conscious as he said, "Good evening, Miss Castleton."

"Good evening." Arabella had flushed a little, and

now she looked at the floor. A silence fell which Anne made no effort to break; she was busy observing the reactions of her two companions. They seemed to have forgotten her presence. They were too aware of one another to think of anything else. But they were also embarrassed and uncomfortable. Anne could not restrain a small smile.

"Have you taken to drinking lemonade?" she asked Laurence to relieve the tension.

"What? Oh, no. It is for Lydia. I must take it to her. Pray excuse me, Anne, Miss Castleton."

He hurried away. Arabella watched him, and Anne watched Bella's face. She did not look happy, and if Anne had not already determined that Laurence should not marry Lydia Branwell, she might have done so in that moment. "I like Laurence more and more," she ventured. "He is not at all what I expected a Debenham to be."

Arabella continued to gaze in his direction. "He is charming."

"Do you think so? I'm glad you like him too."

The other girl started and turned to Anne, her flush deepening. "Indeed, he is all one could wish in a…a brother."

Anne raised her eyebrows but made no reply. It was unfair to tease Bella this way.

They chatted with several acquaintances and had a long satisfying conversation with Alice Worth about dress patterns. Then Mrs. Castleton summoned

Arabella to be introduced to someone, and Anne started across to speak to Edward. But Mariah stopped her before she reached him, saying, "Come over to that sofa. I want to speak to you."

This was so unusual—for Mariah always spent social evenings in a quiet corner—that Anne hastened to comply. The sofa was vacant, and no one stood near it; they were completely private.

"I have been hearing some disturbing stories," Mariah began as soon as they were seated. "Everyone seems to be talking of your friend Miss Castleton."

Anne stiffened and clenched her fists.

"I assume they are not true?"

"Of course not!"

Mariah nodded. "That is what I thought. She seems a nice sort of girl to me. What am I to say?"

Anne gazed at her blankly.

"In response to the gossip," added the other impatiently. "How shall I refute it? You must know all about Miss Castleton. Surely you can provide evidence to contradict the rumors."

This was a new idea. Anne frowned. "What are they saying?"

"Oh, a host of things. But the chief tale seems to be that she was entangled with some unsuitable young man while still at school. Her parents rejected him; there was an elopement, and she was dragged back by her father. Setting aside various absurd embroideries, that is the gist."

"It is a lie!"

Mariah sighed. "Yes, dear, but what am I to say? It is not enough to insist the story is false. One must have some convincing proof to offer."

"Any of her fellow students knows it is not true."

"Yes. Well, we might refer to them." She looked around the room. "Which are they?"

Anne looked down. "Only me."

"Oh. And you are known to be her dearest friend. That won't do."

"How can one stop these dreadful stories once they are started? It is horrible!"

"Yes, I've never cared for gossip. I can't imagine how this rumor was started. It is unusual for a young girl like Arabella, so polite and quiet, to be singled out."

Her heart swelling with rage, Anne told her precisely how it had happened. As she spoke, Mariah's gray eyes hardened and her thin mouth turned down. She showed more emotion than Anne had ever seen her display for anything outside her garden. "That young woman badly needs a lesson," she said when Anne had finished. "Either she does not understand what harm her malice can do, in which case she is a ninnyhammer, or she does."

"She knows," put in Anne. "She knows quite well."

"Then she is contemptible."

"That is what Charles said."

"He was right. But what is to be done?"

"Charles said he would think of something."

Mariah nodded and rose. "I will do my best to discourage the gossip. But we must take decisive action soon."

"I know." Distracted, Anne searched the room for Charles. As Mariah walked away, she saw him. He was still with his friends. They were all smiling, and as she watched, she saw Charles throw back his head and laugh heartily. She clenched her teeth. Despite what he had said about Bella, it was obvious he did not care a straw about her. Anne had wondered lately if Charles was changing—he seemed so much more pleasant than before—but now it seemed to her that he was the same callous, cold man she had hated through her school years. But he had *promised* to help Bella in this instance, and Anne was determined to hold him to that. This was not a case of mere slights to herself; Bella was in real trouble. And Charles was better equipped to get her out of it than anyone else Anne knew. He *would* do it. Her eyes sparkling with rage, Anne walked across to where Charles stood with his friends. She did not wait for a pause in the conversation, but interrupted, "Charles, I must speak to you!"

They all looked surprised. Charles turned slowly and met Anne's eyes. "To me?"

"Yes!"

"You're certain you have finished with everyone else—Edward, Laurence, Mariah, Miss Castleton?"

She gazed up at him, astonished. He sounded almost annoyed. What sort of game was he playing now? "Charles…" she began in an ominous voice.

Seeing her expression, he put a hand under her elbow. "Come, there is a terrace just outside these windows. We can talk there." He opened one of the French doors behind them and urged her outside.

The flagged terrace overhung an uncommonly large garden for a town house. The evening was warm, and a full moon hung in the sky above the nearby rooftops. A climbing rose had flung its branches across the balustrade, filling the air with perfume. But Anne was too preoccupied to notice any of these things. "I am sorry to take you away from your *friends*," she said. "But something has happened. The gossip about Bella has begun; Mariah heard the story, and Bella has been snubbed once already. This will not interest you overmuch, I know, but I came to remind you that you told me you would help."

"Did you indeed? But only after you had consulted everyone else in the ballroom, evidently. Edward must have been a *great* help! I never thought I should see the day that his opinion would be preferred to mine."

"Have you run mad, Charles? And how, may I ask, was I to consult you when you were so engrossed with your *friends* that you had forgotten my existence, let alone Bella's? The way you were laughing—as if you hadn't a care in the world!"

"Certainly I was. Did my advice make such a small impression on you that you do not see why?"

"Advice?"

"I see." He turned away from her and looked out

over the garden. "I suppose you have shown the whole ballroom your distress; that will have redoubled the gossip. My help appears to mean very little to you, since you ignore it at the first test."

Abruptly Anne remembered what he had said about putting a brave face on things. "Oh." She was immediately filled with despair at the thought that she had added to the talk surrounding Bella. "Oh, what a fool I am." Tears formed in her eyes. "What can we do? No one will believe it is a lie now. Poor Bella." A tear slid down her cheek and onto the stone balustrade. "And it is all my fault. If it weren't for me, this would not have happened to her in the first place."

"No," agreed Charles equably. "It probably would have happened to some other girl, someone you didn't know well. That would have been all right, I suppose?"

Startled, Anne looked up at him.

"I am convinced that Laurence would have noticed the difference between the rather formidable Miss Branwell and other young ladies sooner or later," continued the viscount. "And when he did, she would have taken some similar action. It is too bad that the victim happened to be your friend, but I believe things would have developed in much the same way without your intervention."

"You do?" He nodded, and Anne heaved a great sigh.

Her drooping pose softened him. "I don't know if you still care for my help?"

Anne looked up sharply. "Care for it? Are you

joking? I am relying upon it, almost solely. I don't know what you were talking about before, but I certainly do not expect Edward or Mariah to think of anything. Edward does not even know about this yet. Without you, Bella is lost—and so am I."

He moved a little closer to her. "I shan't let that happen."

"But what are we going to do?"

"It is a delicate problem. I have not yet thought of a solution."

She leaned against the balustrade and stared unseeing out over the garden. "There is none, is there? There is no defense against gossip. If you protest, people merely take it as an admission of guilt, as you said before. We are helpless." She pounded on the stone with her fist.

"It is not like you to give up, Anne."

She turned to look at him. "I cannot fight all of society. And even if I could, there is nothing to lay hold of, nothing *real*. It is all *talk*."

He moved to stand beside her. The helpless, broken look in her eyes touched him more than anything he could remember, and his momentary pique vanished. At that moment, she seemed to him a wild gallant creature harried by a host of petty, despicable attackers. Something within him protested violently against this unequal battle. He had no thought of responsibility; he did not see it as his *duty* to rescue Anne. Indeed, he hardly recognized his impulse. He knew only that

that look must be wiped away and replaced by her old blithe mischief. "*I* know something about talk," he replied, "and about the *ton*. I will think of a way to stop the rumors, and to end Laurence's engagement at the same time."

Anne gazed up at him, surprised by the vehemence of his tone. "Do you really think you can?"

"Yes."

"It seems so hopeless to me."

"Have you no faith in my abilities?" he asked, in an attempt at lightness.

She considered the matter. She had never seen Charles fail at anything he truly wanted to do. If he was serious about wanting to help—and, unexpectedly, he seemed so—then perhaps something could be done. Slowly she nodded, gaining confidence. She took a deep breath.

"That's better," he responded, seeing the violet shadow in her eyes lighten. "I shall devote all my time to plotting our revenge."

She smiled a little. Their eyes held, and he put a hand over hers on the balustrade. "Don't worry," he added.

For some reason, Anne suddenly found breathing difficult. She wanted to make some move, but she seemed frozen in place, her hand immobile under his. After a long moment, he smiled and drew it away. "Shall we go back in? It is getting late. Mariah will be wanting to go." He offered his arm. "And do not, under any circumstances, tell her there is a garden here, or we will never get away."

With a self-conscious laugh, Anne took his arm, and together they walked back inside.

Fifteen

WHEN ANNE ENTERED THE DRAWING ROOM AFTER breakfast the next morning, she found Laurence there, bent over a sheet of writing paper at the desk in the corner. When she spoke to him, he started, and turned to stare as if she were a stranger, then hastily folded the paper and put it in his pocket. Anne had only time to see that it looked like a list of some sort. But Laurence's appearance drove the matter from her mind in a moment; his expression was so strained and his skin so pale that she could feel nothing but pity. "Are you all right?" she could not help but ask. "You seem ill."

"No, no," he replied distractedly. "I am perfectly healthy, only a bit anxious."

"Why?" Anne eyed him, wondering if he would mention Lydia Branwell.

"I heard some disturbing, er, gossip last night at the Archers'. Manifestly untrue. It concerned… That is…"

"Bella," finished Anne quietly.

"Did someone dare to mention it to *you*?" He looked outraged.

The temptation to tell him about Lydia's part in this tangle was almost irresistible. Anne struggled with herself. If she revealed what she had overheard, either Laurence would not believe her, in which case she would have accomplished nothing, or he would, and then he would be more miserable than ever—bound to a woman without principle or delicacy. Finally she nodded.

"Infamous! I cannot understand how such a ridiculous story got started in the first place. Anyone who knows Miss Castleton must see how impossible it is."

"Yes. But she is not known to everyone."

"You are remarkably cool!"

"I have known about the rumor for several days, and I mean to do something to stop it."

"What?" asked Laurence eagerly. "I will help in any way I can."

"Well…ah…I am not quite sure yet. Charles promised to think of some plan."

"Charles!"

"Yes. And since he knows far more about society than I, I am confident of our success."

"But what has he to do with the matter? Why should he interfere?"

Anne looked at him. "He feels, as you do, that such gossip is very wicked. He wants to set things right."

"Charles?" He seemed unable to accept this idea.

Anne felt a spark of annoyance. "Is that so hard to believe? Do you think your brother without moral scruples?"

"No, no. I know his principles are good. It is just that I have never known him to exert himself on another's behalf."

For some reason, Anne was suddenly angry. "Have you not? Not even your own?"

Laurence gazed at her in surprise.

"Did he not watch over both you and Edward when you were boys? It must have been a burdensome task for a young man, but I don't suppose he ever complained of it."

Her companion's mouth dropped open.

In the face of his blank astonishment, Anne colored slightly and looked down. "But that is beside the point," she added. "He *has* promised to help put a stop to these ridiculous rumors, and I believe he can, if anyone can. So I am not as angry as I was at first."

"Yes…well…that's all right, then." Laurence seemed a bit stunned. "You must tell me what I can do."

"Of course."

There was a short silence. Anne went to sit on the sofa before the fireplace, and Laurence paced about the room as if he found it impossible to stay still. His face reassumed the expression Anne had noticed when she came in. As she watched him, she frowned with concern. Surely he was thinner than he had been when she came to London, and the beginnings of lines showed in his forehead and down his cheeks. He looked five years older. She wished she could ask him what was wrong—for it must be something more than the gossip—but it did not seem right to mention Lydia. She could not tell him what she planned.

Abruptly he stopped pacing and swung around to face her. "Are you enjoying the season, Anne?" he said.

"Why…yes."

"I have not spoken to you about it. We have been so busy these last weeks. I hope London is all you wished for."

"I have had a splendid time," answered the girl, puzzled. "Until this recent business, everything has been wonderful."

"Good, good." Laurence seemed both uneasy and distracted, and Anne could not make out why. "It is a great change for you, after the quiet life at school."

"Yes," she agreed.

"You haven't… That is… I am not prying, but I cannot help but wonder if you have met anyone you like *particularly*."

"Everyone has been kind," responded Anne, still more perplexed. "I have made a great many new friends."

"Ah, yes, yes." He tapped his hands together nervously. "I was thinking of something more than friendship, however. During the season, one meets a variety of persons of… That is…one has the opportunity to…"

"Do you mean have I met anyone I want to marry?" asked Anne, suddenly comprehending. "I haven't."

Laurence took a deep breath. "Ah. Yes, I was asking that."

"Well, why didn't you, then? Surely you needn't be so indirect with *me*, Laurence."

"No." He sounded doubtful. "But it is a delicate question. I did not wish…" He paused, then seemed to come to a resolution. "What I wanted, Anne, is to offer you some advice. I know I have no real right to do so, but I am a bit older than you, and I have made my…that is, I know a little more about the world, and I thought—"

"I should be happy to hear your views," she interrupted, before he could become hopelessly tangled in his own words.

"Thank you!" But with this, he hesitated so long that she almost thought he had changed his mind. "I only wished to say," he continued finally, "that you should take your time. Serious decisions ought to be made with the utmost care and thought. Do not hurry into an attachment. You are very young. You may have another season, two more, before you choose. Wait until you are certain."

He met her eyes, and Anne swallowed. She did not know how to answer him. It seemed obvious to her that he was regretting his own engagement, and his resigned tone made her throat tight with tears. "I will," she managed finally.

He nodded once briskly and turned away. "I must go. I have letters to write." But before he had taken a step, Fallow entered the drawing room and announced Arabella, who came in on his heels.

"Bella!" said Anne, jumping up and striding toward her friend, hands outstretched. She hoped to cover the lingering awkwardness between her and Laurence with her enthusiasm. "How wonderful of you to call. I particularly wanted to see you today."

Arabella smiled and squeezed Anne's hands quickly, but she did not look as cheerful as usual. She glanced toward Laurence, then away again.

"Good morning, Miss Castleton," he said. "How are you?"

"Very well." Arabella's voice trembled a little. "I...I meant to tell you last night that I enjoyed the book you lent me very much. It was just what I like."

He smiled. "Was it? I thought so."

"Am I so transparent?" To the dismay of everyone in the room, her voice cracked, as if she were about to cry. She quickly turned her back on the others, putting a hand to her mouth. Laurence's expression was agonized; he took one step in Arabella's direction, then stopped. "Letters," he murmured in a strangled voice and rushed from the room.

Anne went to Bella, throwing an arm about her shoulders. "Come and sit down."

They both sat on the sofa. Anne patted Bella's hand. "I'm sorry," whispered the latter. "What a fool I am."

"Nonsense. You are no such thing." But despite her bracing words, Anne did not know how to comfort her friend. Too many important topics were forbidden.

Arabella turned wide dark eyes on her. "Mr. Debenham seemed…angry. I hope I have not done anything to…offend him."

"Of course not! And he wasn't angry. He was, er, thinking of something else, I daresay."

"I would not have him angry with me for the world."

"I tell you, he wasn't, Bella."

The younger girl looked down at her clasped hands. "You don't know whether… That is, he didn't mention that he had…heard anything about me?"

Anne's heart sank. The rumors had reached Arabella, a thing she had prayed would not happen. She hardly knew how to answer. "What do you mean?" she finally, cravenly, replied.

Her friend gazed at her. "I think you know, Anne. People have been talking about me. You must have heard something of it."

Anne slumped, dropping her own eyes. "Yes," she admitted at last.

Arabella's eyes filled with tears, and she pressed her lips tightly together.

"Everyone knows it is nothing but a pack of lies. No one believes a word of it, Bella."

"Jane Thorndale does. So do others. Mrs. Thorndale gave me the cut direct last night."

Anne felt such a mixture of outrage and pity that

she could not speak. She took her friend's hand and squeezed it hard.

"It is the sort of story people *do* believe. They enjoy it."

"They are beastly, then!"

Bella sighed. "It makes me feel better just to talk to you. You never let things pull you down. But I don't know what to do, Anne. I cannot contradict the rumors. I am not supposed to know anything about them. And no one would believe me anyway."

"No, it is very hard; you can do nothing. I, however, can."

Arabella frowned. "What do you mean?"

"I am going to stop the talk, as soon as may be."

"How?" asked the other, looking alarmed. "Anne, you mustn't do anything foolish."

"I shan't. Even if I wished to, Charles won't let me."

"Ch-Charles? Lord Wrenley?"

"Yes, he is planning how we should set about it. Isn't it splendid of—"

"He knows all about this?" Bella put her hands to flaming cheeks. "I suppose *everyone* does. I have never been so mortified in my life."

"But, Bella…"

"He is almost a complete stranger to me, Anne! And people I know even less well are gossiping about my private affairs, perhaps at this very minute? It is horribly humiliating."

Anne nodded, mute before her vehemence.

"Mr...Laurence Debenham must know also, then?"

"He...heard something, I believe."

Arabella burst into tears, putting her face in her hands. "I can't bear it!" she sobbed.

Anne threw her arms around her and let her cry. She could think of nothing else to do. But as the other's tears gradually lessened, she vowed once again to do everything in her power to stop the talk, and to pay back Lydia Branwell to the last degree.

Arabella stayed only long enough to regain her composure and remove the signs of tears from her face. Then she insisted on going, despite Anne's entreaties. When she had seen her to the front door, Anne turned and ran up the stairs, hurrying straight to the library to find Charles. He *must* decide what they were to do at once.

But the library was empty, as were the other parlors on the first floor. She looked in the "garden" and asked Mariah if she had seen Charles, but the reply was negative. "Is anything wrong, dear?" added the other. With a quick negative, Anne returned to the drawing room and rang for Fallow.

"Where is Lord Wrenley?" she asked when he appeared.

"He said he had business in the City this morning, my lady. He expected to return in time for luncheon."

"I see." Anne sighed, half angrily.

"Is anything wrong? Should I send after him?"

"No, Fallow. I shall speak to him later. But if he

should come in soon, will you tell him that I want to see him, please?"

"Certainly, my lady."

"Thank you."

"Is there anything else? Would you care for a cup of tea, perhaps?"

"No." She dismissed him and threw herself down on the sofa once again. But she found it impossible to sit still. Every feeling cried out for instant action, yet there was nothing she could do. She could not bear the thought of reading or sewing or even of talking to Mariah. Why didn't Charles come home? Anne pounded the sofa arm in frustration, stood, and began to pace the room like a caged animal.

She was still pacing when Edward sauntered in half an hour later. He looked fashionably jaunty in yellow pantaloons and a light blue coat, a spotted kerchief knotted round his neck. "Hullo," he cried. "I have good news."

"That would be welcome just now!"

"Harry Hargreaves is practically living in the Branwell's pocket. He called there already and stayed *two* hours."

Anne turned away with a sigh. "That's good, I suppose."

"You suppose! I should think it is."

"I really can't worry about Harry Hargreaves at the moment."

"You can't...?" Edward stared disgustedly at her.

"I don't understand you, Anne. You made a great fuss about helping Laurence, practically forced me to go along, and now that I have made a tremendous effort and things are coming along well, you say you haven't time to worry about it."

"I'm sorry, Edward. Arabella was here this morning."

"Miss Castleton? And so?"

"I can't think of anything but her problem now."

"Dash it, Anne. I know she is your best friend, but her trifling little problems really cannot compare with—"

"Haven't you heard?"

"Heard what? I have been too busy running about London after Hargreaves to hear anything."

She told him the story, including, this time, Lydia Branwell's part in it. When she finished, he was staring at her with his mouth open. "That...that harpy! I didn't like her before, but even I would not have thought her capable of *this*."

"Bella is terribly unhappy."

"I daresay! The deuce. Something must be done."

"Charles is making a plan."

This only increased Edward's stupefaction. "Charles!"

Anne was by now accustomed to this reaction. "Yes, Edward. Why should he not?"

"Because he has never done anything of the kind in his life, that's why. Are you certain you understood him correctly?"

"Of course I am! He was as outraged as you are. I don't see why everyone is so astonished by that."

"Well, perhaps you don't know Charles as I do, then. He never exerts himself for anyone, least of all a girl he hardly knows. I can't believe it."

Anne began a hot retort, then stopped. Edward's, and Laurence's, reaction was really not so odd. She would have thought the same a short time ago. Indeed, she *had* thought it only last night. Charles had convinced her he meant to help, but she had not really considered before *why* he should do so. It *was* unlike him. Anne pondered. He did think Lydia Branwell's actions contemptible; he had clearly said so, in a tone that allowed no doubt. And he liked Bella, a little— perhaps. Anne frowned. Really, Charles had hardly ever spoken to Bella. As her friend had said, they were practically strangers.

"What did he actually say?" asked Edward.

"He said he would think of a way to stop the rumors."

Edward gazed steadily at her, then nodded. "Well, if he says he will do it, he will. He always performs what he promises. But it is astonishing that he is taking an interest in the matter. I wonder what he plans?"

"I don't know. He is out this morning. But I mean to talk to him about it the moment he comes in. We must act soon."

"Yes. The quicker these things are scotched, the better. But, by Jove, Anne, it is more important than ever that we separate Laurence and the Branwell creature now. She is even worse than I thought. Why, if Laurence ever heard of this, he would never get over it.

He has been mad on the subject of honesty since he was six years old." Edward brightened. "Say, perhaps we should tell him. It would sour him on the girl forever."

Anne shook her head. "Even if he believed us, and I suppose he would take Charles's word, what could he do?"

"Break it off, of course!"

"Because Miss Branwell started a rumor? She would say that someone had told her the story. And she would insist, truthfully, that she said it was probably a lie." Anne grimaced. "Of course, that only made it more convincing when she told it."

Edward was frowning. "I suppose you're right."

"I am. I have thought it out. Laurence would simply be more miserable than ever if he knew the truth and our plan did not work. He would be bound to a woman he could not respect, let alone love."

"It's too bad. Nothing would put him off her so thoroughly. But I suppose we can't."

They contemplated this in silence for a moment.

"What *can* I do?" asked Edward then. "It's intolerable she should get away with this."

"I know. Charles must have thought of something by now."

Edward began to pace. "Perhaps we don't need Charles. Surely we can formulate a plan ourselves."

"I have racked my brain. Nothing reasonable comes out."

"Well, approach it rationally. Our problem is to

stop the rumors and to end Laurence's engagement. So. We can't murder Miss Branwell, unfortunately."

Anne giggled. "And it wouldn't stop the talk."

"No. Perhaps I can convince Hargreaves to elope with her. And after they have gone, I'll follow and threaten to reveal all unless she signs a paper confessing that she made up the whole story about Miss Castleton."

"I don't think that would answer."

"Why not?"

"Neither Mr. Hargreaves nor Lydia is the sort to elope, Edward."

His face fell. "No."

"I think we should wait to hear what Charles proposes."

"Kidnap the bishop?" ventured Edward. "Make her do what we want, to get him back?"

"No." Anne began to feel very glad that Charles was on her side. If she had been forced to rely on Edward for help, they would not have gotten very far.

"Well, I suppose all I can do is encourage Hargreaves to haunt the Branwells, then." Edward sighed. "Rather tame."

"But important," replied Anne, eager to keep him thus undangerously occupied. "And you have done so well up to now."

"I think I have," he agreed. "It wasn't much fun dancing attendance on that starched-up prig, you know."

"I do. You have been very good."

Edward grinned. "Trying to turn me up sweet? Don't

worry. I shan't do anything stupid. But you will tell me
what Charles plans, won't you? And let me help?"

"Of course."

He nodded. "I must be off. I'm engaged to play
billiards with Hargreaves at my club. I'll be sure to sing
the Branwell's praises, though the words choke me."

"Thank you, Edward."

"I'd as lief shake her till her ears rattled!"

"I know how you feel. After we overheard her, I
wanted to scratch her eyes out, but Charles stopped me."

"Did he? Too bad. I should have enjoyed seeing that."

Anne laughed. "Wretch! You want me to disgrace
myself before the *ton*?"

"No." He grinned. "But admit it, Anne, it would
have been dashed satisfying!"

"Immensely."

They laughed together, and Edward took his
leave. When he was gone, Anne found that in spite
of everything, she felt a bit better. But the question
of Charles's motives would not be dismissed. As soon
as she was alone, it resurfaced to puzzle her again.
Could it be that some of her remarks had actually
had an effect on him? Was he becoming fonder of his
family? And if he was, did that include her? This idea
sent a thrill through her. Could it be true? "I mustn't
pin too much upon one incident," she told herself
sternly, and she jumped up to go and see if Charles
had come home.

Sixteen

HE HAD NOT. BY THE TIME SHE SAT DOWN TO A luncheon of cold meat and fruit, Anne was entirely out of patience with him. How could he stay away so long at this crucial time? Mariah joined her in the dining room. This was unusual, as she generally ate nothing in the middle of the day, unless perhaps a bit of bread and cheese in her garden. But today she sat down at the table, and as soon as the servants had left them, leaned forward. "I believe I have thought of something that will help," she said.

"Help Bella, you mean? What?"

Mariah looked resolute. "I will offer Bishop Branwell a cutting from my Oriental Sunset." She folded her arms and sat back, awaiting reaction.

"Your...?" replied Anne, uncomprehendingly.

"Yes. It is a great sacrifice, but the cause is good. He hinted about it when I first met him. Of course, I shifted the subject at once, *then*." She shook her head. "Very difficult it was. The man has no delicacy."

"But…ah…"

"No, no, my dear, I am quite determined. You needn't feel hesitant because it is such a great thing. I have thought it all over and am resigned. The offer alone should be enough to move the bishop to discipline his daughter. If he commands her, I daresay she will publicly retract the rumors."

"Mariah, I am sorry, I don't know what your Oriental Sunset is. Is…is it a flower?"

Mariah looked stunned.

"I should know, of course," continued Anne hurriedly. "Did you tell me? I have a shocking memory. I'm sure it is very beautiful, but, er, do you think…?"

"Oriental Sunset," pronounced Mariah in an awful voice, "is my rose!"

Anne tried to look suitably impressed.

"It is the rose I bred from two old strains, a wholly new type. It is the color of the evening sky at its most brilliant."

"It must be lovely."

"My dear Anne." Mariah was overcome with emotion. "It is exquisite, matchless, perfect!"

"Of course. I did not mean…"

"Every horticulturist in the country has been after me for cuttings. I have given out two—*two*—in the last year. They are cherished and envied across England."

"I'm sorry," repeated Anne. "I should have known."

"Well, I don't believe I have mentioned it before," conceded Mariah, calming somewhat. "But I assure you that Bishop Branwell knows." She laughed shortly. "Yes indeed."

"I wonder, though, if giving it to him will really solve the problem. A public declaration from Lydia might simply cause *more* talk. And it would be unfortunate if you gave away your cutting for nothing."

"Unfortunate!" Mariah pondered this. "You think it will not serve?"

"People are so stupid. I'm afraid such a dramatic reversal might make more of them believe the story. They would say that there must be something to it or we would not have gone to such lengths. Also, I do not like the idea of approaching the bishop. I don't trust him."

"I see." She sighed. "Well, I cannot pretend that I am not relieved. The thought of my rose in the hands of that...pruning lunatic was terrible. But I keep the offer open, in case you should think of a way it might be useful."

"That is very kind of you, Mariah."

"Bella Castleton's a sweet gal." They ate in silence for a while. "Say," added Mariah then, "how about her mother?"

"Mrs. Castleton?"

"No, Mrs. Branwell. If you don't like to go to the bishop—and I'd say you're right about that—what about his wife? Someone might speak to her. I can, if it comes to that."

Anne frowned, pondering the idea. "I don't believe

she has any influence over her daughter," she said slowly. "She is so meek and timid."

"Perhaps she is merely shy with strangers."

"No, it is something more than that. I don't know, Mariah. I must think."

"Well, I am ready to try. You need only tell me."

"Thank you," said Anne again. "You really are very good."

The other woman smiled, her gray eyes lighting. "Most people would say that I am, in fact, an extremely careless chaperone and a hopeless eccentric, dear."

Anne smiled back. "We have seen the stupidity of 'most people.'"

Mariah laughed aloud. "You are a fine girl, Anne. Watching over you has been much less burdensome than I expected. You must come to visit me in Devon; I will show you my garden."

"And give me a cutting from your rose?" inquired the girl mischievously.

"No. You don't care a whit for horticulture, and you don't deserve one."

Anne laughed too. "True enough. But you are talking as if you will be leaving me soon."

"Oh, I shan't go until all is settled."

"What do you mean?"

Mariah surveyed her, then shrugged, a twinkle lingering in her eye. "Never mind. I see I am premature."

"I don't understand."

"I see that you don't." Mariah rose. "I must get back to my border. The lavender is doing worse and worse. What do you think about mirrors? Is reflected sunlight efficacious? I have never been required to find out."

"But, Mariah…"

"I shall try, however. It cannot hurt. There are too many mirrors in the parlor, in any case." She went out, muttering to herself.

Anne remained in her chair, puzzled over her remarks. What, precisely, was to be "settled"? She could not imagine.

It was here that Charles found her, frowning, elbows on the table on either side of her plate. She was so deep in thought that he had to speak before she noticed him. "You look pensive."

Anne jumped, startled. "Charles! At last!"

He strolled into the room, putting his driving gloves on the dining table. He still wore his many-caped coat, and his blond hair was ruffled by the wind. He looked very handsome. "A gratifying reception," he replied, smiling. "Fallow said you wished to see me at once. Is anything wrong?"

"Only that I have had such a morning as I would not wish to repeat—first Laurence, then Bella, then Edward, and finally Mariah!"

"Indeed? You have my sincere sympathy."

Taken aback, Anne looked at him. Then she started to laugh. "It was the subject of conversation that wearied me, not the people. Charles, you are the most complete hand."

He returned her smile. "Believe me, I should find that procession in itself too much. What did you talk about?"

Anne's smile faded. "Need you ask?"

"The rumors?"

"Yes. Bella has begun to hear them, too." Quickly she told about him her talk with Arabella. "She is very unhappy."

"Poor girl."

"Charles, we must do something at once!"

"Yes, it would be best to act soon. I have been thinking over the problem, and I believe I have an idea. There are difficulties, but…"

"What is it?" cried Anne, bouncing in her chair with impatience.

He smiled again. "You must let me explain at my own plodding pace. And I should like to be rid of my coat. Shall we go to the library? Are you finished eating?"

"Yes, yes." She rose, and they went upstairs, leaving the viscount's things with Fallow. In the library, Anne plumped down in an armchair while Charles took another. "Tell me," she demanded then.

He leaned a little forward. "Our problem is complex. Indeed, we are faced with not one puzzle, but two—to stop the talk, and to end Laurence's engagement. They are quite separate."

She nodded impatiently, eliciting another smile.

"It seems to me also that the first is more pressing.

Miss Castleton must be relieved of anxiety as soon as possible. If we cannot disentangle Laurence at the same time, then we cannot, though I hope one plan may accomplish both objectives."

"You are talking like a history book," objected Anne. "Can't you just tell me your idea?"

"I am doing my best," he answered wryly. "A history book!"

"Well, plans of campaign, you know, and…what was the phrase, 'parameters of action.' Was it Richelieu who said that, or someone else? I've forgotten."

"I haven't the faintest notion. And I am astonished that you have."

Anne made a face. "Oh, yes, I know that you think me 'a hopeless student.' Miss Millington showed me that letter you wrote to her."

"Betrayed," exclaimed Charles. "Will all my past sins come back to haunt me?"

"They will if you do not go on immediately!"

Laughing, he held up his hands. "Very well. So, our first concern is to end the rumors. And that is not an easy task. There is nothing more persistent than gossip, yet it is at the same time elusive. No one ever knows where they heard a thing or what the basis was; they simply take up a scandalous story and pass it on, twisting it a bit in the process. I had a good deal of trouble thinking of a way we might stop that, but it seems to me that there are two steps to take. First, a sure way of destroying a rumor is to replace it with another. Stale gossip is the most despised commodity. No one wishes to be caught spreading an old story."

"You don't mean we should start a rumor about Lydia Branwell?" asked Anne, surprised.

"No, but we shall replace hers with our own, nevertheless, if we succeed."

"How?"

"I'm coming to that. The second part of our attack is to get the story about Miss Castleton definitely retracted. Though the effect may be small, it must be clearly stated that it was a lie."

"But won't that simply attract more attention to the matter? Edward and Mariah both suggested something like that, and I—"

"It might," interrupted Charles, "if it were done improperly. But I hope to manage both steps at once, in a way that will convince everyone the retraction is true."

"How?" said Anne again.

"That is, of course, the difficulty. Here is my idea. Miss Branwell must be maneuvered into a position where she thinks she is safe, then confronted with her deed and made to admit she fabricated the whole. However, unbeknownst to her, there will be an audience to her admission. The resulting scandal will supplant the present one."

Anne pondered this, frowning. "But how will we get her in such a position? And even if we do, why should she confess?"

"You have stated the obstacles succinctly. It will be simple to gather a small, carefully selected audience to spread the story of her perfidy. Leaving aside your first objection for a moment, I think she might be made to speak if you, and you alone, were present and goaded her. She seems to have a marked antipathy to you." He smiled slightly.

"I? Oh, Charles, I couldn't. I would make a mull of it somehow!"

"Nonsense. I have complete faith in your abilities."

"But what would I say? How would I get her to—"

"These questions may be left until later. Our chief difficulty at the outset is setting the scene. How can we be sure Miss Branwell is where we want her to be at the proper time, when our audience is in place?"

Anne was still distracted. "Perhaps Edward or Mariah could bring her."

"I don't like to trust such a delicate mission to Edward. Mariah might do, but Miss Branwell is likely to refuse either of them. We need someone closer to her."

Uneasily considering her own projected role in this, Anne merely shook her head.

"The problem of Laurence's engagement *may* be solvable by this means as well," Charles went on. "We can easily include Laurence in our audience, and what he hears will no doubt make him wish to break it off, but—"

"He already does," put in Anne.

"What?"

"Wish to break it off. He does wish to."

"He told you so?"

"Not directly, but I could tell."

"Well, then, we need only persuade Miss Branwell, a daunting prospect."

"What if she thought Laurence responsible for our confrontation?" suggested Anne. "She might be angry enough to end the engagement."

Charles gazed at her in astonishment. "A splendid idea. It could very well work. You must give her the impression that Laurence is in on the plot, of course."

Anne nodded.

"Then we must arrange for them to meet just afterward. That should not be too hard. Edward can manage it, I would think."

"Yes. But, Charles, I cannot believe I am the right person to face her. I'll make a mistake. And anyway, I... I don't want to. Couldn't...?" She hesitated. She hated to ask anything of him when he was doing so much, but her part was so frightening. "Couldn't *you* do it?"

Charles did not recoil. "I *would* gladly, to spare you the unpleasantness," he replied. "But I do not think it would answer. It will be difficult enough for you to get her to speak. You will have to rely on her temper to loosen her tongue. But she would take too much care with me, as the head of Laurence's family. I'm certain I would fail."

Anne frowned and, after a moment, nodded slowly. "I suppose you're right."

"I'm afraid you are the only logical person for the job. You have a talent for enraging Miss Branwell."

She smiled. "And others. I never thought to be grateful for it."

Looking into her eyes, he laughed. "So, what do you think of my plan?"

"I like it. I think it has a strong chance of working."

"I am only concerned about ensuring Miss Branwell's presence. She is a headstrong girl. And you say Laurence no longer worships at her feet. No doubt she is annoyed at all of us for that."

"Oh, lud!" exclaimed Anne. "I forgot Harry Hargreaves."

"Harry… Is he the young man you and Edward found?"

"Yes, and he may be a nuisance now. Edward says he is always at the Branwells', and I suppose Lydia likes that. He could spoil our whole scheme. Oh, why did we ever begin it?"

"On the contrary, I think it very lucky you did. If Miss Branwell has another suitor on tap, she will be much more ready to break with Laurence. But we must take Mr. Hargreaves into our calculations by all means." He grinned. "Perhaps we could leave him to Mariah?"

Slowly Anne began to smile. "She could handle him, I daresay."

"I cannot imagine the young man she could *not* handle."

"Yes, that should do."

"So we are left with only the problem of maneuvering the lady. I wish we could be as certain of that."

Suddenly Anne had an idea. "Perhaps we can; perhaps there is something I can do about that."

"What?"

"I won't tell you until I try. It may very well come to nothing."

Charles eyed her a bit skeptically. "You are not thinking of the bishop, are you? Because I don't…"

"No. Not even with the inducement of Mariah's rose."

"I beg pardon?"

Absently Anne recounted Mariah's offer. Charles lapsed into helpless laughter. "It was really *very* kind of her," Anne finished.

"Heroic. But it would not serve."

"So I told her. Oh, and Edward volunteered to kidnap the bishop and hold him to ransom."

The viscount's laughter died. "I hope you dissuaded him."

"I did."

"But what do *you* mean to do?"

"I am not so rash as Edward. You must trust me." She looked over at him. "Do you?"

He met her eyes, his own steady and clear. "Unreservedly."

Emboldened by his look, Anne added, "Why are you doing this, Charles?"

"Doing what?"

"Making such an effort to help Bella, inconveniencing yourself for a near-stranger?"

"You are forgetting Laurence."

"No, I'm not. I am remembering what you said to me when I first decided to help him."

Lord Wrenley smiled wryly. "Ah, yes."

Anne leaned forward. "You like him better now, don't you?"

"You know, I believe I do. Edward, too."

"Oh, Charles!"

"But that is not my only reason for joining this melee." Their chairs were not far apart. He reached across and put a hand over hers where it rested on the chair arm. "We are getting on better than we once did, aren't we, Anne?"

Her throat suddenly tight, Anne swallowed. "Yes."

"Have you forgotten some of the…bitterness you once felt?" She started to reply, but he added, "You had a right, do not mistake me. I made some, er, unwise choices in my youth."

This subject, and Charles's warm tone, were making it very difficult for Anne to speak, but she felt she must. "I *have* forgotten," she insisted. "I made at least as many errors as you."

"Hardly. It is kind of you to say so, but even if true, it would not excuse my negligence. You were not responsible—"

"Don't use that word," interrupted the girl quickly. He raised one eyebrow. "I don't like it."

For a long moment he was silent, seeming to think over her remark with growing understanding and realization. "Perhaps you're right," he murmured finally. "It is not a good word for us to use."

"Ever!" finished Anne.

He gazed at her bemusedly. "What an extraordinary girl you are." She flushed and looked down. His hand still covered hers. "Do you have any idea how extraordinary?"

Gazing at him from under her eyelashes, she replied, "People have always called me an 'original.'"

Charles began to laugh. "Indeed they have. How right they were! And that is part of the answer to your question—perhaps the whole answer."

Anne watched him, suddenly feeling a vast contentment. It was as if she could visualize a great many future moments just like this one, when they would sit together alone and Charles would break into laughter. It was the same merriment, she realized then, that he showed so often with his intimate friends, and so seldom with his family. But now he was sharing it with her.

"Ah, Anne," he said when he regained control, "how could I have missed so much about you for so long? I'm not nearly as intelligent as my vanity would have me believe. A dull fellow, in fact."

"They say," answered Anne, greatly daring, "that one often overlooks what is closest."

Holding her gaze, he nodded, then gave her hand

a gentle squeeze. "An astute proverb. But when one becomes aware…" He paused. "We shall have a good deal to talk about once this Branwell problem is settled," he added. "I am inclined to leave it till then."

Anne's heart was beating very fast, but a spark of mischief remained in her gray-violet eyes. "Why?" she asked demurely.

Charles looked up sharply, and began to smile. "I don't quite know. A desire to have everything neatly in place, perhaps. Or perhaps a wish to prove something. Can you understand that?"

She nodded, very serious now. Her throat was tight again.

"Yes," continued the viscount meditatively, "I believe that's it. What a curious sensation."

"Thank you," whispered Anne very softly.

His head jerked round and he rose. Still holding her hand, he gazed down at her, his expression a mixture of tenderness and chagrin. "You mustn't thank *me*, Anne," he said unsteadily, and tightening his hold, he pulled her to her feet and into his arms. They stood still for a long moment, he searching her eyes; then he bent his head and kissed her very gently on the lips.

Anne had never felt anything remotely like it. She trembled in his clasp, and a thrill seemed to run down along her spine. Her hands moved automatically up his arms to twine round his neck as she gave herself up wholly to the kiss.

It ended too soon, as Charles drew away, holding her at arm's length. "I should not have done that," he said.

She looked up at him, startled.

"Not while you live in my house, under my protection."

"Pooh," replied Anne.

He threw back his head and laughed once more. "Well, not, at any rate, before I asked you—"

The library door was flung open with a crash, and Mariah burst in. Charles quickly let his hands drop. "That blasted girl has let Augustus out again," she cried. "He's flown downstairs and is fighting the cook's cat. You'd best come and help me recapture him."

Anne started to giggle. Charles gazed at her sternly. "Go and remove your detestable pet," he ordered. "We will return to this subject when things are calm again."

Seventeen

ANNE TOOK THIS AS A PROMISE, BUT UNFORTUNATELY, calm did not return for some time. Separating an enraged Augustus from the thoroughly embittered kitchen cat, even in that low-ceilinged room, proved a lengthy task. And by the time it was done, Charles had to go out. "I'm sorry," he apologized when he left her. "I have been promised to Alvanley for this afternoon these two weeks."

"It doesn't matter," replied Anne, and she spoke no more than the truth. She neither felt nor wanted to feel any hurry over this matter.

"We will meet at dinner, then," he added tenderly.

"Yes."

He took her hand and kissed it briefly before striding out.

Anne went to the window to watch him ride away, a meditative smile on her lips. But once he was out of sight, a plan that had been forming in her mind since their earlier talk surfaced once more. The single weakness in their proposed course of action could, she thought, be removed if she could convince a certain person to help them. The chances of success were small, but she was determined to try; she wanted to contribute something of her own to the conspiracy.

Accordingly, she went up to her room and fetched a bonnet and light pelisse. She avoided Crane, who would certainly be scandalized if she discovered that Anne meant to go out alone. Mariah was again shut up in her garden, and the front hall was empty when she slipped down. No one saw her leave the house and hail a hackney cab on the corner.

She directed the driver to an address on King Street and sat back to compose her thoughts and decide what to say. All of her persuasive powers would be called upon in the next hour or so, and she wanted to put her case as well as possible. The approach would be very delicate.

After what seemed to her a very short time, the cab pulled up. She paid her fare and stepped down onto the pavement before the Branwell town house. For a long moment Anne gazed up at the facade. She knew that Lydia was out; Laurence had mentioned that he was driving her to Richmond Park this afternoon. And she felt tolerably certain that the bishop did not sit with his wife during the day. Callers were equally unlikely, in view of the lady's shyness. She expected to find Mrs. Branwell alone.

Anne stepped up to the front door and plied the

knocker briskly. It was opened by the butler, and she asked for Mrs. Branwell. "I'm sorry, Mrs. Branwell is not at home," was the reply. But the tone the man used told Anne that her quarry was in, though not receiving visitors.

"This is very important," she said. "I will just run up and speak to her. You needn't announce me." And before the butler could do more than gape at her in astonishment, she slipped past him and ran lightly up the stairs to the first floor.

She looked quickly into the drawing room. It was empty. Hearing the servant's heavy tread ascending the staircase, she swiftly tried two doors farther along the corridor; both opened to reveal empty parlors, and she hurried on. She must find Mrs. Branwell soon if she wished to avoid an unpleasant dispute. She heard the butler call, "Miss! Excuse me, miss, but you cannot…"

She thrust open a third door, and found the lady—cozily settled in an armchair before a crackling fire, with a pot of tea, a plate of biscuits, and a novel open before her. It was an attractive picture, and Anne could not help smiling slightly; it was so clear that Mrs. Branwell was reveling in a solitary retreat from her formidable family.

When the older woman saw Anne, her mouth fell open in astonishment and chagrin, and an almost laughable disappointment showed in her face. She looked like a little girl deprived of a promised treat. Anne felt sorry for her, but her errand was too important for more than a hurried apology as she shut the door in the face of the scandalized butler. "Pardon me for disturbing you, Mrs. Branwell," she said, "but I must speak to you about something." She sank into the armchair opposite her hostess.

Regret turned to alarm and bewilderment in Mrs. Branwell's features.

"You will think it odd of me to have come," acknowledged Anne. "We are not very well acquainted, but we are connections of a kind, through your daughter and Laurence Debenham."

The mention of Lydia made Mrs. Branwell shrink back slightly. "Lydia is out," she murmured so softly that Anne scarcely heard it.

The girl surveyed her. What could have made this woman so timid and frightened? Had she always been so? And was it a mistake to think that she could help them? She had expected a difficult conversation. It would be very hard to explain Lydia's conduct to her mother without offending, and even more so to enlist the aid of this painfully retiring creature. But she was determined to try. She leaned forward. "Tell me, Mrs. Branwell, are you pleased with your daughter's engagement? Do you think they will be happy?"

Her companion looked more alarmed.

"You needn't mind about Laurence; you may say what you like to me. Do you truly think they will suit?"

"Wh-why not?" stammered the other.

"Well, to my mind, their temperaments are

antagonistic. It seems to me that your daughter has strong opinions and does not enjoy having them contradicted. And she prefers to make most of the decisions. Now, Laurence is very kind and considerate, but he will expect to rule his own household. I fear they may not agree on that, and you know, the happiness of each party is essential to a successful marriage."

Mrs. Branwell stared at her like a bird fascinated by a snake.

"I honestly believe that both of them might be better off with different sorts of partners. Your daughter, for example, seems to have many more common interests with a man like Mr. Hargreaves. Do you like him?"

A spark showed briefly in Mrs. Branwell's eyes. Anne could not tell what emotion it signified, but she felt she was making an impression. Her listener no longer looked quite so timorous and downtrodden.

"Something that happened recently made me see all this more clearly," continued the girl, choosing her words with great care. "I believe your daughter misunderstood Laurence's politeness to a friend of mine, and as a consequence she passed on a false story about her, which is doing a great deal of harm." She paused, watching Mrs. Branwell. This was the best possible construction she could put on Lydia's behavior.

The older woman straightened in her chair. Her thin lips turned down. "Did *Lydia* start those rumors about Miss Arabella Castleton?" she asked in a voice Anne had never heard her use before.

Anne colored; she did not know exactly how to answer this. She could not lie, but she did not want to antagonize Lydia's mother. "Well...er...I'm not certain she..."

"She *did*!" The woman's nervous expression faded entirely. "I knew she was using them. That was bad enough, but if she deliberately spread a lie!" Mrs. Branwell stood and faced the fire, seeming to struggle with herself. "If she did that, then I can be silent no longer," she finished. And she sighed so heartrendingly that Anne held out a comforting hand. Mrs. Branwell did not take it. Turning to face her, she continued, "You are absolutely certain of what you say? I do not like to believe this of my own daughter."

Slowly Anne nodded. "I overheard her. And I *know* the story is false!"

Her hostess scanned her face in silence for a long moment, then nodded and sank into her chair again. "I did not think it had gone so far with her. I tried in the beginning, you know. I set out to be a good mother. But Lydia was always headstrong, and so attached to her father, who is...a man of strong opinions. And then, when there were no more children..." She trailed off, but Anne built a vivid picture from these few phrases, and felt sorrier for the other woman than ever.

A silence stretched between them. Mrs. Branwell seemed lost in thought, and Anne was overcome by her suddenly broadened vision of the world. She had not quite realized what life could be like in a loveless marriage.

"Why did you come here?" asked Mrs. Branwell finally. "I suppose you want something from me."

"No! You have borne enough."

The other looked surprised, then smiled thinly. "Very kind. But I wonder if you will feel the same when you have returned home without whatever you came for?"

Seeing Anne's horrified expression, her smile widened. "Come, my dear, I am very ready to make what amends I can for Lydia's behavior. You needn't look so stricken. None of this is *your* fault, I suppose."

"I...I mean to break up the match," stammered Anne. "And I came to ask you to help me."

Some of her former timidity seemed to return as Mrs. Branwell contemplated this idea. She looked distinctly alarmed, but resolved. "H-how do you hope to accomplish this? And what part am I to play?"

"You would only have to see that Lydia comes to a particular room at a set time," replied Anne eagerly. "You would not have to stay, or to...to do anything else. Oh, except make it seem that Laurence is behind it."

The other woman eyed her. "You must tell me a little more than that. We are talking of my daughter, after all."

Nodding, Anne explained their plan in some detail.

"I see." She thought it all over. "Very well, I will do what you ask."

Anne held out her hands. "Thank you!"

Mrs. Branwell merely looked at her. "That is *all* I will do, mind. And I agree only because Lydia has acted very badly and deserves a lesson." She sighed. "I daresay she would rather marry Mr. Hargreaves in any case; she seems to like him. Now, if there is nothing else, I wish you would go."

This was spoken in such a tired, hopeless voice that Anne could not be offended. She rose at once. "Of course. I will write to you when we have made our final plans. Thank you, Mrs. Branwell. I think you are doing the right thing."

Her companion smiled slightly again. "Indeed? How could you not?"

As she walked down the stairs to the door, Anne felt very subdued, and she was too preoccupied even to notice the butler's freezing courtesy as he bowed her out. Poor Mrs. Branwell; how did she bear it? Then Anne remembered the fire, the tea, the novel— perhaps she knew.

She reached home in the late afternoon and had just taken off her bonnet and come back down to the drawing room when Laurence came in. He looked angry. "Anne, I want to speak to you!"

She raised her eyebrows. "Here I am."

"Something must be done about this ridiculous gossip!"

"I have told you that—"

"Yes, but it is worse than I realized. Lydia was telling me—"

"She mentioned it to you?"

Anne's tone was so outraged that Laurence frowned at her. "Yes, it has reached her as well. She was very shocked and didn't seem to credit it when I told her it was, of course, a total fabrication."

"Did she not?" The girl laughed scornfully.

"No, Anne, she did not. And many others, who do not know Miss Castleton as you do, will feel the same. We must do something!"

Nearly speechless with rage at Lydia Branwell's new offense, Anne replied, "We? What do *you* propose to do, Laurence?"

"What is the matter with you? I thought you would be as upset as I over the way this story is spreading."

"But I am. And I asked you what you mean to do." The words came out harshly. But Anne was too angry to care that she was blaming Laurence for his fiancée's fault and expecting him to behave as if he knew the truth when he did not.

"I shall tell everyone I know that it is a lie," he retorted. "But that will not be enough. Rumors are pernicious; they stick even in the absence of evidence. We must try some more dramatic measure soon. This could make Miss Castleton bitterly unhappy!"

"It already has," responded Anne.

"She does not know!"

"Yes, indeed. Some kind soul told her."

Laurence struck the palm of his hand with his fist. "Monstrous! I must go at once and tell her..."

"Tell her what?" asked the girl sweetly when he paused.

He seemed to struggle with himself, every limb vibrating with tension. "No," he added finally. "But you will tell her, please, when you see her next, that I do not believe a word of it. I find it inconceivable."

"I'm sure that will make her feel a great deal better," answered Anne sarcastically.

"What *is* the matter with you?" said Laurence again. "You are acting as if this were my fault somehow."

Realizing that he was right, she tried to regain her composure. When she thought of Lydia Branwell's poisonous tongue, she nearly screamed with vexation, but it was, after all, none of Laurence's doing. "I'm sorry. I am upset. It has been very hard to see Bella treated so."

"I should say so!"

"And we have worked out a plan, so you needn't worry."

"What is it?"

This time Anne cursed her own tongue; she couldn't tell Laurence without spoiling everything. "Really, Laurence, you needn't be concerned." Suddenly inspired, she added, "Indeed, I don't think you *should* be, considering." She gave him a meaningful look.

He colored a little. "What do you mean?"

"You are very taken with Bella, are you not? But of course, you are an engaged man."

His flush deepened. He seemed to search for a reply. Finally he said, "I am," in a strangled voice.

"Well, then, you'd best leave it to others to defend her." Anne shrugged. She did not wish to be unkind to Laurence, but she must divert him from the subject of their plan.

"You *promise* that something will be done?"

"Oh, yes."

"And if I can help in *any* way, even the smallest, you will tell me."

"Of course."

"Very well," he replied curtly, and he turned and walked out of the room without another word.

When he was gone, Anne's first thought was to find Charles and tell him of recent developments. But he had not yet returned home, and as it was nearly time to change for dinner in any case, she went up to her room and curled up in the window seat, looking out over the rooftops and chimney pots of London and thinking over the dramatic events of the past few days.

She was still angry whenever she thought of Lydia Branwell. That girl was utterly unscrupulous, and she obviously cared for no one in the world but herself. Anne could hardly wait to see her forced to retract her lies about Bella. And poor Bella! How low she must be feeling, and how helpless. That would perhaps be the worst, to know about the rumors and not to be able to *do* anything.

Anne clenched her fists in frustration, then told herself that something *was* being done. She and Charles were doing something. And it was all settled now;

everything was ready. As she insisted upon this, she seemed to realize it fully for the first time. Their plan was made, except for the final details; she had seen to the last element today. All was ready, and in a short time, Bella would be cleared.

With a sigh, Anne relaxed, leaning back against the side of the window. She had been so worried about her friend for what seemed such a long time that she had not been able to consider anything else. But now that she knew what action would be taken, she could think of other things, and the first that occurred to her, quite naturally, was Charles.

When she remembered how she had viewed him just months ago, she was amazed. She had come home from school intent on making him miserable, and getting revenge, certain that he was the most odious man alive. But the more she saw of him, the less she believed that. Either he had changed radically during the years she was away or she had been mistaken from the first.

Anne frowned. Perhaps neither was precisely true, for Charles had seemed to have two personalities when she first came home—one for his family and another for his close friends. She still did not understand how he had become that way. However, he had abandoned his "family" manner almost completely as time passed, until she had nearly forgotten it.

Anne smiled to herself and drew a finger lightly across her lips. She now had some notion of why that change had come. Who could ever have predicted that Charles would fall in love with her? Or she with him? It was the oddest thing. But Anne had known since this morning that it was indeed true. When Charles had kissed her, a great many things had suddenly come clear. She knew in that instant that what she had been feeling for him was not simple respect and liking. His gradually changed behavior and recent sympathy and help when her friend was threatened had led Anne step by step deep into love. And what of him? She had no doubt of his feelings; she was filled with a calm certainty whenever she thought of him. But what had made him love her? She was still the mercurial, unconventional girl he had sent away so long ago. Why, she wondered, had he changed his opinion of her so radically?

After a while Anne abandoned this question with a shrug and a smile. Perhaps she would ask Charles when an opportunity came, or perhaps she wouldn't. It would depend. She reviewed their meeting in the library once again; how strange and wonderful that kiss had been. A dreamy smile crossed Anne's face as she imagined telling Charles that it had made her wish strongly for another.

The door opened, and Crane came bustling in. She did not notice Anne at first, curled in the corner window seat, but went about her business getting out an evening dress and laying it across the bed. Then Anne moved slightly, making a small noise, and the maid started and whirled around. "My lady! I nearly jumped out of my skin, I was that startled!"

Anne rose. "I'm sorry, Crane. I was here the whole time."

"I didn't see you." She sounded accusing. "And you're never upstairs so early. Are you feeling well?"

"Yes, indeed, *very* well."

The maid eyed her, suspicious of the enthusiasm in her voice.

Anne grinned. "We shall all be wonderfully happy before very long, Crane. Wait and see!"

The other turned away and went to fetch a pair of Anne's evening slippers. "That'll be a rare thing, my lady," she replied. "I shall look forward to it." Her expression merely became more severe when Anne started to laugh.

Eighteen

LAURENCE WAS OUT TO DINNER THAT EVENING, SO Charles and Anne were able to explain their scheme to Mariah as soon as the servants were gone. They lingered at table going over the details, and in the end, Mariah was delighted. "How clever you are!" she exclaimed. "Mr. Hargreaves, eh? Oh, I shall have no trouble with *him*. I shall tell him precisely what is wrong with the bishop's theories of pruning; that will occupy a great deal of time." She laughed, and the others joined in.

"If Lydia Branwell comes to him after all is over, however," replied Anne, "you must go away and leave them alone." When Charles glanced at her sharply, she added, "Well, even Miss Branwell deserves another chance."

"Poor Mr. Hargreaves," he murmured.

"I think Mr. Hargreaves is as careful of his own interest as she."

He shrugged.

"But when is it to be?" interrupted Mariah. "The sooner the better, I should think."

Charles agreed. "I suggest Lady Huntington's ball two nights from now. I know her house well, and she is a friend of mine; she will let us do what we like. And two days should give us ample time to arrange everything."

"Two days," echoed Anne uneasily. She had carefully avoided thinking much about her part in the proposed plan. The idea of a confrontation with Lydia was too unnerving, but with the time so short, she was forced to face it. Would she manage? Would her temper get the best of her and ruin the whole?

"All will go well," said Charles, as if reading her thoughts. "We will rehearse what you must say until you are comfortable."

Anne smiled gratefully at him.

"Still, it will be a delicate business," said Mariah. "All those comings and goings. I hope we can carry it off."

"I shall play stage manager," answered Charles. "I have every confidence in my ability to steer people where I want them at the proper moment."

The two women looked at him; they could not but agree.

"So," he continued, "it remains only to speak to Edward—"

"Speak to me about what?" replied Captain Debenham, striding into the room. "Are you still at table? What sluggards!"

"We are discussing what is to be done about Bella," responded Anne.

"Ah." Edward pulled out a chair and sat down. "I see why you want to speak to me, then. What's the scheme?"

Charles smiled. "You sound ready for anything."

"Absolutely!"

Anne met Charles's amused eyes and grinned. "Well, then you will not mind when we tell you that we have decided you should marry Bella in order to put a stop to the rumors."

Edward had taken a grape from a plate on the table and popped it into his mouth. Now he choked so violently that Mariah leaned over and pounded him on the back. "You must be joking," he croaked the moment he could form words. Anne and Charles both burst out laughing, and he eyed them with disgust. "Very amusing. I suppose you would have found it even funnier if that grape had done for me once and for all."

"Oh, Edward, I'm sorry." Anne laughed. "You looked so eager; I couldn't resist."

Edward, who had just become fully aware of his older brother's pleasant expression, nodded absently. "Never mind. Suppose you tell me the real plan, though."

Anne proceeded to do so, occasionally seconded by Charles. When they were finished, Edward stared from one to the other for a full minute, then exclaimed, "First-rate! So I am to manage Laurence? I can do that, no fear." He gazed at his brother. "You thought of this, Charles?"

The viscount shrugged slightly.

"He did," said Anne, "all except for Mrs. Branwell." The others turned to gaze at her, and she suddenly remembered that she had neglected to tell them of her success this afternoon. She did so now.

"That makes things easier," mused Charles when she was done. "I can leave Miss Branwell to her mother. Splendid, Anne!"

The girl colored slightly.

"You really went and asked her?" said Edward. "You always were a plucky girl, Anne. But I am amazed she agreed to help you; the woman always looks so browbeaten."

"She has more character than people know," answered Anne very quietly. Charles looked at her.

"Well, so, all is ready, then." Captain Debenham rubbed his hands together. "This will be a pleasure, if it works."

"It will!" insisted Anne. "Won't it, Charles?"

"I think our chances are very good."

"A toast," cried Edward, pouring himself a glass of wine and standing with it held high. "To success!"

Laughing, the other three raised their glasses and drank. Edward drained his and made as if to throw it into the fireplace. "Not the Limoges!" exclaimed Charles, and his brother grinned and set the goblet gently down on the cloth.

For Anne, the next two days flew by. She wrote to Mrs. Branwell and received a guarded affirmative reply. And she spent a great deal of time going over what she was to say to Lydia Branwell. Edward was constantly underfoot, and Laurence suddenly seemed much more in evidence than usual, so that they had to sneak about to make their final plans. There seemed to be no opportunity for Charles and Anne to be alone, and after one abortive attempt that had been interrupted four times in the first five minutes, Charles ruefully abandoned the effort. "We will talk as soon as this thing is over," he told her. "The very minute!" She had nodded and smiled, almost as amused by his impatience as frustrated by the circumstances that caused it.

At last, all was ready, and the day arrived. Anne spent it fidgeting, alternately longing for the time to come and be over and wishing the minutes were longer before her ordeal. But the day passed at the customary speed, and by the time she went up to her room to dress for the Huntingtons' ball, she was screwed up to an extremely high pitch of excitement.

"Do stop squirming, my lady," complained Crane as she buttoned Anne into a ball gown of white satin trimmed with pearls. "I can't do up all these fastenings if you keep moving about. I declare there must be forty buttons on this dress."

With an audible sigh, Anne tried to be still. When she had chosen this gown she had thought the long row of pearl buttons down the back lovely. Now she wondered how she could have been so stupid. "Do hurry, Crane," she said, shifting restlessly again.

Her maid stopped altogether and put her hands on her hips. "I *could*, my lady, if you would stay still!"

Making an enormous effort, Anne controlled her nervousness until the dress was closed. Then she rushed Crane through the dressing of her hair and the finding of her gloves, wrap, and other necessities. When she strode out the door ten minutes later, the maid could be heard muttering, "I can't do a proper job all in a minute. That fan was wrong; the dear knows where she put the other one. This is not what I'm used to, I must say."

Anne and Mariah drove to the ball together. Charles had gone ahead to make certain arrangements at the Huntington town house, and raise Lady Huntington's curiosity to fever pitch. The two women greeted their hostess briefly and went directly into the ballroom, where the first set had not yet begun. Charles, standing on the other side of the floor, nodded to them but did not approach. Anne saw Edward lounging in the far corner and Laurence standing with the Branwell party nearby, his expression far from happy. Lydia was chatting animatedly with Harry Hargreaves. Everything was in place, and the time they had chosen, directly after the second set, would soon arrive.

Anne danced the opening set with a friend of Edward's, but when another officer solicited her for the next, she refused abstractedly. Charles was to be her partner, both to finalize their plans and to ensure that she could get away.

Just before the music started, he came. It was a waltz, and he encircled her waist with an expert arm as they joined the revolving couples on the floor. "All is ready," he told her.

"Good." She hesitated, then added, "I think."

"Don't worry. I'm sure you will do very well."

"I wish I were. It is so important, and I must do it all alone."

"I would help if I could."

"Oh, I know that. I wasn't… It is just that I have a great knot in my stomach."

He smiled a little. "The best thing for that is to get it over. It is time you were in position, in any case." He steered their steps in the direction of the ballroom door.

"Already?"

He nodded as Anne swallowed nervously. Soon they were beside the doorway, and in another moment they had slipped through it into the corridor beyond. "This way," added Charles, leading her to a small parlor toward the back of the house. A fire was burning in the grate, and candles were lit. "You will confront her here," he said. "This door communicates with a larger room, as you see." He showed her. "We will leave it ajar, and I will make sure that several of the greatest gossips in the *ton* are there to hear what you and Miss Branwell have to say. She won't notice because of this curtain." As he spoke, he drew a light drapery over the doorway, disguising it completely. Then he turned to gaze at Anne. "I must go and gather the audience. Will you be all right alone?"

She nodded, though her expression was not very happy.

"It will be done with very soon," he added encouragingly and, with a quick squeeze of her hand, went out.

Anne walked over to the fireplace and held out her hands to the blaze. The house was not cold, but she felt shivery. So much depended upon her words in the next few minutes.

After what seemed to her a long time, she heard people come into the other parlor. Their conversation was a bare murmur, but she began to worry that Lydia would hear it as soon as she came in, spoiling everything. But before she could do more than frown, the sound diminished. Charles must have done something. Now there was just the barest hint of noise, and she heard that only because she knew to listen for it. She smiled, then immediately was serious again. Footsteps were approaching along the corridor.

"Why would Laurence ask us to come *here*?" she heard Lydia Branwell's resonant voice asking. "I think you've muddled things, Mother, as usual." Her disrespectful tone strengthened Anne's resolve. "Indeed, I think I saw him in the ballroom as we left."

Mrs. Branwell made an inaudible reply, and in the

next moment Lydia appeared in the doorway of the small parlor. She checked when she saw Anne. "You!"

"Good evening, Miss Branwell." Anne saw the girl's mother slip away along the corridor as Lydia came farther into the room.

"What are you doing here? Where is Laurence?"

"Laurence?" Anne tried to make her tone sound falsely innocent.

"Did he send you here to meet me? Why? He has been very annoying lately, and if this is—"

"He has been uneasy about my friend Bella, I know," interrupted Anne. "Particularly after you spoke to him about the rumors."

Lydia paused, a slight smile curving her lips; Anne felt like strangling her. "I?"

"Yes, he mentioned it to me." Their eyes met squarely. "Where did you hear it originally?"

Miss Branwell shrugged. "Who can remember such things?"

"*I* remember hearing you tell it to Lady Duncan some time ago. Indeed, it was the first night the story was mentioned."

"Do you?" Lydia's voice was honeyed poison.

"Yes. In fact, I believe you started the rumor yourself, out of spite because Laurence seemed to like Bella. And because Bella is my friend, and you dislike me!"

Lydia Branwell seemed to make some inner calculation. Then she smiled again. "You are quite right," she admitted.

"You know the story is a contemptible lie!" Anne felt her temper rising and sternly controlled it.

"A lie, certainly. But contemptible?" She shrugged. In the brief pause, Anne heard the slight scrape of footsteps in the corridor behind them. Was Edward performing his part? She hoped so. "I thought it a very fine lie," continued Lydia. "It was so effective. Nothing Miss Castleton or her 'friends' could say or do. Nothing unpleasantly overt. But in that one stroke I finished her, as a rival or anything else. And I had my revenge on *you* as well." Her smile widened. "You see where your silly little schemes got you. I warned you to leave me alone. Starting that gossip was the neatest thing I ever did." Seeing Anne's outraged expression, she added, "And you needn't think you will tell everyone what I have said, because no one will believe you. I shall deny it, and they will think you are clumsily trying to help your friend."

Simultaneously, Anne heard the hidden door click shut and a rush of movement behind her. She turned to see Laurence standing there, his face flushed with rage, his figure trembling. "You...you...monster!" he sputtered. "I could hardly believe my ears! *You* began that dreadful lie?"

Lydia Branwell glared furiously at Anne, but there was also, for the first time, a spark of fear in her dark eyes. "Laurence! What do you mean? I have just been joking with Lady Anne. We—"

"You needn't try to cover it up. I heard what you

said. You are the most contemptible woman I have ever met, Lydia. I had some doubts about your character before this, but I never *imagined* you could behave with such an utter want of principle or delicacy or… or any admirable quality."

"H–how dare you talk to me this way?" gasped his fiancée.

Laurence stepped farther into the room, facing her. Anne unobtrusively moved back; she didn't want to be a distraction in this confrontation. "I?" Laurence laughed harshly. "I, dare? That is amusing. You say that to me when you have dared to behave like the lowest woman of the streets."

Lydia gasped again. "*You*… Our engagement is at an end, Laurence Debenham!" She tossed her head. "My father shall hear of the way you have spoken to me!"

He laughed. "Splendid. I shall tell him precisely why I did so. Do not trouble yourself about the announcement. I will inform *The Morning Post* first thing tomorrow."

Looking chagrined, Lydia Branwell turned on her heel and stormed out of the room. She nearly collided with Edward as she did so, throwing him a searing glance and twitching her skirts to the side as if to avoid contamination.

"Hurrying straight to Harry Hargreaves, I wager," said Edward as he strolled into the room. "Wants to make sure of him at once. I daresay the announcement of their engagement will be just below the one calling yours off."

Laurence stared at him incredulously. He was still breathing hard after his confrontation with his intended. He turned his head to look at Anne. "Did you plan this?" he said finally.

Anne nodded, eyeing him apprehensively. She was uncertain how he would take their interference in his affairs.

"We took care of the rumors, too," put in Edward. "Charles gathered all the old cats in the next room and saw to it that they overhead the Branwell's confession."

"Overheard?" Laurence looked dazed.

"There is a door behind that curtain," explained Anne. As a horrified expression crossed Laurence's face, she added, "It is shut now. Charles closed it when you came in."

"I see." The Reverend Debenham still looked bewildered, but he was also quite obviously relieved.

"They're probably spreading this juicy new tidbit around the *ton* already," commented Edward with satisfaction. "Before the night is out, everyone will know that Lydia started the lie about Miss Castleton."

Laurence shook his head as if to clear it. "I can't quite take it in. You arranged all of this?"

"The three of us," agreed Edward. "Oh, and Mariah. She's done heroic duty with Hargreaves. Kept him talking for an hour." He chuckled. "I daresay he knows as much about roses as his future father-in-law by now."

"I...I don't know what to say." Laurence sighed.

"I have a suggestion," replied Anne.

"What?"

"I think you should go and tell Bella what has happened. Not about Miss Branwell, of course, though she'll hear that soon enough, I suppose. But you could tell her that the rumors have stopped *and* that your engagement is at an end."

Laurence met her eyes, realization dawning slowly in his own. He began to smile, then to nod. "I believe I will," he agreed. "Yes, I believe that is what I will do." Anne and Edward exchanged a grin as he hurried out of the room.

Nineteen

THE HUNTINGTON BALL MOVED TO ITS CONCLUSION in the customary fashion. The gossip was perhaps a bit more animated than usual, and the Branwell party left very early, but otherwise all was more or less predictable. The Debenham group had no opportunity to gather and discuss the night's events. Anne was asked to dance the moment she reentered the ballroom, and though she wanted very much to speak to Charles, she felt she must accept. Her absence had already caused some remark, for in soliciting her hand, the gentleman had said, "Where the deuce have you been, Lady Anne? We've all been looking for you." She saw Edward join the set, then watched Laurence lead a radiant Arabella into it. With a sigh, she resigned herself to wait for the end of the ball.

At the first interval, Arabella sought her out. "Anne!" she exclaimed. "Have you heard?"

"Heard?" repeated the other girl, smiling.

"That Laurence is no longer…that is…his engagement is broken off."

"Oh, yes."

Arabella smiled tremulously up at her, and Anne nodded, her smile widening. All the necessary communication passed between them in that moment. Then Anne took her friend's arm. "Let us get some lemonade, shall we? I am terribly thirsty."

The evening ended at last. All three Debenham brothers rode home in the coach with Mariah and Anne, and the party was very merry despite the crowding. "The Branwell's face as she went past me out of that parlor was worth twenty guineas," declared Edward. "She knew we'd given her her own back."

Seeing Laurence frown, Anne nodded. "I am sorry it was necessary, but I fear she brought it on herself."

"I should say so!" cried Edward.

"I have a great deal to thank you for," said Laurence quietly. "All of you. And I do thank you. I have not quite…recovered from the events of the evening." He put his forehead in one hand. Edward closed his mouth with a snap and after a moment, Charles laid a hand on his brother's shoulder. Anne felt tears start in her eyes.

"Here we are," said Mariah cheerfully as they pulled up before the house. "And I, for one, am exhausted. I am going straight up to bed."

"I'm not at all sleepy," protested Anne. The brothers smiled at her.

"Perhaps a last drink in the library?" suggested Charles.

"Oh, yes!"

So the younger members of the party settled in the library, the gentlemen with brandies and Anne with a rare glass of Madeira, which soon made her feel the slightest bit light-headed.

"So," sighed Edward after a quarter hour of desultory talk, "all is well again. It is hard to believe."

"Not quite all," answered Anne, a glint in her gray-violet eyes. Charles looked sharply over at her.

"What do you mean?" asked Captain Debenham. "The rumors are stopped, Laurence is a free man, and he has told me that he means to offer for Miss Castleton after a decent interval. What remains?"

Anne had continued to hold Charles's eyes during this speech. "There is something to be settled between Charles and me," she said.

"Couldn't that wait until tomorrow?" replied Charles.

Anne giggled. "No!"

"Good Lord, she's foxed!" Edward laughed. "Drunk as a wheelbarrow. We shouldn't have given her the Madeira."

"I'm not!" asserted Anne.

Laurence nodded. "She's not used to it. We should have thought. I'll ring for her maid to take her up to bed."

"No," exclaimed Anne, who was not really drunk but merely recklessly elated by the wine. "I want *everything* settled. Charles!"

The two younger Debenhams turned puzzled eyes on the viscount, expecting him to be annoyed at Anne's persistence. But Charles was smiling at her. "Are you certain you wish me to ask *now*?" he said. "It is not very private."

"Yes."

Still smiling, he walked over and took her hand. "Very well. Will you be my wife, Anne?"

"Of course I will!"

"By Jove!" cried Edward.

"My dear Charles!" exclaimed Laurence.

The viscount smiled indulgently at them both. "Now perhaps you would leave us…"

"Congratulations, old man," added Captain Debenham. "A capital notion."

Laurence nodded slowly. "I suspected something of the sort, and I…I am very glad." He went and shook Charles's hand, dropping a brief kiss on Anne's cheek. "I am delighted that you are to be truly our sister at last."

"This calls for another round!" urged Edward, picking up the brandy bottle and beginning to fill his glass. "And toasts!"

"No, it does not," replied Charles firmly, causing him to pause with the bottle tilted in midair. "I will endure all the toasts you like when we announce this publicly, but now I wish you would both go home."

"Laurence lives here," protested Edward.

"Then I wish you would go home and he would go

to bed," retorted Charles. "Really, can't you see that you are both de trop?" He softened this rebuke with a wry smile.

"Of course," agreed Laurence, taking Edward's arm and urging him toward the library door. "Come, I'll see you out. Fallow's gone to bed."

"But I haven't even—" Edward's protest was cut off by the closing door, and Anne and Charles were left alone.

"Now you can kiss me again," suggested the girl, smiling saucily up at him.

He laughed. "I am much more likely to beat you. Why did you insist that I propose before my wretched brothers?"

"You have all been getting on so well together. I thought it would be nice to share it with them."

"Did you indeed?"

"Yes. And it was. But I am glad they're gone now. Aren't you going to kiss me?"

"I am not in the habit of kissing inebriated ladies."

"Oh? What sort do you kiss?"

"Anne!"

"Charles?"

He laughed and swept her into his arms, kissing her long and hard.

"Oh," breathed Anne when he drew back. "That was even nicer than the first time!"

"I'm so happy you're pleased."

She looked up at him. "Are *you* pleased, Charles?"

He returned her regard in silence for a moment. "I am far more than that."

"Really? You aren't daunted at the prospect of spending years and years with me?"

His arms tightened round her waist. "Daunted? I am overjoyed. I ask nothing more from life than to care for you."

"*Care* for me? Oh, no, I won't have you feeling *responsible*!" She wrinkled her nose at him. "You must think of another word."

He laughed again. "Then I shall say, rather, I love you, Anne, with all my heart."

She considered. "That will do very well."

He kissed her again, so thoroughly that she was left breathless and shaken. "I love you too, Charles," she whispered when they drew apart. She stroked the place where his hair curled on the back of his neck. "I truly do."

He was bending to kiss her yet again when the library door opened and Mariah looked in, clad in a nightgown and wrapper. "I just wanted..." she had begun when she saw them embracing. Her eyebrows rose; then she smiled. "Oh, good, it is settled. I can take my lavender home for some proper sun."

Anne giggled. "You may take that blasted parrot as well." Charles laughed.

"Augustus?" protested Anne.

"Yes, my love."

"I don't mind," responded Mariah. "I shall hang

his cage in the dining-room window, where he can see my roses."

"Splendid," answered Charles. "Good night!"

Mariah withdrew. "I thought you liked Augustus," protested Anne.

"Then you are much less intelligent than I thought you, my darling."

"What if I want to keep him?"

"Do you?"

Anne considered. "No, but I might have. You didn't even ask me!"

"I thought I knew what you would like, and you see that I was right."

She thought again. "Next time, you must ask." Anne's gray-violet eyes met his seriously. "I am *not* your responsibility, Charles. I am your love; it's quite different."

Very slowly he started to nod. "Yes, I begin to see that it is."

Her arms still around his neck, she leaned back and smiled up at him. "Good. It's much more fun."

He laughed as he pulled her to him again.

Brand-new Regency romance
from bestselling author

JANE ASHFORD

Married to a Perfect Stranger

Coming in Spring 2015
from Sourcebooks Casablanca

Read on for a sneak peek

One

JOHN BEXLEY STOOD AT THE RAIL OF THE HMS *ALCESTE* and watched the gray water race by. Foam streaked the waves under an overcast sky. The sails belled out in a fresh wind, and the current in these narrowing straits, halfway across the world from England and home, pushed them even faster. It wasn't a full-fledged storm, but the weather was certainly what the navy men called "lively." And the roll and heeling of the ship made the small cabin he shared below feel like a cage being shaken by gigantic hands. Far better to brace yourself on deck, endure the salt spray and the roar, feel the full thrill of their swift progress. It was like flying.

He tightened his grip on the rigging as a gust tilted the ship further toward the sea. Rushing water gurgled and hissed along the timbers. The exultation of this run before the wind was a scrap of compensation for the failure of their mission. They were heading home with nothing accomplished, due to intransigence of the Chinese emperor. And as a junior clerk on the diplomatic mission, he'd had no great role to play in their thwarted attempt to sway the monarch. Still, he'd seen and experienced things he would never have been able to imagine. His mind teemed with new ideas. John grinned in the teeth of the wind. The huge expanse and buffeting energy of sea and sky matched his mood. He had the oddest sense that something had come to life inside him on this long voyage.

There was a crack like a cannon shot. The ship shuddered all along its length and stopped dead in the water, throwing John to his knees. Then the vessel slewed around until it wallowed broadside in the waves, sails snapping like pistol fire. John sprang up and looked wildly around for the source of the attack. The masts shook. There was a grating splintering sound, as of tortured wood. They'd hit something in the sea.

Clinging to rail and ropes, John peered over the side. Foam sucked and surged over a rock just below the surface. The wind pushed at the sails and shoved them harder against it. He could see that the hull was breached, water pouring in. They must have veered out of the channel through the straits. He straightened. Sailors swarmed the deck, some getting in each other's way. Where was the captain? The first mate? Someone should do something, give orders.

He remembered that the senior officers were dining with Lord Amherst and the top members of diplomatic group. But why hadn't they come up on deck? John looked to the helmsman. He was leaning against the big ship's wheel. The impact had apparently stunned him.

The prow of the ship sagged and dipped. They were sinking. He was going to die thousands of miles from home, his fate unknown to his family and friends for weeks. And Mary. He and his newlywed wife were just beginning to get acquainted when they'd been separated by this voyage. Now he would leave her a widow, pulled down into these cold foreign seas. John clutched the rigging so tight his nails dug into his palms.

By God, he was not! Denial rose in John, fierce and fiery, along with a surge of confidence stronger than any he'd ever felt before. He knew what to do. The *Lyra* was following not far behind them. It could pick them up. "Ready the dinghies," he shouted to the nearest sailors. "Everyone must get off the ship. We're going down."

Some of the crew had already gone to the pulleys. At his command, others joined them. John ran for the hatch to see what was keeping Lord Amherst and the others.

The moment he entered the narrow gangway, his fellow clerk Edmund Fordyce careened into him. "Where is Lord Amherst?" John asked.

"How the devil would I know?" replied Fordyce. He pushed John against the wall, trying to get by him. "Get out of my way, you idiot. There's water pouring into my cabin."

"We've struck a rock. We have to find the…"

"All I'm finding is a way off this crate." Fordyce shoved harder, squeezing past John and heading for the hatch.

"Fordyce! We need to…"

"*I* need to not risk my neck. *You* can do as you like." His tone suggested that he thought John was a fool. Fordyce staggered as the ship leaned, then lunged out onto the deck. The hatch slammed shut behind him.

John pushed off the wall and moved farther into the ship. Timbers groaned, and the floor heaved under his feet. Water sloshed out of a cabin on the left. At the end of the corridor, the door to the captain's cabin was shut. A long sliver of wood had somehow become jammed under it, John saw, preventing it from opening. Fists pounded on the inside. A chorus of voices shouted for aid. A knife jabbed through the boards at shoulder height, once, and again.

"Wait a moment," he called. He bent and yanked at the piece of wood. At first, it wouldn't shift, but when he kicked it, it moved and finally came loose. John jerked it free and pushed at the door.

The panels burst open. The captain surged out first, cursing. His first mate and other crewmen were right behind him. Then came Lord Amherst and the senior diplomatic staff. En masse, they jostled toward the hatch. "We hit a rock," John said. He wasn't sure whether anyone heard.

When the knot of men had rushed past, John followed. Water coursed over the toes of his boots. As he went, he checked quickly inside the cabins that lined the corridor. All were empty except the last. Reynolds, one of the troopers accompanying their group, was there, dazed and bleeding from a knock on the head. John put an arm around him and helped him up to the deck.

The scene there had become a more organized chaos. The captain was shouting orders. The helmsman had recovered. The ship's dinghies were being lowered into the thrashing sea. John saw Lord Amherst climbing down into one. The deck was listing badly now, the stern rising as water filled the front holds. John helped Reynolds across the shuddering planks. The grating of timber on rock was even louder now, audible even over the confused shouting.

A crewman gave him a hand him with Reynolds. And then John was sliding down a rope into a heaving longboat. He could see their sister ship, the *Lyra*, standing off not far away, waiting to take them aboard. Dinghies dotted the waves, rowing toward her. He grabbed an oar himself as the last men dropped into the boat, and they pulled hard toward rescue. Curiously, along with relief, John felt a rising excitement. He was intensely aware of the pull of his muscles as he rowed, the lash of spray, salty on his lips, the whistle of the wind. Had he ever felt this alive, this clear and certain? All his senses united to tell him there would be no turning back from this profound moment. From now on, everything was different.

Minutes later, they made it to the *Lyra*. Crewmen reached down to help them climb to safety. John vaulted over the rail and turned to look back at the *Alceste*. The ship that had carried them from England to the ports of China, and part way back again, was going down. Most of his possessions, including gifts he'd purchased for people back home, were going with it. Waves washed over the foredeck. Spars and coils of rope floated free. The prow went under. The hull tipped and seemed to hesitate, then slipped beneath the surging sea. It seemed fitting to bow his head briefly, as if saying farewell to a friend.

"Well, I had to see to it that we got everyone off, sir," said a voice behind him. "Couldn't leave anyone behind."

John turned and discovered Fordyce, speaking to Lord Amherst.

"One has to do one's duty whatever the risk," added his fellow clerk.

Lord Amherst nodded, eyes on the spot where the *Alceste* had disappeared. John stared at Fordyce, amazed at the man's effrontery. Surely someone had seen him, rushing to the dinghies ahead of everyone else?

As if sensing his gaze, Fordyce's pale blue eyes flicked at John, then away. "I suppose it's just bred in the bone, sir," he said to Lord Amherst. "Family tradition and all that."

John didn't hear what Amherst murmured in response. He was distracted by the captain of the *Lyra*, ordering his helmsman to steer well away from the hidden shoals.

∽

The small Somerset manor house lazed under the June sun, its red brick mellow with age, its bow windows and ruddy chimney pots aglow. Bees hummed in the garden, where summer blooms perfumed the air. Foliage hung heavy in the small park; lawns glowed green.

But in a pleasant parlor at the back of the house, Mary Fleming Bexley felt far from peaceful. Though she had asked her mother to come, indeed insisted that she must, the visit was not going well. "I've been living with Aunt Lavinia for eighteen months, Mama," she said. "I know what she…"

"Well, we had to put you somewhere," said her mother indulgently. "Married a month, and then your husband goes haring off to China." She said it as if the mission that had taken John away was Mary's fault somehow.

What would she have answered, Mary wondered, if John had said, "Will you marry me and then go live with your great-aunt for months and months while I sail off on an important diplomatic journey to China?" Her reply might have been a bit more complicated than "yes." She'd had less than a month as a wife, actually, and then he was gone to the other side of the world and she was packed off to Somerset.

Packed off; there was the crux of it. It seemed she was always being packed off in one way or another. As if she was a misaddressed parcel or a stray shawl left behind at the end of a house party. "I'm twenty-four years old," she began. "A married woman…"

"At last," interrupted her mother. "Thanks to me. Well, and Mrs. Bexley, of course."

Of course, thought Mary. Their families had come up with the match and pushed for it in a united front. Mary understood now, as she hadn't then, that the Flemings and the Bexleys saw their offspring as two of a kind. She, the least promising of five sisters, short on common sense. John, overshadowed by his three brothers' loud accomplishments, stuck in a junior position at the Foreign Office. Mary had actually overheard her mother and John's discussing their similar shortcomings, not long after he'd departed on his voyage. That had been when they were deciding what to "do" with her. She and John had been hustled into marriage like backward children being sent off to school. Why had she let that happen? "Aunt Lavinia is not herself," she tried.

"Really? Who is she then?" Her mother laughed. "Do you remember how your father used to compare her to a frigate under full sail—'prow jutting well out, a nose fit for cleaving waves.' I had to scold him so. I was afraid one of you children would repeat it."

Mary did remember. Her four sisters had feared Lavinia when she visited, sweeping in like a scudding ship, shedding pronouncements and odd gifts and errant barks of laughter. Mary alone had been fascinated, trailing in the older woman's wake like an inquisitive seabird. But sadly, this was not the Great-Aunt Lavinia she'd found when she arrived to stay here. "She's older," Mary said. "And...confused." Worse than confused—uncharacteristically anxious, a shell of her former, formidable self.

Her mother frowned. "Confused about what? She seemed fine to me. A bit tired, perhaps, but as you say, she's nearly eighty. I'm sure her nap will restore her."

Aunt Lavinia had been having a good day. Mary could not regret this, though it did make it harder to convince her mother.

"Really, Mary, don't you think you're the one who's confused? You call me here at a moment's notice, saying I must come, and I still have no idea why. I'm quite busy at home, you know."

Her mother was always busy. She descended like a striking hawk whenever the least disorder threatened. Mary searched for the right words. But in the face of Mama's all-too-familiar impatience, she couldn't find them. "Let me show you something." Her hand trembled slightly as she reached for her sketch pad.

"Oh, Mary." Her mother sighed and shook her head. "I don't have the time to look at drawings. Please tell me you did not drag me thirty miles over bumpy roads to show me a book of sketches. It's all very well for a *child* to be slow and dreamy and lose herself in fancies, but…" She rubbed her forehead.

Mary felt an old despair. She couldn't stop drawing, any more than she could stop eating. Her mother would never understand this; she'd given up arguing with her about it years ago. She started to put the sketchbook away. But no. Then her mother would leave without agreeing to her plan. And what would become of Great-Aunt Lavinia when Mary left this house? John had to come home *sometime*. "Please, Mama, if you would just look."

Her mother's tone grew sharper. "Mary, as you have pointed out, you are grown up. You must stop wasting time on such stuff and settle down to more useful pursuits."

Part of her wanted to wilt and slink away, hide the drawings, hide herself, as she had so often done back home. Then, from somewhere, rose a determination that would not be denied. Mary had learned something important in these last chaotic months. In fact, her enforced sojourn in Somerset had brought her a revelation. She'd finally understood that in order to truly understand a situation, she had to draw the people involved. Drawing was her key to understanding the world. Only then did she see the truth of things. Only then could she figure out what to do and find the proper words to communicate it.

She'd known that her drawings captured emotion

as well as appearances, through contrast perhaps, or juxtaposition. She couldn't explain how it happened. Sometimes, she had a hint about the feelings already. Other times, she had no idea until the drawing was done. For some reason, she learned subtle things with her hands, as they moved. Not through books, or lectures. No matter how hard she tried, words slipped out of her mind, while shapes and shadows illuminated it. Her mother, her sisters, could look and grasp and comprehend words all in a moment. They could remember all they read with ease. Her sisters found her inability to do so hilarious. Her mother just found it irritating. She looked vastly irritated now. But though Mary trembled under that well-known glare, she had to take the leap. "No, you must look."

Before her mother could object again, Mary flipped open the sketchbook and put two drawings side by side before her.

The first was a watercolor portrait of a middle-aged woman. The face gazed out at the viewer with calm authority. Determination edging toward stubbornness showed in the lines bracketing her lips; pride and imagination in the fashionable cut of her gray curls. Mary had caught a subtle twinkle in the blue eyes, a persistent curiosity in the tilt of the head. More than the sum of its parts, the painting conveyed the essence of a strong personality.

The second portrait showed the same woman, and yet not the same. In this one, the sharp eyes had blurred; though painted, they seemed to shift with uncertainty under the viewer's gaze. This woman's mouth looked ready to quiver with uncertainty. The skin sagged not just with greater age, but with an uncomprehending anxiety as well. Around this face, the well-kept gray hair and modish lace cap seemed incongruous.

Mary looked from one image to the other, her heart aching for her great-aunt.

"Yes, very well," said her mother. "You've drawn Aunt Lavinia. What do you wish me to say? That it is a good likeness?"

"Can you *really* look, Mama? Please? Try?"

The pleading in her voice seemed to reach her mother at last. She considered the pages again. Her stare went from one portrait to the other. Back again. Gradually, she began to frown.

And Mary felt freed to speak. "She's very forgetful, even of familiar people's names or her own history. The servants were at their wits' end when I arrived." It had been daunting, to be tossed into a floundering household, suddenly surrounded by people looking to her for leadership. She'd had to fumble her way to the idea that she could take charge, if she did it in her own way. "I believe we must find her a companion. Someone who is more than a housekeeper, though she will have to manage the household, too. Someone... patient and kind. We should pay quite well, I think, well enough to attract just the right sort of person."

She would fight for this plan, Mary thought. Great-Aunt Lavinia deserved the best.

"We?" said her mother.

"Well, it would come out of Aunt's income, naturally. But as she is not really capable of approving the expenditure, I thought I should speak to you. As her only close relation."

Her mother was looking at her oddly. "You have considered this."

Now that Mary had begun, the words poured out. "I drafted an advertisement that sets forth just what we need." She took the folded paper from the pocket of her gown. "The butler here says there is an agency in London that provides ladies' companions. We must be very clear that we require someone...special." Mary unfolded the page and extended it. She was pleased to see that it did not shake in her hand.

Her mother took it and read. "Well expressed," she commented, sounding surprised.

"I thought, if you agreed, we could send it right off."

"Perhaps I should talk to Aunt Lavinia before..." Her mother paused, looked down at the portraits again. "No. That is, I *shall* talk to her. But I daresay you are right. You may put it in the mail." She looked up. "Or...what do you intend to do with the replies?"

"I...I thought I would invite the best candidates here for a visit." Mary faltered a bit under her parent's close examination. "Unless you would prefer to interview...?"

Her mother cocked her head. "You would have to pay their coach fares."

Mary nodded.

"They must be asked about their previous positions and show a complete set of references."

"Yes, Mama."

"Do you really think *you* can find the proper person?" Years of doubt tinged her tone.

Mary sat straighter and met her skeptical gaze. "I do."

The pause that followed went on longer than Mary would have liked, but at last her mother said, "Very well. I shall let you try."

"Th-thank you, Mama," Mary replied, her spirit swelling with triumph.

"I'll give you a list of important questions," her mother added sharply. "And I shall expect a full report on each possibility before the final decision is made."

Mary nodded, her elation a little dimmed. How odd that this success made her feel more lonely, rather than less so.

༄

John Bexley strode down the gangplank onto the Southampton dock and paused to look over the busy port town. For the first time since he'd left English shores in February 1816, everything felt familiar—the shape of the buildings, the faces and dress of the people, the sounds and scents and voices. And yet, they also felt strangely changed. His twenty-month journey to the other side of the world had reduced England to just one corner of a vast globe. A noble corner, without a doubt, a corner with a proud history and admirable ideals, but still just a smallish island among continents. And so his home looked not only natural and welcoming, but also a bit…constricted.

Speaking of constricted, John wiggled his shoulders, trying to get more comfortable in a coat that no longer fit. He'd gained more muscle than his clothes could accommodate. The binding cloth contributed to the mixed emotions of this moment. He'd outgrown his raiment. What about his old routines, or the wife he'd left behind?

John looked at the English faces on the docks around him, pale even under the August sun. For almost two years, he and Mary had led separate lives—his active and public, hers domestic and small. So many things had happened to him that she would never comprehend. And a thousand domestic details that newly married persons usually shared had gone by on opposite sides of the world.

Worse, John wondered now whether he'd done the right thing, giving in to his family's plan for him. The young man he'd been before this voyage had let them urge him into a lifetime bond without really thinking. If the foreign secretary's letter about the China mission had come a few weeks sooner, would he have offered for Mary? The answer was too uncomfortable to contemplate.

John looked around out over the town. His world of two years ago seemed like a dream to him now, pale and insubstantial, the people distant shadows. Swept away on a grand journey, he'd found inner continents as surprising as the discoveries of ancient explorers. The impulses that had risen in him and answered the challenge of storm-wracked seas still burned—more vibrant perceptions, fiercer ambition, a determination to make his mark.

But a suitable wife—one with important connections and social skills—was practically required for advancing through the ranks of the Foreign Office.

A bale of silks rose from the ship's hold, pulley creaking as the navvies hauled on the rope. The heavy cargo swung out over the dock and plunged down just as a street urchin emerged from between two stacks of crates. John took three steps, snatched the boy from its path. and pulled him well out of the way. "Careful there," he said.

Pale and wide-eyed, the grimy child nodded his thanks and scampered away.

The planks of the dock vibrated as the bale thumped to the boards. A brawny dockworker rounded the corner of a warehouse and hefted it; no easy task, John knew. He should head into town, find transport, and begin the last sixty miles of his journey. To Mary. But his tumbled thoughts kept him standing near the ship.

He remembered his first sight of her at the Bath Assembly. Neither of them came from the sort of grand families who went to London for the Season; Bath was the center of their social world. She'd stood with her mother by the wall—a small, delicate girl with chestnut brown hair and huge dark eyes; a full lower lip that seemed made for kissing; pretty little hands. She'd looked as sweet and timid as a sparrow. In that moment—which now seemed long ages ago— his family's mandate that she was the wife for him had seemed no burden at all. He'd walked over, been presented. Mary had smiled at him…

After that, events were a bit of a blur. They'd danced, walked the streets of Bath together, taken teas and dinners at their families' tables. He had offered for her; that moment had been between the two of them. At the time, it hadn't seemed as if he had a choice. But once the words were spoken, and she had accepted, their mothers had swooped in and taken over. He didn't remember being consulted about a single item after that. He was simply told things. Mary's father had lectured him about how the combination of their two inherited incomes would allow them to live very comfortably, as if he couldn't work that out for himself. His brothers had teased him relentlessly, as usual. He'd overheard his parents agreeing that this was a good enough match—for him, for Mary—and for some reason, incomprehensible to him now, he'd made no remark.

There'd been a whirl of a wedding and a seaside week in Weston-super-Mare, with dolorous rain and intimacies that had been clumsier than he'd have liked. Then the Foreign Office summons had arrived to take over his thoughts and change his life.

John sighed. His life, not Mary's. What would a little sparrow like Mary think of the intricacies of Foreign Office etiquette? What would she think of him now that he'd...come alive. He took a deep breath of the seaside air. That's how it felt—as if he'd been half asleep for years and finally woken. Now, he intended to plunge into the drive for advantage and jostling rivalries he'd generally ignored in his three years on the job. Work was going to occupy much of his time. Where did Mary fit in all this?

John loosened his shoulders, chafing at the tightness of his coat once again. Done was done. Mary was his wife. She would have to fit. She was young, unformed, eager to please. Though she didn't have the family connections that were so useful in government work, she was a taking little thing. She'd welcome his guidance. Indeed, she would probably be awed by his new sophistication. That was a curiously attractive notion.

John fell into a pleasant reverie. In the long months at sea, men had talked, and inevitably one of their topics had been women. John had heard a lot of nonsense and endured a load of empty boasting. But some of it had been eye-opening, and when one winnowed through the sources, considered the characters of the speakers, quite intriguing. He looked forward to trying out some of the...

"Ah, here he is!"

John stiffened at the sound of that affected voice. He'd thought he was the last passenger off the ship.

"Bexley can deal with the trunks," the voice drawled on. "It's just the sort of thing he's good at."

John turned to face the two men stepping off the *Lyra*'s gangplank. Beside Lord Amherst's admirable, capable private secretary sauntered the recent bane of John's existence, The Honorable Edmund Fordyce.

Since the shipwreck, Fordyce had made it his mission to harass John. Before that, they'd had little to do with each other, despite the smallness of their party. Fordyce, equally junior in the diplomatic group, had pursued more exalted company. A foppish, supercilious, son of an earl—as John had learned in recent weeks—Fordyce had constantly dropped names and attempted to reminisce with Lord Amherst about lavish country house parties and fashionable town balls.

But following their encounter in that narrow gangway of a sinking ship, the man had focused almost obsessively on John. He'd created opportunities to highlight the difference in their backgrounds, or cast doubt on John's abilities. It was wildly irritating. And ridiculous. What did he think John was going to do—run and tattle about his cowardice like a sniveling schoolboy? Try to tell their superiors that he, John, had made sure the *Alceste* was clear? That Fordyce had misrepresented his own behavior? There was no way to initiate such a conversation, even if he wished to.

John had even tried to say something like this to Fordyce, with no effect. It was as if the fellow didn't even hear him. By this time, the mere sound of his voice affected John like the screech of tortured metal.

"If you wouldn't mind, Bexley," said the secretary. His expression showed a certain amount of sympathy. "I must follow Amherst to London immediately, and there are a number of confidential items still in the hold."

"John will be happy to play footman," said Fordyce. "Won't you, John? Oh, I didn't think. Are you familiar with footmen? They stand about front halls in *important* houses, waiting to run errands and carry packages, that sort of thing." He smiled, the picture of toothy falsity.

Fordyce laced his arm with the secretary's as if they were bosom friends. The secretary didn't quite shake him off. But John read distaste in his face, which took some of the sting out of Fordyce's words. Confidential items required careful handling, by someone who could be trusted. The task was significant, whatever Fordyce's silly prejudices. "Certainly, sir," John said.

The secretary nodded his thanks as the two men moved off down the dock. "See you in London, Bexley," he added.

John's spirits rose at this acknowledgment. More than his own inner landscape had changed with this voyage. He was known now; from amongst the vast army of junior functionaries in the Foreign

Office, he'd been noticed. His future prospects were immeasurably brighter than they had been before this journey. That, and Fordyce's sour expression, considerably lightened the job of seeing that each trunk was properly labeled and sent off with a reliable carrier to its correct destination.

What a Lady Needs for Christmas

The MacGregor Series
by Grace Burrowes

New York Times and *USA Today* Bestselling Author

The best gifts are the unexpected ones...

To escape a scandal, Lady Joan Flynn flees to her family's estate in the Scottish Highlands. She needs a husband by Christmas, or the holidays will ring in nothing but ruin.

Practical, ambitious mill owner Dante Hartwell offers to marry Joan, because a wellborn wife is his best chance of gaining access to aristocratic investors.

As Christmas—and trouble—draw nearer, Dante and Joan discover that true love often hides beneath the most unassuming holiday wrapping...

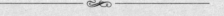

Praise for Grace Burrowes:

"Burrowes is superb at creating connections that feel honest and real." —*Publishers Weekly*

"The stories she tells have depth and emotion that will capture your heart and mind." —*Night Owl Reviews*

For more Grace Burrowes, visit:

www.sourcebooks.com

The Captive

Book 1 in the Captive Hearts series

by Grace Burrowes

New York Times and *USA Today* bestseller

———— ❧ ————

He'll never be free...

Captured and tortured by the French, Christian Severn, Duke of Mercia, survives by vowing to take revenge. Before the duke can pursue justice, Gillian, Countess of Greendale, reminds him that his small daughter needs her papa desperately.

Until he surrenders his heart...

Christian's devotion to his daughter and his kindness toward Gilly give her hope of a future with him, for surely he shares her loathing for violence. Little does Gilly know, the battle for Christian's heart is only beginning.

———— ❧ ————

"Burrowes deftly builds the romantic tension amid lovely layers of domestic tranquillity and honest conversations." —*Publishers Weekly*

"This is a beautiful story of redemption and love's power over evil that wrenches readers' emotions, yet leaves them utterly satisfied." —*RT Books Reviews*

For more Grace Burrowes, visit:

www.sourcebooks.com

The Traitor

Book 2 in the Captive Hearts series

by Grace Burrowes

New York Times and *USA Today* Bestselling Author

———— ❧ ————

The past will overtake him...

Abandoned in France since boyhood, despite being heir to an English barony, Sebastian St. Clair makes the impossible choice to serve in the French Army. When he returns to England, old enemies challenge him on the field of honor, one after another.

But this time, he will not fight alone...

Millicent Danforth desperately needs her position as companion to the Traitor Baron's aunt, but grieves to learn that Sebastian must continually fight a war long over. As Sebastian and Milly explore their growing passion, they uncover a plot that will cost Sebastian his life and his honor, unless he does battle once more...

———— ❧ ————

"It takes a skilled storyteller to turn a ruthless interrogator into a man worthy of readers' respect and adoration. Burrowes steps outside the box and readers are gifted with a memorable love story." —*RT Book Reviews*

For more Grace Burrowes, visit:

www.sourcebooks.com

The Laird

Book 3 in the Captive Hearts series
by Grace Burrowes

New York Times and *USA Today* Bestselling Author

He left his bride to go to war...

After years of soldiering, Michael Brodie returns to his Highland estate to find that the bride he left behind has become a stranger. Brenna is self-sufficient, competent, confident—and furious. But despite Michael's prolonged absence, Brenna has remained loyal.

Now his most important battle will be for her heart.

Michael left Brenna when she needed him most, and then stayed away even after the war ended. Even though Michael has come home a seemingly wiser, more patient, and honorable husband, Brenna is wary of entrusting him with the truths she's been guarding.

"Readers seeking a sweet, sensitive romance will savor this tale." —*RT Book Reviews*

"Burrowes's straightforward, sensual love story is intelligent and tender, rising above the crowd with deft dialogue and delightful characters." —*Publishers Weekly*

For more Grace Burrowes, visit:

www.sourcebooks.com

A Winter Wedding

The Marriage Mart Series
by Amanda Forester

This adventurous duke

The Duke of Marchford requires a suitable bride, but catching spies for the Foreign Office takes up most of his time. Not wanting to face another London season as an eligible man, he employs the notorious Madame X to find him a match.

Has met his match

Miss Penelope Rose's own unsuccessful attempts at matrimony did not stop her from becoming London's most exclusive matchmaker. Marchford proves to be a difficult client, but as he draws on her social expertise to help him flush out a dangerous traitor, they find that falling in love may be the riskiest adventure of all.

"Pure ambrosia... Readers will delight in one of Forester's happiest offerings to date." —*Publishers Weekly*

"Forester's latest sparkles with charming repartee and just enough humor to spice up the romance and intrigue." —*RT Book Reviews*, 4 Stars

For more Amanda Forester, visit:

www.sourcebooks.com